The Pict, staggering under the impact of the corpse against him, made no attempt to parry the dripping axe; the instinct to slay submerging even the instinct to live, he drove his spear ferociously at his enemy's broad breast. The Cimmerian had the advantage of a greater intelligence, and a weapon in each hand. The hatchet, checking its downward sweep, struck the spear aside, and the knife in the Cimmerian's left hand ripped upward into the painted belly.

An awful howl burst from the Pict's lips as he crumpled, disembowelled—a cry not of fear or of pain, but of baffled, bestial fury, the death-screech of a panther. It was answered by a wild chorus of yells some distance east of the glade. The Cimmerian started convulsively, wheeled, crouching like a wild thing at bay, lips asnarl, shaking the sweat from his face. Blood trickled down his forearm from under the bandage.

ECHOES OF VALOR

ROBERT E. HOWARD
FRITZ LEIBER ★ HENRY KUTTNER

ECHOES OF VALOR

EDITED BY
KARL
EDWARD
WAGNER

TOR

A TOM DOHERTY ASSOCIATES BOOK

ECHOES OF VALOR

Copyright © 1987 by Karl Edward Wagner

First printing: February 1987

A TOR Book

Published by Tom Doherty Associates, Inc.
49 West 24 Street
New York, N.Y. 10010

Cover art by Ken Kelly

ISBN: 0-812-55750-6
CAN. ED.: 0-812-55751-4

Printed in the United States of America

0 9 8 7 6 5 4 3 2 1

ACKNOWLEDGMENTS

The Black Stranger by Robert E. Howard. Copyright © 1953 by Future Publications, Inc., for *Fantasy Magazine*, March 1953. This version copyright © 1987 by Conan Properties, Inc. Published by permission of Conan Properties, Inc.

Adept's Gambit by Fritz Leiber. Copyright © 1947 by Fritz Leiber, Jr., for *Night's Black Agents*. Reprinted by permission of the author and the author's agent, Richard Curtis Assoc.

Wet Magic by Henry Kuttner. Copyright © 1942 by Street & Smith Publications, Inc., for *Unknown Worlds*, February 1943. Reprinted by permission of Don Congdon Assoc., agent for the author's estate.

Table of Contents

Editor's Introduction to

"The Black Stranger"

*W*hile *the origins of epic fantasy are as old as mankind itself, it was Robert E. Howard who crystallized the various elements that formed this genre's pulp traditions. Born January 22, 1906, in Peaster, Texas, Howard grew up in various small towns across Texas until his father and mother settled in Cross Plains. In poor health as a child (there are good indications that he had rheumatic fever and later suffered from rheumatic heart disease), the young Howard found escape through his intense imagination— creating magical realms of fantastic adventure from such books of ancient history and myths as he was able to find. At the same time, he was fascinated by the tales of gunfights and Indian wars still vividly recalled by survivors of those lawless days. It was this fusion of Old World myth and Old West legend that directed the emergence of a new approach to epic fantasy in Howard's writing.*

By age 15 Howard had determined to become a writer. Undaunted by rejection slips, he managed to make his first sale to Weird Tales—*a story of primitive man entitled "Spear and Fang" (July 1925). Sales were pitifully slow in coming, but by the close of the 1920s Howard's stories were beginning to attract notice in* Weird Tales. *Most popular were his stories involving series characters: Solo-*

*mon Kane, a Puritan adventurer in the age of Elizabeth;
Bran Mak Morn, a Pictish king in the early years of third-
century Roman Britain; King Kull, a savage who became
king in the age of lost Atlantis.*

With the December 1932 issue of Weird Tales *appeared
Howard's most famous creation, Conan. This first story,
"The Phoenix on the Sword," was actually a rewrite of a
King Kull story that editor Farnsworth Wright had earlier
rejected, and it takes place quite late in Conan's career.
Howard would quickly fill in the gaps of Conan's saga,
with tales of Conan as a thief, a pirate, a mercenary, an
adventurer, a king—and always a barbarian, no matter
what his role. While a great popular success with the
readers of* Weird Tales, *Conan was not a commercial
success.* Weird Tales *was a poor-paying market when it
did manage to pay, and at the time of Howard's death the
magazine owed him $1350 for stories already published.
Financial necessities forced Howard to abandon Conan in
1935 and to write for better-paying markets. On June 12,
1936, during a spell of profound depression, Howard shot
himself.*

*Robert E. Howard completed twenty-one Conan stories
during those four years. Of these, seventeen were published in* Weird Tales, *while four were rejected by Wright
and remained unpublished until many years after Howard's death. "The Black Stranger" is one of this latter
group, first published in an abridged form in the March
1953 issue of* Fantasy Magazine. *It is one of the last
Conan stories that Howard wrote, and in terms of Conan's
career it takes place immediately following "Beyond the
Black River"* (Weird Tales, *May and June 1935).*

*These two stories mark a departure from Howard's
usual milieu for the Conan stories. Commenting on this,
Howard wrote: "My latest sales to Weird Tales have been
a two-part Conan serial, 'Beyond the Black River'—a*

frontier story, and a novelet dealing with Mississippi negroes, etc. . . . In the Conan story I've attempted a new style and setting entirely—abandoned the exotic settings of lost cities, decaying civilizations, golden domes, marble palaces, silk-clad dancing girls, etc., and thrown my story against a background of forests and rivers, log cabins, frontier outposts, buckskin-clad settlers, and painted tribesmen. Some day I'm going to try my hand at a longer yarn of the same style, a serial of four or five parts."

Howard did try his hand at this, and "The Black Stranger" was the result. Unfortunately, Wright rejected the piece. Howard made an unsuccessful attempt to salvage the story by rewriting it as a pirate story, "Swords of the Red Brotherhood," substituting his swashbuckling hero, Black Vulmea, for Conan. This version was eventually published as part of a hardcover collection, Black Vulmea's Vengeance (Grant, 1976). There has been some confusion as to which is the original version. I have the photocopy of Howard's original manuscript of "The Black Stranger," which clearly shows Howard's efforts to change the story from the Conan to the Black Vulmea version. This version here follows Howard's original manuscript. This is the first time the complete form of "The Black Stranger" has appeared in print.

The Black Stranger

Robert E. Howard

Chapter 1
The Painted Men

One moment the glade lay empty; the next, a man stood poised warily at the edge of the bushes. There had been no sound to warn the grey squirrels of his coming. But the gay-hued birds that flitted about in the sunshine of the open space took fright at his sudden appearance and rose in a clamoring cloud. The man scowled and glanced quickly back the way he had come, as if fearing their flight had betrayed his position to some one unseen. Then he stalked across the glade, placing his feet with care. For all his massive, muscular build he moved with the supple certitude of a panther. He was naked except for a rag twisted about his loins, and his limbs were criss-crossed with scratches from briars, and caked with dried mud. A brown-crusted bandage was knotted about his thickly-muscled left arm. Under his matted black mane his face was drawn and gaunt, and his eyes burned like the eyes of a wounded panther. He limped slightly as he followed the dim path that led across the open space.

Half-way across the glade he stopped short and whirled, catlike, facing back the way he had come, as a long-drawn call quavered out across the forest. To another man it would have seemed merely the howl of a wolf. But this man knew it was no wolf. He was a Cimmerian and understood the voices of the wilderness as a city-bred man understands the voices of his friends.

Rage burned redly in his bloodshot eyes as he turned once more and hurried along the path, which, as it left the glade, ran along the edge of a dense thicket that rose in a solid clump of greenery among the trees and bushes. A massive log, deeply embedded in the grassy earth, paralleled the fringe of the thicket, lying between it and the path. When the Cimmerian saw this log he halted and looked back across the glade. To the average eye there were no signs to show that he had passed; but there was evidence visible to his wilderness-sharpened eyes, and therefore to the equally keen eyes of those who pursued him. He snarled silently, the red rage growing in his eyes—the berserk fury of a hunted beast which is ready to turn at bay.

He walked down the trail with comparative carelessness, here and there crushing a grass-blade beneath his foot. Then, when he had reached the further end of the great log, he sprang upon it, turned and ran lightly back along it. The bark had long been worn away by the elements. He left no sign to show the keenest forest-eyes that he had doubled on his trail. When he reached the densest point of the thicket he faded into it like a shadow, with hardly the quiver of a leaf to mark his passing.

The minutes dragged. The grey squirrels chattered again on the branches—then flattened their bodies and were suddenly mute. Again the glade was invaded. As silently as the first man had appeared, three other men materialized out of the eastern edge of the clearing. They were dark-skinned men of short stature, with thickly-muscled chests and arms. They wore beaded buckskin loin-cloths, and an eagle's feather was thrust into each black mane. They were painted in hideous designs, and heavily armed.

They had scanned the glade carefully before showing themselves in the open, for they moved out of the bushes without hesitation, in close single-file, treading as softly as leopards, and bending down to stare at the path. They were following the trail of the Cimmerian, but it was no easy task even for these human bloodhounds. They moved slowly across the glade, and then one stiffened, grunted and pointed with his broad-bladed stabbing spear at a crushed grass-blade where the path entered the forest again. All halted instantly and their beady black eyes quested the forest walls. But their quarry was well hidden; they saw nothing to awake their suspicion, and presently they moved on, more rapidly, following the faint marks that seemed to indicate their prey was growing careless through weakness or desperation.

They had just passed the spot where the thicket crowded closest to the ancient trail when the Cimmerian bounded into the path behind them and plunged his knife between the shoulders of the last man. The attack was so quick and unexpected the Pict had no chance to save himself. The blade was in his heart before he knew he was in peril. The other two whirled with the instant, steel-trap quickness of savages, but even as his knife sank home, the Cimmerian struck a tremendous blow with the war-axe in his right hand. The second Pict was in the act of turning as the axe fell. It split his skull to the teeth.

The remaining Pict, a chief by the scarlet tip of his eagle-feather, came savagely to the attack. He was stabbing at the Cimmerian's breast even as the killer wrenched his axe from the dead man's head. The Cimmerian hurled the body against the chief and followed with an attack as furious and desperate as the charge of a wounded tiger. The Pict, staggering under the impact of the corpse against him, made no attempt to parry the dripping axe; the instinct to slay submerging even the instinct to live, he drove his spear ferociously at his enemy's broad breast. The Cimmerian had the advantage of a greater intelligence, and a weapon in each hand. The hatchet, checking its downward sweep, struck the spear aside, and the knife in the Cimmerian's left hand ripped upward into the painted belly.

An awful howl burst from the Pict's lips as he crumpled, disembowelled—a cry not of fear or of pain, but of baffled, bestial fury, the death-screech of a panther. It was answered by a wild chorus of yells some distance east of the glade. The Cimmerian started convulsively, wheeled, crouching like a wild thing at bay, lips asnarl, shaking the sweat from his face. Blood trickled down his forearm from under the bandage.

With a gasping, incoherent imprecation he turned and fled westward. He did not pick his way now, but ran with all the speed of his long legs, calling on the deep and all but inexhaustible reservoirs of endurance which are Nature's compensation for a barbaric existence. Behind him for a space the woods were silent, then a demoniacal howling burst out at the spot he had recently left, and he knew his pursuers had found the bodies of his victims. He had no breath for cursing the blood-drops that kept spilling to the ground from his freshly opened wound, leaving a trail a child could follow. He had thought that perhaps these three Picts were all that still pursued him of the war-party which had followed him for over a hundred miles. But he might have known these human wolves never quit a blood-trail.

The woods were silent again, and that meant they were racing after him, marking his path by the betraying blood-drops he could not check. A wind out of the west blew against his face, laden with a salty dampness he recog-

nized. Dully he was amazed. If he was that close to the sea
the long chase had been even longer than he had realized.
But it was nearly over. Even his wolfish vitality was
ebbing under the terrible strain. He gasped for breath and
there was a sharp pain in his side. His legs trembled with
weariness and the lame one ached like the cut of a knife in
the tendons each time he set the foot to earth. He had
followed the instincts of the wilderness which bred him,
straining every nerve and sinew, exhausting every subtlety
and artifice to survive. Now in his extremity he was
obeying another instinct, looking for a place to turn at bay
and sell his life at a bloody price.

He did not leave the trail for the tangled depths on either
hand. He knew that it was futile to hope to evade his
pursuers now. He ran on down the trail while the blood
pounded louder and louder in his ears and each breath he
drew was a racking, dry-lipped gulp. Behind him a mad
baying broke out, token that they were close on his heels
and expected to overhaul their prey swiftly. They would
come as fleet as starving wolves now, howling at every
leap.

Abruptly he burst from the denseness of the trees and
saw, ahead of him, the ground pitching upward, and the
ancient trail winding up rocky ledges between jagged boulders. All swam before him in a dizzy red mist, but it was a
hill he had come to, a rugged crag rising abruptly from the
forest about its foot. And the dim trail wound up to a
broad ledge near the summit.

That ledge would be as good a place to die as any. He
limped up the trail, going on hands and knees in the
steeper places, his knife between his teeth. He had not yet
reached the jutting ledge when some forty painted savages
broke from among the trees, howling like wolves. At the
sight of their prey their screams rose to a devil's crescendo, and they raced toward the foot of the crag, loosing

arrows as they came. The shafts showered about the man who doggedly climbed upward, and one stuck in the calf of his leg. Without pausing in his climb he tore it out and threw it aside, heedless of the less accurate missiles which splintered on the rocks about him. Grimly he hauled himself over the rim of the ledge and turned about, drawing his hatchet and shifting knife to hand. He lay glaring down at his pursuers over the rim, only his shock of hair and blazing eyes visible. His chest heaved as he drank in the air in great shuddering gasps, and he clenched his teeth against a tendency toward nausea.

Only a few arrows whistled up at him. The horde knew its prey was cornered. The warriors came on howling, leaping agilely over the rocks at the foot of the hill, war-axes in their hand. The first to reach the crag was a brawny brave whose eagle feather was stained scarlet as a token of chieftainship. He halted briefly, one foot on the sloping trail, arrow notched and drawn half-way back, head thrown back and lips parted for an exultant yell. But the shaft was never loosed. He froze into motionlessness, and the blood-lust in his black eyes gave way to a look of startled recognition. With a whoop he gave back, throwing his arms wide to check the rush of his howling braves. The man crouching on the ledge above them understood the Pictish tongue, but he was too far away to catch the significance of the staccato phrases snapped at the warriors by the crimson-feathered chief.

But all ceased their yelping, and stood mutely staring up—not at the man on the ledge, it seemed to him, but at the hill itself. Then without further hesitation, they unstrung their bows and thrust them into buckskin cases at their girdles; turned their backs and trotted across the open space, to melt into the forest without a backward look.

The Cimmerian glared in amazement. He knew the Pictish nature too well not to recognize the finality ex-

pressed in the departure. He knew they would not come
back. They were heading for their villages, a hundred
miles to the east.

But he could not understand it. What was there about
his refuge that would cause a Pictish war-party to abandon
a chase it had followed so long with all the passion of
hungry wolves? He knew there were sacred places, spots
set aside as sanctuaries by the various clans, and that a
fugitive, taking refuge in one of these sanctuaries, was
safe from the clan which raised it. But the different tribes
seldom respected sanctuaries of other tribes; and the men
who had pursued him certainly had no sacred spots of their
own in this region. They were the men of the Eagle,
whose villages lay far to the east, adjoining the country of
the Wolf-Picts.

It was the Wolves who had captured him, in a foray
against the Aquilonian settlements along Thunder River,
and they had given him to the Eagles in return for a
captured Wolf chief. The Eaglemen had a red score against
the giant Cimmerian, and now it was redder still, for his
escape had cost the life of a noted war-chief. That was
why they had followed him so relentlessly, over broad
rivers and hills and through long leagues of gloomy forest,
the hunting grounds of hostile tribes. And now the survivors of that long chase turned back when their enemy was
run to earth and trapped. He shook his head, unable to
understand it.

He rose gingerly, dizzy from the long grind, and scarcely
able to realize that it was over. His limbs were stiff, his
wounds ached. He spat dryly and cursed, rubbing his
burning, bloodshot eyes with the back of his thick wrist.
He blinked and took stock of his surroundings. Below him
the green wilderness waved and billowed away and away
in a solid mass, and above its western rim rose a steel-blue
haze he knew hung over the ocean. The wind stirred his

black mane, and the salt tang of the atmosphere revived
him. He expanded his enormous chest and drank it in.

Then he turned stiffly and painfully about, growling at
the twinge in his bleeding calf, and investigated the ledge
whereon he stood. Behind it rose a sheer rocky cliff to the
crest of the crag, some thirty feet above him. A narrow
ladder-like stair of hand-holds had been niched into the
rock. And a few feet from its foot there was a cleft in the
wall, wide enough and tall enough for a man to enter.

He limped to the cleft, peered in, and grunted. The
sun, hanging high above the western forest, slanted into the
cleft, revealing a tunnel-like cavern beyond, and rested a
revealing beam on the arch at which this tunnel ended. In
that arch was set a heavy iron-bound oaken door!

This was amazing. This country was howling wilderness. The Cimmerian knew that for a thousand miles this
western coast ran bare and uninhabited except by the
villages of the ferocious sea-land tribes, who were even
less civilized than their forest-dwelling brothers.

The nearest outposts of civilization were the frontier
settlements along Thunder River, hundreds of miles to the
east. The Cimmerian knew he was the only white man
ever to cross the wilderness that lay between that river and
the coast. Yet that door was no work of Picts.

Being unexplainable, it was an object of suspicion, and
suspiciously he approached it, axe and knife ready. Then
as his bloodshot eyes became more accustomed to the soft
gloom that lurked on either side of the narrow shaft of
sunlight, he noticed something else—thick iron-bound chests
ranged along the walls. A blaze of comprehension came
into his eyes. He bent over one, but the lid resisted his
efforts. He lifted his hatchet to shatter the ancient lock,
then changed his mind and limped toward the arched door.
His bearing was more confident now, his weapons hung at

his sides. He pushed against the ornately carven door and it swung inward without resistance.

Then his manner changed again, with lightning-like abruptness; he recoiled with a startled curse, knife and hatchet flashing as they leaped to positions of defense. An instant he poised there, like a statue of fierce menace, craning his massive neck to glare through the door. It was darker in the large natural chamber into which he was looking, but a dim glow emanated from the great jewel which stood on a tiny ivory pedestal in the center of the great ebony table about which sat those silent shapes whose appearance had so startled the intruder.

They did not move, they did not turn their heads toward him.

"Well," he said harshly; "are you all drunk?"

There was no reply. He was not a man easily abashed, yet now he felt disconcerted.

"You might offer me a glass of that wine you're swigging," he growled, his natural truculence roused by the awkwardness of the situation. "By Crom, you show damned poor courtesy to a man who's been one of your own brotherhood. Are you going to—" his voice trailed into silence, and in silence he stood and stared awhile at those bizarre figures sitting so silently about the great ebon table.

"They're not drunk," he muttered presently. "They're not even drinking. What devil's game is this?" He stepped across the threshold and was instantly fighting for his life against the murderous, unseen fingers that clutched his throat.

Chapter 2
Men From the Sea

Belesa idly stirred a sea-shell with a daintily slippered toe, mentally comparing its delicate pink edges to the first pink haze of dawn that rose over the misty beaches. It was not dawn now, but the sun was not long up, and the light, pearl-grey clouds which drifted over the waters had not yet been dispelled.

Belesa lifted her splendidly shaped head and stared out over a scene alien and repellent to her, yet drearily familiar in every detail. From her dainty feet the tawny sands ran to meet the softly lapping waves which stretched westward to be lost in the blue haze of the horizon. She was standing on the southern curve of the wide bay, and south of her the land sloped upward to the low ridge which formed one horn of that bay. From that ridge, she knew, one could look southward across the bare waters—into infinities of distance as absolute as the view to the westward and to the northward.

Glancing listlessly landward, she absently scanned the fortress which had been her home for the past year. Against a vague pearl and cerulean morning sky floated the golden and scarlet flag of her house—an ensign which awakened no enthusiasm in her youthful bosom, though it had flown triumphantly over many a bloody field in the far South. She made out the figures of men toiling in the gardens and fields that huddled near the fort, seeming to shrink from the gloomy rampart of the forest which fringed the open belt on the east, stretching north and south as far as she could see. She feared that forest, and that fear was shared by every one in that tiny settlement. Nor was it an idle fear—death lurked in those whispering depths, death swift and terrible, death slow and hideous, hidden, painted, tireless, unrelenting.

She sighed and moved listlessly toward the water's edge, with no set purpose in mind. The dragging days were all of one color, and the world of cities and courts and gaiety seemed not only thousands of miles but long ages away. Again she sought in vain for the reason that had caused a Count of Zingara to flee with his retainers to this wild coast, a thousand miles from the land that bore him, exchanging the castle of his ancestors for a hut of logs.

Her eyes softened at the light patter of small bare feet across the sands. A young girl came running over the low sandy ridge, quite naked, her slight body dripping, and her flaxen hair plastered wetly on her small head. Her wistful eyes were wide with excitement.

"Lady Belesa!" she cried, rendering the Zingaran words with a soft Ophirean accent. "Oh, Lady Belesa!"

Breathless from her scamper, she stammered and made incoherent gestures with her hands. Belesa smiled and put an arm about the child, not minding that her silken dress came in contact with the damp, warm body. In her lonely, isolated life Belesa bestowed the tenderness of a naturally affectionate nature on the pitiful waif she had taken away from a brutal master encountered on that long voyage up from the southern coasts.

"What are you trying to tell me, Tina? Get your breath, child."

"A ship!" cried the girl, pointing southward. "I was swimming in a pool that the sea-tide left in the sand, on the other side of the ridge, and I saw it! A ship sailing up out of the south!"

She tugged timidly at Belesa's hand, her slender body all aquiver. and Belesa felt her own heart beat faster at the mere thought of an unknown visitor. They had seen no sail since coming to that barren shore.

Tina flitted ahead of her over the yellow sands, skirting the tiny pools the outgoing tide had left in shallow depressions. They mounted the low undulating ridge, and Tina poised there, a slender white figure against the clearing sky, her wet flaxen hair blowing about her thin face, a frail quivering arm outstretched.

"Look, my Lady!"

Belesa had already seen it—a billowing white sail, filled with the freshening south wind, beating up along the coast, a few miles from the point. Her heart skipped a beat. A small thing can loom large in colorless and isolated lives; but Belesa felt a premonition of strange and violent events. She felt that it was not by chance that this sail was beating up this lonely coast. There was no harbor town to the north, though one sailed to the ultimate shores of ice; and the nearest port to the south was a thousand miles away. What brought this stranger to lonely Korvela Bay?

Tina pressed close to her mistress, apprehension pinching her thin features.

"Who can it be, my Lady?" she stammered, the wind whipping color to her pale cheeks. "Is it the man the Count fears?"

Belesa looked down at her, her brow shadowed.

"Why do you say that, child? How do you know my uncle fears anyone?"

"He must," returned Tina naively, "or he would never have come to hide in this lonely spot. Look, my Lady, how fast it comes!"

"We must go and inform my uncle," murmured Belesa. "The fishing boats have not yet gone out, and none of the men have seen that sail. Get your clothes, Tina. Hurry!"

The child scampered down the low slope to the pool where she had been bathing when she sighted the craft,

and snatched up the slippers, tunic and girdle she had left
lying on the sand. She skipped back up the ridge, hopping
grotesquely as she donned her scanty garments in mid-flight.

Belesa, anxiously watching the approaching sail, caught
her hand, and they hurried toward the fort. A few moments after they had entered the gate of the log palisade
which enclosed the building, the strident blare of a trumpet
startled the workers in the gardens, and the men just
opening the boat-house doors to push the fishing boats
down their rollers to the water's edge.

Every man outside the fort dropped his tool or abandoned whatever he was doing and ran for the stockade
without pausing to look about for the cause of the alarm.
The straggling lines of fleeing men converged on the
opened gate, and every head was twisted over its shoulder
to gaze fearfully at the dark line of woodland to the east.
Not one looked seaward.

They thronged through the gate, shouting questions at
the sentries who patrolled the firing-ledges built below the
up-jutting points of the upright palisade logs.

"What is it? Why are we called in? Are the Picts
coming?"

For answer one taciturn man-at-arms in worn leather and
rusty steel pointed southward. From his vantage-point the
sail was now visible. Men began to climb up on the
ledges, staring toward the sea.

On a small lookout tower on the roof of the manor
house, which was built of logs like the other buildings,
Count Valenso watched the on-sweeping sail as it rounded
the point of the southern horn. The Count was a lean, wiry
man of medium height and late middle age. He was dark,
somber of expression. Trunk-hose and doublet were of
black silk, the only color about his costume the jewels that
twinkled on his sword hilt, and the wine-colored cloak
thrown carelessly over his shoulder. He twisted his thin

black mustache nervously, and turned his gloomy eyes on
his seneschal—a leather-featured man in steel and satin.

"What do you make of it, Galbro?"

"A carack," answered the seneschal. "It is a carack
trimmed and rigged like a craft of the Barachan pirates—
look there!"

A chorus of cries below them echoed his ejaculation; the
ship had cleared the point and was slanting inward across
the bay. And all saw the flag that suddenly broke forth
from the masthead—a black flag, with a scarlet skull
gleaming in the sun.

The people within the stockade stared wildly at that
dread emblem; then all eyes turned up toward the tower,
where the master of the fort stood somberly, his cloak
whipping about him in the wind.

"It's a Barachan, all right," grunted Galbro. "And
unless I am mad, it's Strom's *Red Hand*. What is he doing
on this naked coast?"

"He can mean no good for us," growled the Count. A
glance below showed him that the massive gates had been
closed, and that the captain of his men-at-arms, gleaming
in steel, was directing his men to their stations, some to
the ledges, some to the lower loop-holes. He was massing
his main strength along the western wall, in the midst of
which was the gate.

Valenso had been followed into exile by a hundred men:
soldiers, vassals and serfs. Of these some forty were
men-at-arms, wearing helmets and suits of mail, armed
with swords, axes and crossbows. The rest were toilers,
without armor save for shirts of toughened leather, but
they were brawny stalwarts, and skilled in the use of their
hunting bows, woodsmen's axes, and boar-spears. They
took their places, scowling at their hereditary enemies.
The pirates of the Barachan Isles, a tiny archipelago off

the southwestern coast of Zingara, had preyed on the people of the mainland for more than a century.

The men on the stockade gripped their bows or boar-spears and stared somberly at the carack which swung inshore, its brass work flashing in the sun. They could see the figures swarming on the deck, and hear the lusty yells of the seamen. Steel twinkled along the rail.

The Count had retired from the tower, shooing his niece and her eager protégée before him, and having donned helmet and cuirass, he betook himself to the palisade to direct the defense. His subjects watched him with moody fatalism. They intended to sell their lives as dearly as they could, but they had scant hope of victory, in spite of their strong position. They were oppressed by a conviction of doom. A year on that naked coast, with the brooding threat of that devil-haunted forest looming for ever at their backs, had shadowed their souls with gloomy forebodings. Their women stood silently in the doorways of their huts, built inside the stockade, and quieted the clamor of their children.

Belesa and Tina watched eagerly from an upper window in the manor house, and Belesa felt the child's tense little body all aquiver within the crook of her protecting arm.

"They will cast anchor near the boat-house," murmured Belesa. "Yes! There goes their anchor, a hundred yards off-shore. Do not tremble so, child! They can not take the fort. Perhaps they wish only fresh water and supplies. Perhaps a storm blew them into these seas."

"They are coming ashore in long boats!" exclaimed the child. "Oh, my Lady, I am afraid! They are big men in armor! Look how the sun strikes fire from their pikes and burgonets! Will they eat us?"

Belesa burst into laughter in spite of her apprehension.

"Of course not! Who put that idea into your head?"

"Zingelito told me the Barachans eat women."

"He was teasing you. The Barachans are cruel, but they are no worse than the Zingaran renegades who call themselves buccaneers. Zingelito was a buccaneer once."

"He was cruel," muttered the child. "I'm glad the Picts cut his head off."

"Hush, child." Belesa shuddered slightly. "You must not speak that way. Look, the pirates have reached the shore. They line the beach, and one of them is coming toward the fort. That must be Strom."

"Ahoy, the fort there!" came a hail in a voice gusty as the wind. "I come under a flag of truce!"

The Count's helmeted head appeared over the points of the palisade; his stern face, framed in steel, surveyed the pirate somberly. Strom had halted just within good earshot. He was a big man, bare-headed, his tawny hair blowing in the wind. Of all the sea-rovers who haunted the Barachans, none was more famed for deviltry than he.

"Speak!" commanded Valenso. "I have scant desire to converse with one of your breed."

Strom laughed with his lips, not with his eyes.

"When your galleon escaped me in that squall off the Trallibes last year I never thought to meet you again on the Pictish Coast, Valenso!" said he. "Although at the time I wondered what your destination might be. By Mitra, had I known, I would have followed you then! I got the start of my life a little while ago when I saw your scarlet falcon floating over a fortress where I had thought to see naught but bare beach. You have found it, of course?"

"Found what?" snapped the Count impatiently.

"Don't try to dissemble with me!" The pirate's stormy nature showed itself momentarily in a flash of impatience. "I know why you came here—and I have come for the same reason. I don't intend to be balked. Where is your ship?"

"That is none of your affair."

"You have none," confidently asserted the pirate. "I see pieces of a galleon's masts in that stockade. It must have been wrecked, somehow, after you landed here. If you'd had a ship you'd have sailed away with your plunder long ago."

"What are you talking about, damn you?" yelled the Count. "My plunder? Am I a Barachan to burn and loot? Even so, what would I loot on this naked coast?"

"That which you came to find," answered the pirate coolly. "The same thing I'm after—and mean to have. But I'll be easy to deal with—just give me the loot and I'll go my way and leave you in peace."

"You must be mad," snarled Valenso. "I came here to find solitude and seclusion, which I enjoyed until you crawled out of the sea, you yellow-headed dog. Begone! I did not ask for a parley, and I weary of this empty talk. Take your rogues and go your ways."

"When I go I'll leave that hovel in ashes!" roared the pirate in a transport of rage. "For the last time—will you give me the loot in return for your lives? I have you hemmed in here, and a hundred and fifty men ready to cut your throats at my word."

For answer the Count made a quick gesture with his hand below the points of the palisade. Almost instantly a shaft hummed venomously through a loop-hole and splintered on Strom's breastplate. The pirate yelled ferociously, bounded back and ran toward the beach, with arrows whistling all about him. His men roared and came on like a wave, blades gleaming in the sun.

"Curse you, dog!" raved the Count, felling the offending archer with his iron-clad fist. "Why did you not strike his throat above the gorget? Ready with your bows, men— here they come!"

But Strom had reached his men, checked their headlong rush. The pirates spread out in a long line that overlapped

the extremities of the western wall, and advanced warily,
loosing their shafts as they came. Their weapon was the
longbow, and their archery was superior to that of the
Zingarans. But the latter were protected by their barrier.
The long arrows arched over the stockade and quivered
upright in the earth. One struck the window-sill over which
Belesa watched, wringing a cry of fear from Tina, who
cringed back, her wide eyes fixed on the venomous vibrating shaft.

The Zingarans sent their bolts and hunting arrows in
return, aiming and loosing without undue haste. The women
had herded the children into their huts and now stoically
awaited whatever fate the gods had in store for them.

The Barachans were famed for their furious and headlong style of battling, but they were wary as they were
ferocious, and did not intend to waste their strength
vainly in direct charges against the ramparts. They maintained their wide-spread formation, creeping along and
taking advantage of every natural depression and bit of
vegetation—which was not much, for the ground had been
cleared on all sides of the fort against the threat of Pictish
raids.

A few bodies lay prone on the sandy earth, back-pieces
glinting in the sun, quarrel shafts standing up from arm-pit
or neck. But the pirates were quick as cats, always shifting
their position, and were protected by their light armor.
Their constant raking fire was a continual menace to the
men in the stockade. Still, it was evident that as long as
the battle remained an exchange of archery, the advantage
must remain with the sheltered Zingarans.

But down at the boat-house on the beach, men were at
work with axes. The Count cursed sulphurously when he
saw the havoc they were making among his boats, which
had been built laboriously of planks sawn out of solid logs.

"They're making a mantlet, curse them!" he raged. "A

sally now, before they complete it—while they're scattered—''

Galbro shook his head, glancing at the bare-armed henchmen with their clumsy pikes.

''Their arrows would riddle us, and we'd be no match
for them in hand-to-hand fighting. We must keep behind
our walls and trust to our archers.''

''Well enough,'' growled Valenso. ''If we can keep
them outside our walls.''

Presently the intention of the pirates became apparent to
all, as a group of some thirty men advanced, pushing
before them a great shield made out of the planks from the
boats, and the timbers of the boat-house itself. They had
found an ox-cart, and mounted the mantlet on the wheels,
great solid disks of oak. As they rolled it ponderously
before them it hid them from the sight of the defenders
except for glimpses of their moving feet.

It rolled toward the gate, and the straggling line of
archers converged toward it, shooting as they ran.

''Shoot!'' yelled Valenso, going livid. ''Stop them before they reach the gate!''

A storm of arrows whistled across the palisade, and
feathered themselves harmlessly in the thick wood. A
derisive yell answered the volley. Shafts were finding
loop-holes now, as the rest of the pirates drew nearer, and
a soldier reeled and fell from the ledge, gasping and
choking, with a clothyard shaft through his throat.

''Shoot at their feet!'' screamed Valenso; and then—
''Forty men at the gate with pikes and axes! The rest hold
the wall!''

Bolts ripped into the sand before the moving shield. A
blood-thirsty howl announced that one had found its target
beneath the edge, and a man staggered into view, cursing
and hopping as he strove to withdraw the quarrel that

skewered his foot. In an instant he was feathered by a dozen hunting arrows.

But, with a deep-throated shout, the mantlet was pushed to the wall, and a heavy, iron-tipped boom, thrust through an aperture in the center of the shield, began to thunder on the gate, driven by arms knotted with brawny muscles and backed with blood-thirsty fury. The massive gate groaned and staggered, while from the stockade bolts poured in a steady hail and some struck home. But the wild men of the sea were afire with the fighting-lust.

With deep shouts they swung the ram, and from all sides the others closed in, braving the weakened fire from the walls, and shooting fast and hard.

Cursing like a madman, the Count sprang from the wall and ran to the gate, drawing his sword. A clump of desperate men-at-arms closed in behind him, gripping their spears. In another moment the gate would cave in and they must stop the gap with their living bodies.

Then a new note entered the clamor of the melee. It was a trumpet, blaring stridently from the ship. On the cross-trees a figure waved his arms and gesticulated wildly.

That sound registered on Strom's ears, even as he lent his strength to the swinging ram. Exerting his mighty thews he resisted the surge of the other arms, bracing his legs to halt the ram on its backward swing. He turned his head, sweat dripping from his face.

"Wait!" he roared. "Wait, damn you! *Listen!*"

In the silence that followed that bull's bellow, the blare of the trumpet was plainly heard, and a voice that shouted something unintelligible to the people inside the stockade.

But Strom understood, for his voice was lifted again in profane command. The ram was released, and the mantlet began to recede from the gate as swiftly as it had advanced.

"Look!" cried Tina at her window, jumping up and down in her wild excitement. "They are running! All of them! They are running to the beach! Look! They have abandoned the shield just out of range! They are leaping into the boats and rowing for the ship! Oh, my Lady, have we won?''

"I think not!" Belesa was staring sea-ward. "Look!"

She threw the curtains aside and leaned from the window. Her clear young voice rose above the amazed shouts of the defenders, turned their heads in the direction she pointed. They sent up a deep yell as they saw another ship swinging majestically around the southern point. Even as they looked she broke out the royal golden flag of Zingara.

Strom's pirates were swarming up the sides of their carack, heaving up the anchor. Before the stranger had progressed half-way across the bay, *The Red Hand* was vanishing around the point of the northern horn.

Chapter 3
The Coming of the Black Man

"Out, quick!" snapped the Count, tearing at the bars of the gate. "Destroy that mantlet before these strangers can land!"

"But Strom has fled," expostulated Galbro, "and yonder ship is Zingaran."

"Do as I order!" roared Valenso. "My enemies are not all foreigners! Out, dogs! Thirty of you, with axes, and make kindling wood of that mantlet. Bring the wheels into the stockade."

Thirty axemen raced down toward the beach, brawny men in sleeveless tunics, their axes gleaming in the sun. The manner of their lord had suggested a possibility of peril in that oncoming ship, and there was panic in their haste. The splintering of the timbers under their flying axes came plainly to the people inside the fort, and the axemen were racing back across the sands, trundling the great oaken wheels with them, before the Zingaran ship had dropped anchor where the pirate ship had stood.

"Why does not the Count open the gate and go down to meet them?" wondered Tina. "Is he afraid that the man he fears might be on that ship?"

"What do you mean, Tina?" Belesa demanded uneasily. The Count had never vouchsafed a reason for this self-exile. He was not the sort of a man to run from an enemy, though he had many. But this conviction of Tina's was disquieting; almost uncanny.

Tina seemed not to have heard her question.

"The axemen are back in the stockade," she said. "The gate is closed again and barred. The men still keep their places along the wall. If that ship was chasing Strom, why did it not pursue him? But it is not a war-ship. It is a carack, like the other. Look, a boat is coming ashore. I see a man in the bow, wrapped in a dark cloak."

The boat having grounded, this man came pacing leisurely up the sands, followed by three others. He was a tall, wiry man, clad in black silk and polished steel.

"Halt!" roared the Count. "I will parley with your leader, alone!"

The tall stranger removed his morion and made a sweeping bow. His companions halted, drawing their wide cloaks about them, and behind them the sailors leaned on their oars and stared at the flag floating over the palisade.

When he came within easy call of the gate: "Why, surely," said he, "there should be no suspicion between gentlemen in these naked seas!"

Valenso stared at him suspiciously. The stranger was dark, with a lean, predatory face, and a thin black mustache. A bunch of lace was gathered at his throat, and there was lace on his wrists.

"I know you," said Valenso slowly. "You are Black Zarono, the buccaneer."

Again the stranger bowed with stately elegance.

"And none could fail to recognize the red falcon of the Korzettas!"

"It seems this coast has become the rendezvous of all the rogues of the southern seas," growled Valenso. "What do you wish?"

"Come, come, sir!" remonstrated Zarono. "This is a churlish greeting to one who has just rendered you a service. Was not that Argossean dog, Strom, just thundering at your gate? And did he not take to his sea-heels when he saw me round the point?"

"True," grunted the Count grudgingly. "Though there is little to choose between a pirate and a renegade."

Zarono laughed without resentment and twirled his mustache.

"You are blunt in speech, my Lord. But I desire only leave to anchor in your bay, to let my men hunt for meat and water in your woods, and perhaps, to drink a glass of wine myself at your board."

"I see not how I can stop you," growled Valenso. "But understand this, Zarono: no man of your crew comes within this palisade. If one approaches closer than a hundred feet, he will presently find an arrow through his gizzard. And I charge you do no harm to my gardens or the cattle in the pens. Three steers you may have for fresh meat, but no more. And we can hold this fort against your ruffians, in case you think otherwise."

"You were not holding it very succesfully against Strom," the buccaneer pointed out with a mocking smile.

"You'll find no wood to build mantlets unless you chop down trees, or strip it from your own ship," assured the

Count grimly. "And your men are not Barachan archers; they're no better bowmen than mine. Besides, what little loot you'd find in this castle would not be worth the price."

"Who speaks of loot and warfare?" protested Zarono. "Nay, my men are sick to stretch their legs ashore, and nigh to scurvy from chewing salt pork. I guarantee their good conduct. May they come ashore?"

Valenso grudgingly signified his consent, and Zarono bowed, a thought sardonically, and retired with a tread as measured and stately as if he trod the polished crystal floor of the Kordava royal court, where indeed, unless rumor lied, he had once been a familiar figure.

"Let no man leave the stockade," Valenso ordered Galbro. "I do not trust that renegade dog. Because he drove Strom from our gate is no guarantee that he would not cut our throats."

Galbro nodded. He was well aware of the enmity which existed between the pirates and the Zingaran buccaneers. The pirates were mainly Argossean sailors, turned outlaw; to the ancient feud between Argos and Zingara was added, in the case of the freebooters, the rivalry of opposing interests. Both breeds preyed on the shipping and the coastal towns; and they preyed on one another with equal rapacity.

So no one stirred from the palisade while the buccaneers came ashore, dark-faced men in flaming silk and polished steel, with scarfs bound about their heads and gold hoops in their ears. They camped on the beach, a hundred and seventy-odd of them, and Valenso noticed that Zarono posted lookouts on both points. They did not molest the gardens, and only the three beeves designated by Valenso, shouting from the palisade, were driven forth and slaughtered. Fires were kindled on the strand, and a wattled cask of ale was brought ashore and broached.

Other kegs were filled with water from the spring that
rose a short distance south of the fort, and men began to
straggle toward the woods, crossbows in their hands. Seeing
this, Valenso was moved to shout to Zarono, striding back
and forth through the camp: "Don't let your men go into
the forest. Take another steer from the pens if you haven't
enough meat. If they go trampling into the woods they
may fall foul of the Picts.

"Whole tribes of the painted devils live back in the
forest. We beat off an attack shortly after we landed, and
since then six of my men have been murdered in the
forest, at one time or another. There's peace between us
just now, but it hangs by a thread. Don't risk stirring them
up."

Zarono shot a startled glance at the lowering woods, as
if he expected to see hordes of savage figures lurking
there. Then he bowed and said: "I thank you for the
warning, my Lord." And he shouted for his men to come
back, in a rasping voice that contrasted strangely with his
courtly accents when addressing the Count.

If Zarono could have penetrated the leafy mask he would
have been more apprehensive, if he could have seen the
sinister figure that lurked there, watching the strangers
with inscrutable black eyes—a hideously painted warrior,
naked but for a doe-skin breech-clout, with a toucan feather
drooping over his left ear.

As evening drew on, a thin skim of grey crawled up
from the sea-rim and overcast the sky. The sun sank in a
wallow of crimson, touching the tips of the black waves
with blood. Fog crawled out of the sea and lapped at the
feet of the forest, curling about the stockade in smoky
wisps. The fires on the beach shone dull crimson through
the mist, and the singing of the buccaneers seemed dead-
ened and far away. They had brought old sail-canvas from
the carack and made them shelters along the strand, where

beef was still roasting, and the ale granted them by their captain was doled out sparingly.

The great gate was shut and barred. Soldiers stolidly tramped the ledges of the palisade, pike on shoulder, beads of moisture glistening on their steel caps. They glanced uneasily at the fires on the beach, stared with greater fixity toward the forest, now a vague dark line in the crawling fog. The compound lay empty of life, a bare, darkened space. Candles gleamed feebly through the cracks of the huts, and light streamed from the windows of the manor. There was silence except for the tread of the sentries, the drip of water from the eaves, and the distant singing of the buccaneers.

Some faint echo of this singing penetrated into the great hall where Valenso sat at wine with his unsolicited guest.

"Your men make merry, sir," grunted the Count.

"They are glad to feel the sand under their feet again," answered Zarono. "It has been a wearisome voyage—yes, a long, stern chase." He lifted his goblet gallantly to the unresponsive girl who sat on his host's right, and drank ceremoniously.

Impassive attendants ranged the walls, soldiers with pikes and helmets, servants in satin coats. Valenso's household in this wild land was a shadowy reflection of the court he had kept in Kordava.

The manor house, as he insisted on calling it, was a marvel for that coast. A hundred men had worked night and day for months building it. Its log-walled exterior was devoid of ornamentation, but, within, it was as nearly a copy of Korzetta Castle as was possible. The logs that composed the walls of the hall were hidden with heavy silk tapestries, worked in gold. Ship beams, stained and polished, formed the beams of the lofty ceiling. The floor was covered with rich carpets. The broad stair that led up from

the hall was likewise carpeted, and its massive balustrade
had once been a galleon's rail.

A fire in the wide stone fireplace dispelled the dampness
of the night. Candles in the great silver candelabrum in the
center of the broad mahogany board lit the hall, throwing
long shadows on the stair. Count Valenso sat at the head
of that table, presiding over a company composed of his
niece, his piratical guest, Galbro, and the captain of the
guard. The smallness of the company emphasized the pro-
portions of the vast board, where fifty guests might have
sat at ease.

"You followed Strom?" asked Valenso. "You drove
him this far afield?"

"I followed Strom," laughed Zarono, "but he was not
fleeing from me. Strom is not the man to flee from anyone. No; he came seeking for something; something I too
desire."

"What could tempt a pirate or a buccaneer to this naked
land?" muttered Valenso, staring into the sparkling contents of his goblet.

"What could tempt a count of Kordava?" retorted Zarono,
and an avid light burned an instant in his eyes.

"The rottenness of a royal court might sicken a man of
honor," remarked Valenso.

"Korzettas of honor have endured its rottenness with
tranquillity for several generations," said Zarono bluntly.
"My Lord, indulge my curiosity—why did you sell your
lands, load your galleon with the furnishings of your castle
and sail over the horizon out of the knowledge of the king
and the nobles of Zingara? And why settle here, when
your sword and your name might carve out a place for you
in any civilized land?"

Valenso toyed with the golden seal-chain about his
neck.

"As to why I left Zingara," he said, "that is my own

affair. But it was chance that left me stranded here. I had
brought all my people ashore, and much of the furnishings
you mentioned, intending to build a temporary habitation.
But my ship, anchored out there in the bay, was driven
against the cliffs of the north point and wrecked by a
sudden storm out of the west. Such storms are common
enough at certain times of the year. After that there was
naught to do but remain and make the best of it.''

"Then you would return to civilization, if you could?''

"Not to Kordava. But perhaps to some far clime—to
Vendhya, or Khitai—''

"Do you not find it tedious here, my Lady?'' asked
Zarono, for the first time addressing himself directly to
Belesa.

Hunger to see a new face and hear a new voice had
brought the girl to the great hall that night. But now she
wished she had remained in her chamber with Tina. There
was no mistaking the meaning in the glance Zarono turned
on her. His speech was decorous and formal, his expression sober and respectful; but it was but a mask through
which gleamed the violent and sinister spirit of the man.
He could not keep the burning desire out of his eyes when
he looked at the aristocratic young beauty in her low-
necked satin gown and jeweled girdle.

"There is little diversity here,'' she answered in a low
voice.

"If you had a ship,'' Zarono bluntly asked his host,
"you would abandon this settlement?''

"Perhaps,'' admitted the Count.

"I have a ship,'' said Zarono. "If we could reach an
agreement—''

"What sort of an agreement?'' Valenso lifted his head
to stare suspiciously at his guest.

"Share and share alike,'' said Zarono, laying his hand
on the board with the fingers spread wide. The gesture was

curiously reminiscent of a great spider. But the fingers quivered with curious tension, and the buccaneer's eyes burned with a new light.

"Share what?" Valenso stared at him in evident bewilderment. "The gold I brought with me went down in my ship, and unlike the broken timbers, it did not wash ashore."

"Not that!" Zarono made an impatient gesture. "Let us be frank, my Lord. Can you pretend it was chance which caused you to land at this particular spot, with a thousand miles of coast from which to choose?"

"There is no need for me to pretend," answered Valenso coldly. "My ship's master was one Zingelito, formerly a buccaneer. He had sailed this coast, and persuaded me to land here, telling me he had a reason he would later disclose. But this reason he never divulged, because the day after we landed he disappeared into the woods, and his headless body was found later by a hunting party. Obviously he was ambushed and slain by the Picts."

Zarono stared fixedly at Valenso for a space.

"Sink me," quoth he at last, "I believe you, my Lord. A Korzetta has no skill at lying, regardless of his other accomplishments. And I will make you a proposal. I will admit when I anchored out there in the bay I had other plans in mind. Supposing you to have already secured the treasure, I meant to take this fort by strategy and cut all your throats. But circumstances have caused me to change my mind—" He cast a glance at Belesa that brought the color into her face, and made her lift her head indignantly.

"I have a ship to carry you out of exile," said the buccaneer, "with your household and such of your retainers as you shall choose. The rest can fend for themselves."

The attendants along the walls shot uneasy glances sidelong at each other. Zarono went on, too brutally cynical to conceal his intentions.

"But first you must help me secure the treasure for which I've sailed a thousand miles."

"What treasure, in Mitra's name?" demanded the Count angrily. "You are yammering like that dog Strom, now."

"Did you ever hear of Bloody Tranicos, the greatest of the Barachan pirates?" asked Zarono.

"Who has not? It was he who stormed the island castle of the exiled prince Tothmekri of Stygia, put the people to the sword and bore off the treasure the prince had brought with him when he fled from Khemi."

"Aye! And the tale of that treasure brought the men of the Red Brotherhood swarming like vultures after a carrion—pirates, buccaneers, even the black corsairs from the South. Fearing betrayal by his captains, he fled northward with one ship, and vanished from the knowledge of men. That was nearly a hundred years ago.

"But the tale persists that one man survived that last voyage, and returned to the Barachans, only to be captured by a Zingaran war-ship. Before he was hanged he told his story and drew a map in his own blood, on parchment, which he smuggled somehow out of his captor's reach. This was the tale he told: Tranicos had sailed far beyond the paths of shipping, until he came to a bay on a lonely coast, and there he anchored. He went ashore, taking his treasure and eleven of his most trusted captains who had accompanied him on his ship. Following his orders, the ship sailed away, to return in a week's time, and pick up their admiral and his captains. In the meantime Tranicos meant to hide the treasure somewhere in the vicinity of the bay. The ship returned at the appointed time, but there was no trace of Tranicos and his eleven captains, except the rude dwelling they had built on the beach.

"This had been demolished, and there were tracks of naked feet about it, but no sign to show there had been any fighting. Nor was there any trace of the treasure, or any sign to show where it was hidden. The pirates plunged into the forest to search for their chief and his captains, but were attacked by wild Picts and driven back to their ship. In despair they heaved anchor and sailed away, but before they raised the Barachans, a terrific storm wrecked the ship and only that one man survived.

"That is the tale of the Treasure of Tranicos, which men have sought in vain for nearly a century. That the map exists is known, but its whereabouts have remained a mystery.

"I have had one glimpse of that map. Strom and Zingelito were with me, and a Nemedian who sailed with the Barachans. We looked upon it in a hovel in a certain Zingaran sea-port town, where we were skulking in disguise. Somebody knocked over the lamp, and somebody howled in the dark, and when we got the light on again, the old miser who owned the map was dead with a dirk in his heart, and the map was gone, and the night-watch was clattering down the street with their pikes to investigate the clamor. We scattered, and each went his own way.

"For years thereafter Strom and I watched one another, each supposing the other had the map. Well, as it turned out, neither had it, but recently word came to me that Strom had departed northward, so I followed him. You saw the end of that chase.

"I had but a glimpse at the map as it lay on the old miser's table, and could tell nothing about it. But Strom's actions show that he knows this is the bay where Tranicos anchored. I believe that they hid the treasure somewhere in that forest and returning, were attacked and slain by the Picts. The Picts did not get the treasure. Men have traded up and down this coast a little, knowing nothing of the treasure, and no gold ornament or rare jewel has ever been seen in the possession of the coastal tribes.

"This is my proposal: let us combine our forces. Strom

is somewhere within striking distance. He fled because he feared to be pinned between us, but he will return. But allied, we can laugh at him. We can work out from the fort, leaving enough men here to hold it if he attacks. I believe the treasure is hidden near by. Twelve men could not have conveyed it far. We will find it, load it in my ship, and sail for some foreign port where I can cover my past with gold. I am sick of this life. I want to go back to a civilized land, and live like a noble, with riches, and slaves, and a castle—and a wife of noble blood.''

"Well?" demanded the Count, slit-eyed with suspicion.

"Give me your niece for my wife," demanded the buccaneer bluntly.

Belesa cried out sharply and started to her feet. Valenso likewise rose, livid, his fingers knotting convulsively about his goblet as if he contemplated hurling it at his guest. Zarono did not move; he sat still, one arm on the table and the fingers hooked like talons. His eyes smoldered with passion, and a deep menace.

"You dare!" ejaculated Valenso.

"You seem to forget you have fallen from your high estate, Count Valenso," growled Zarono. "We are not at the Kordavan court, my Lord. On this naked coast nobility is measured by the power of men and arms. And there I rank you. Strangers tread Korzetta Castle, and the Korzetta fortune is at the bottom of the sea. You will die here, an exile, unless I give you the use of my ship.

"You will have no cause to regret the union of our houses. With a new name and a new fortune you will find that Black Zarono can take his place among the aristocrats of the world and make a son-in-law of which not even a Korzetta need be ashamed.''

"You are mad to think of it!" exclaimed the Count violently. "You—who is that?"

A patter of soft-slippered feet distracted his attention.

Tina came hurriedly into the hall, hesitated when she saw the Count's eyes fixed angrily on her, curtsied deeply, and sidled around the table to thrust her small hands into Belesa's fingers. She was panting slightly, her slippers were damp, and her flaxen hair was plastered down on her head.

"Tina!" exclaimed Belesa anxiously. "Where have you been? I thought you were in your chamber, hours ago."

"I was," answered the child breathlessly, "but I missed my coral necklace you gave me—" She held it up, a trivial trinket, but prized beyond all her other possessions because it had been Belesa's first gift to her. "I was afraid you wouldn't let me go if you knew—a soldier's wife helped me out of the stockade and back again—please, my Lady, don't make me tell who she was, because I promised not to. I found my necklace by the pool where I bathed this morning. Please punish me if I have done wrong."

"Tina!" groaned Belesa, clasping the child to her. "I'm not going to punish you. But you should not have gone outside the palisade, with these buccaneers camped on the beach, and always a chance of Picts skulking about. Let me take you to your chamber and change these damp clothes—"

"Yes, my Lady," murmured Tina, "but first let me tell you about the black man—"

"*What?*" The startling interruption was a cry that burst from Valenso's lips. His goblet clattered to the floor as he caught the table with both hands. If a thunderbolt had struck him, the lord of the castle's bearing could not have been more subtly or horrifyingly altered. His face was livid, his eyes almost starting from his head.

"What did you say?" he panted, glaring wildly at the child who shrank back against Belesa in bewilderment. "What did you say, wench?"

"A black man, my Lord," she stammered, while Belesa, Zarono and the attendants stared at him in amazement. "When I went down to the pool to get my necklace, I saw him. There was a strange moaning in the wind, and the sea whimpered like a thing in fear, and then he came. I was afraid, and hid behind a little ridge of sand. He came from the sea in a strange black boat with blue fire playing all about it, but there was no torch. He drew his boat up on the sands below the south point, and strode toward the forest, looking like a giant in the fog—a great, tall man, black like a Kushite—"

Valenso reeled as if he had received a mortal blow. He clutched at his throat, snapping the golden chain in his violence. With the face of a madman he lurched about the table and tore the child screaming from Belesa's arms.

"You little slut," he panted. "You lie! You have heard me mumbling in my sleep and have told this lie to torment me! Say that you lie before I tear the skin from your back!"

"Uncle!" cried Belesa, in outraged bewilderment, trying to free Tina from his grasp. "Are you mad? What are you about?"

With a snarl he tore her hand from his arm and spun her staggering into the arms of Galbro who received her with a leer he made little effort to disguise.

"Mercy, my Lord!" sobbed Tina. "I did not lie!"

"I said you lied!" roared Valenso. "Gebbrelo!"

The stolid serving man seized the trembling youngster and stripped her with one brutal wrench that tore her scanty garments from her body. Wheeling, he drew her slender arms over his shoulders, lifting her writhing feet clear of the floor.

"Uncle!" shrieked Belesa, writhing vainly in Galbro's lustful grasp. "You are mad! You can not—oh, you can not—!" The voice choked in her throat as Valenso caught

up a jewel-hilted riding whip and brought it down across
the child's frail body with a savage force that left a red
weal across her naked shoulders.

Belesa moaned, sick with the anguish in Tina's shriek.
The world had suddenly gone mad. As in a nightmare she
saw the stolid faces of the soldiers and servants, beast-
faces, the faces of oxen, reflecting neither pity nor sympathy. Zarono's faintly sneering face was part of the nightmare.
Nothing in that crimson haze was real except Tina's naked
white body, criss-crossed with red welts from shoulders to
knees; no sound real except the child's sharp cries of
agony, and the panting gasps of Valenso as he lashed away
with the staring eyes of a madman, shrieking: "You lie!
You lie! Curse you, you lie! Admit your guilt, or I will
flay your stubborn body! *He* could not have followed me
here—"

"Oh, have mercy, my Lord!" screamed the child, writhing vainly on the brawny servant's back, too frantic with
fear and pain to have the wit to save herself by a lie. Blood
trickled in crimson beads down her quivering thighs. "I
saw him! I do not lie! Mercy! Please! Ahhhh!"

"You fool! *You fool!*" screamed Belesa, almost beside
herself. "Do you not see she is telling the truth? Oh, you
beast! Beast! Beast!"

Suddenly some shred of sanity seemed to return to the
brain of Count Valenso Korzetta. Dropping the whip he
reeled back and fell up against the table, clutching blindly
at its edge. He shook as with an ague. His hair was
plastered across his brow in dank strands, and sweat dripped
from his livid countenance which was like a carven mask
of Fear. Tina, released by Gebbrelo, slipped to the floor in
a whimpering heap. Belesa tore free from Galbro, rushed
to her, sobbing, and fell on her knees, gathering the pitiful
waif into her arms. She lifted a terrible face to her uncle,
to pour upon him the full vials of her wrath—but he was

not looking at her. He seemed to have forgotten both her and his victim. In a daze of incredulity, she heard him say to the buccaneer: "I accept your offer, Zarono; in Mitra's name, let us find this accursed treasure and begone from this damned coast!"

At this the fire of her fury sank to sick ashes. In stunned silence she lifted the sobbing child in her arms and carried her up the stair. A glance backward showed Valenso crouching rather than sitting at the table, gulping wine from a huge goblet he gripped in both shaking hands, while Zarono towered over him like a somber predatory bird—puzzled at the turn of events, but quick to take advantage of the shocking change that had come over the Count. He was talking in a low, decisive voice, and Valenso nodded mute agreement, like one who scarcely heeds what is being said. Galbro stood back in the shadows, chin pinched between forefinger and thumb, and the attendants along the walls glanced furtively at each other, bewildered by their lord's collapse.

Up in her chamber Belesa laid the half-fainting girl on the bed and set herself to wash and apply soothing ointments to the weals and cuts on her tender skin. Tina gave herself up in complete submission to her mistress's hands, moaning faintly. Belesa felt as if her world had fallen about her ears. She was sick and bewildered, overwrought, her nerves quivering from the brutal shock of what she had witnessed. Fear of and hatred for her uncle grew in her soul. She had never loved him; he was harsh and apparently without natural affection, grasping and avid. But she had considered him just, and fearless. Revulsion shook her at the memory of his staring eyes and bloodless face. It was some terrible fear which had roused this frenzy; and because of this fear Valenso had brutalized the only creature she had to love and cherish; because of that fear he was selling her, his niece, to an infamous outlaw. What

was behind this madness? Who was the black man Tina
had seen?

The child muttered in semi-delirium.

"I did not lie, my Lady! Indeed I did not! It was a black
man, in a black boat that burned like blue fire on the
water! A tall man, black as a negro, and wrapped in a
black cloak! I was afraid when I saw him, and my blood
ran cold. He left his boat on the sands and went into the
forest. Why did the Count whip me for seeing him?"

"Hush, Tina," soothed Belesa. "Lie quiet. The smarting
will soon pass."

The door opened behind her and she whirled, snatching
up a jeweled dagger. The Count stood in the door, and her
flesh crawled at the sight. He looked years older; his face
was grey and drawn, and his eyes stared in a way that
roused fear in her bosom. She had never been close to
him; now she felt as though a gulf separated them. He was
not her uncle who stood there, but a stranger come to
menace her.

She lifted the dagger.

"If you touch her again," she whispered from dry lips,
"I swear before Mitra I will sink this blade in your breast."

He did not heed her.

"I have posted a strong guard about the manor," he
said. "Zarono brings his men into the stockade tomorrow.
He will not sail until he has found the treasure. When he
finds it we shall sail at once for some port not yet decided
upon."

"And you will sell me to him?" she whispered. "In
Mitra's name—"

He fixed upon her a gloomy gaze in which all considerations but his own self-interest had been crowded out. She
shrank before it, seeing in it the frantic cruelty that possessed the man in his mysterious fear.

"You will do as I command," he said presently, with

no more human feeling in his voice than there is in the ring of flint on steel. And turning, he left the chamber. Blinded by a sudden rush of horror, Belesa fell fainting beside the couch where Tina lay.

Chapter 4
A Black Drum Droning

Belesa never knew how long she lay crushed and senseless. She was first aware of Tina's arms about her and the sobbing of the child in her ear. Mechanically she straightened herself and drew the girl into her arms; and she sat there, dry-eyed, staring unseeingly at the flickering candle. There was no sound in the castle. The singing of the buccaneers on the strand had ceased. Dully, almost impersonally she reviewed her problem.

Valenso was mad, driven frantic by the story of the mysterious black man. It was to escape this stranger that he wished to abandon the settlement and flee with Zarono. That much was obvious. Equally obvious was the fact that he was ready to sacrifice her in exchange for that opportunity to escape. In the blackness of spirit which surrounded her she saw no glint of light. The serving men were dull or callous brutes, their women stupid and apathetic. They would neither dare nor care to help her. She was utterly helpless.

Tina lifted her tear-stained face as if she were listening to the prompting of some inner voice. The child's understanding of Belesa's inmost thoughts was almost uncanny, as was her recognition of the inexorable drive of Fate and the only alternative left to the weak.

"We must go, my Lady!" she whispered. "Zarono

shall not have you. Let us go far away into the forest. We shall go until we can go no further, and then we shall lie down and die together."

The tragic strength that is the last refuge of the weak entered Belesa's soul. It was the only escape from the shadows that had been closing in upon her since that day when they fled from Zingara.

"We shall go, child."

She rose and was fumbling for a cloak, when an exclamation from Tina brought her about. The girl was on her feet, a finger pressed to her lips, her eyes wide and bright with terror.

"What is it, Tina?" The child's expression of fright induced Belesa to pitch her voice to a whisper, and a nameless apprehension crawled over her.

"Someone outside in the hall," whispered Tina, clutching her arm convulsively. "He stopped at our door, and then went on, toward the Count's chamber at the other end."

"Your ears are keener than mine," murmured Belesa. "But there is nothing strange in that. It was the Count himself, perchance, or Galbro." She moved to open the door, but Tina threw her arms frantically about her neck, and Belesa felt the wild beating of her heart.

"No, no, my Lady! Do not open the door! I am afraid! I do not know why, but I feel that some evil thing is skulking near us!"

Impressed, Belesa patted her reassuringly, and reached a hand toward the gold disk that masked the tiny peep-hole in the center of the door.

"He is coming back!" shivered the girl. "I hear him!"

Belesa heard something too—a curious stealthy pad which she knew, with a chill of nameless fear, was not the step of anyone she knew. Nor was it the step of Zarono, or any booted man. Could it be the buccaneer gliding along the hallway on bare, stealthy feet, to slay his host while he slept? She remembered the soldiers who would be on guard below. If the buccaneer had remained in the manor for the night, a man-at-arms would be posted before his chamber door. But who was that sneaking along the corridor? None slept upstairs besides herself, Tina and the Count, except Galbro.

With a quick motion she extinguished the candle so it would not shine through the hole in the door, and pushed aside the gold disk. All the lights were out in the hall, which was ordinarily lighted by candles. Someone was moving along the darkened corridor. She sensed rather than saw a dim bulk moving past her doorway, but she could make nothing of its shape except that it was manlike. But a chill wave of terror swept over her; so she crouched dumb, incapable of the scream that froze behind her lips. It was not such terror as her uncle now inspired in her, or fear like her fear of Zarono, or even of the brooding forest. It was blind unreasoning terror that laid an icy hand on her soul and froze her tongue to her palate.

The figure passed on to the stairhead, where it was limned momentarily against the faint glow that came up from below, and at the glimpse of that vague black image against the red, she almost fainted.

She crouched there in the darkness, awaiting the outcry that would announce that the soldiers in the great hall had seen the intruder. But the manor remained silent; somewhere a wind wailed shrilly. That was all.

Belesa's hands were moist with perspiration as she groped to relight the candle. She was still shaken with horror, though she could not decide just what there had been about that black figure etched against the red glow that had roused this frantic loathing in her soul. It was manlike in shape, but the outline was strangely alien—abnormal— though she could not clearly define that abnormality. But she knew that it was no human being that she had seen, and she knew that the sight had robbed her of all her new-found resolution. She was demoralized, incapable of action.

The candle flared up, limning Tina's white face in the yellow glow.

"It was the black man!" whispered Tina. "I know! My blood turned cold, just as it did when I saw him on the beach. There are soldiers downstairs; why did they not see him? Shall we go and inform the Count?"

Belesa shook her head. She did not care to repeat the scene that had ensued upon Tina's first mention of the black man. At any event, she dared not venture out into that darkened hallway.

"We dare not go into the forest!" shuddered Tina. "He will be lurking there—"

Belesa did not ask the girl how she knew the black man would be in the forest; it was the logical hiding-place for any evil thing, man or devil. And she knew Tina was right; they dared not leave the fort now. Her determination, which had not faltered at the prospect of certain death, gave way at the thought of traversing those gloomy woods with that black shambling creature at large among them. Helplessly she sat down and sank her face in her hands.

Tina slept, presently, on the couch, whimpering occasionally in her sleep. Tears sparkled on her long lashes. She moved her smarting body uneasily in her restless slumber. Toward dawn Belesa was aware of a stifling quality in the atmosphere. She heard a low rumble of thunder somewhere off to sea-ward. Extinguishing the candle, which had burned to its socket, she went to a window whence she could see both the ocean and a belt of the forest behind the fort.

The fog had disappeared, but out to sea a dusky mass

was rising from the horizon. From it lightning flickered and the low thunder growled. An answering rumble came from the black woods. Startled, she turned and stared at the forest, a brooding black rampart. A strange rhythmic pulsing came to her ears—a droning reverberation that was not the roll of a Pictish drum.

"The drum!" sobbed Tina, spasmodically opening and closing her fingers in her sleep. "The black man—beating on a black drum—in the black woods! Oh, save us—!"

Belesa shuddered. Along the eastern horizon ran a thin white line that presaged dawn. But that black cloud on the western rim writhed and billowed, swelling and expanding. She stared in amazement, for storms were practically unknown on that coast at that time of the year, and she had never seen a cloud like that one.

It came pouring up over the world-rim in great boiling masses of blackness, veined with fire. It rolled and billowed with the wind in its belly. Its thundering made the air vibrate. And another sound mingled awesomely with the reverberations of the thunder—the voice of the wind, that raced before its coming. The inky horizon was torn and convulsed in the lightning flashes; afar to sea she saw the white-capped waves racing before the wind. She heard its droning roar, increasing in volume as it swept shoreward. But as yet no wind stirred on the land. The air was hot, breathless. There was a sensation of unreality about the contrast: out there wind and thunder and chaos sweeping inland; but here stifling stillness. Somewhere below her a shutter slammed, startling in the tense silence, and a woman's voice was lifted, shrill with alarm. But most of the people of the fort seemed sleeping, unaware of the on-coming hurricane.

She realized that she still heard that mysterious droning drum-beat and she stared toward the black forest, her flesh crawling. She could see nothing, but some obscure instinct or intuition prompted her to visualize a black hideous figure squatting under black branches and enacting a nameless incantation on something that sounded like a drum—

Desperately she shook off the ghoulish conviction, and looked sea-ward, as a blaze of lightning fairly split the sky. Outlined against its glare she saw the masts of Zarono's ship; she saw the tents of the buccaneers on the beach, the sandy ridges of the south point and the rock cliffs of the north point as plainly as by midday sun. Louder and louder rose the roar of the wind, and now the manor was awake. Feet came pounding up the stair, and Zarono's voice yelled, edged with fright.

Doors slammed and Valenso answered him, shouting to be heard above the roar of the elements.

"Why didn't you warn me of a storm from the west?" howled the buccaneer. "If the anchors don't hold—"

"A storm never came from the west before, at this time of year!" shrieked Valenso, rushing from his chamber in his night-shirt, his face livid and his hair standing stiffly on end. "This is the work of—" His words were drowned as he raced madly up the ladder that led to the lookout tower, followed by the swearing buccaneer.

Belesa crouched at her window, awed and deafened. Louder and louder rose the wind, until it drowned all other sound—all except that maddening droning that now rose like an inhuman chant of triumph. It roared inshore, driving before it a foaming league-long crest of white—and then all hell and destruction was loosed on that coast. Rain fell in driving torrents, sweeping the beaches with blind frenzy. The wind hit like a thunder-clap, making the timbers of the fort quiver. The surf roared over the sands, drowning the coals of the fires the seamen had built. In the glare of lightning Belesa saw, through the curtain of the slashing rain, the tents of the buccaneers whipped to ribbons and washed away, saw the men themselves staggering toward the fort, beaten almost to the sands by the fury of torrent and blast.

And limned against the blue glare she saw Zarono's ship, ripped loose from her moorings, driven headlong against the jagged cliffs that jutted up to receive her . . .

Chapter 5
A Man From the Wilderness

The storm had spent its fury. Full dawn rose in a clear blue rain-washed sky. As the sun rose in a blaze of fresh gold, bright-hued birds lifted a swelling chorus from the trees on whose broad leaves beads of water sparkled like diamonds, quivering in the gentle morning breeze.

At a small stream which wound over the sands to join the sea, hidden beyond a fringe of trees and bushes, a man bent to lave his hands and face. He performed his ablutions after the manner of his race, grunting lustily and splashing like a buffalo. But in the midst of these splashings he lifted his head suddenly, his tawny hair dripping and water running in rivulets over his brawny shoulders. He crouched in a listening attitude for a split second, then was on his feet and facing inland, sword in hand, all in one motion. And there he froze, glaring wide-mouthed.

A man as big as himself was striding toward him over the sands, making no attempt at stealth; and the pirate's eyes widened as he stared at the close-fitting silk breeches, high flaring-topped boots, wide-skirted coat and head-gear of a hundred years ago. There was a broad cutlass in the stranger's hand and unmistakable purpose in his approach.

The pirate went pale, as recognition blazed in his eyes.

"You!" he ejaculated unbelievingly. "By Mitra! *You!*"

Oaths streamed from his lips as he heaved up his cutlass. The birds rose in flaming showers from the trees as
the clang of steel interrupted their song. Blue sparks flew
from the hacking blades, and the sand grated and ground
under the stamping boot heels. Then the clash of steel
ended in a chopping crunch, and one man went to his
knees with a choking gasp. The hilt escaped his nerveless
hand and he slid full-length on the sand which reddened
with his blood. With a dying effort he fumbled at his
girdle and drew something from it, tried to lift it to his
mouth, and then stiffened convulsively and went limp.

The conqueror bent and ruthlessly tore the stiffening
fingers from the object they crumpled in their desperate
grasp.

Zarono and Valenso stood on the beach, staring at the
driftwood their men were gathering—spars, pieces of
masts, broken timbers. So savagely had the storm ham-
mered Zarono's ship against the low cliffs that most of the
salvage was match-wood. A short distance behind them
stood Belesa, listening to their conversation, one arm about
Tina. The girl was pale and listless, apathetic to whatever
Fate held in store for her. She heard what the men said,
but with little interest. She was crushed by the realization
that she was but a pawn in the game, however it was to be
played out—whether it was to be a wretched life dragged
out on that desolate coast, or a return, effected somehow,
to some civilized land.

Zarona cursed venomously, but Valenso seemed dazed.

"This is not the time of year for storms from the west,"
he muttered, staring with haggard eyes at the men dragging the wreckage up on the beach. "It was not chance
that brought that storm out of the deep to splinter the ship
in which I meant to escape. Escape? I am caught like a

rat in a trap, as it was meant. Nay, we are all trapped rats—''

"I don't know what you're talking about," snarled Zarono, giving a vicious yank at his mustache. "I've been unable to get any sense out of you since that flaxen-haired slut upset you so last night with her wild tale of black men coming out of the sea. But I do know that I'm not going to spend my life on this cursed coast. Ten of my men went to hell in the ship, but I've got a hundred and sixty more. You've got a hundred. There are tools in your fort, and plenty of trees in yonder forest. We'll build a ship. I'll set men to cutting down trees as soon as they get this drift dragged up out of the reach of the waves.''

"It will take months," muttered Valenso.

"Well, is there any better way in which we could employ our time? We're here—and unless we build a ship we'll never get away. We'll have to rig up some kind of a sawmill, but I've never encountered anything yet that balked me long. I hope that storm smashed Strom to bits—the Argossean dog! While we're building the ship we'll hunt for old Tranicos's loot.''

"We will never complete your ship," said Valenso somberly.

"You fear the Picts? We have enough men to defy them.''

"I do not speak of the Picts. I speak of a black man.''

Zarona turned on him angrily. "Will you talk sense? *Who* is this accursed black man?''

"Accursed indeed," said Valenso, staring sea-ward. "A shadow of mine own red-stained past risen up to hound me to hell. Because of him I fled Zingara, hoping to lose my trail in the great ocean. But I should have known he would smell me out at last.''

"If such a man came ashore he must be hiding in the

woods," growled Zarono. "We'll rake the forest and hunt him out."

Valenso laughed harshly.

"Seek for a shadow that drifts before a cloud that hides the moon; grope in the dark for a cobra; follow a mist that steals out of the swamp at midnight."

Zarono cast him an uncertain look, obviously doubting his sanity.

"Who is this man? Have done with ambiguity."

"The shadow of my own mad cruelty and ambition; a horror come out of the lost ages; no man of mortal flesh and blood, but a—"

"Sail ho!" bawled the lookout on the north point.

Zarono wheeled and his voice slashed the wind.

"Do you know her?"

"Aye!" the reply came back faintly. "It's *The Red Hand*!"

Zarono cursed like a wild man.

"Strom! The devil takes care of his own! How could he ride out that blow?" The buccaneer's voice rose to a yell that carried up and down the strand. "Back to the fort, you dogs!"

Before *The Red Hand*, somewhat battered in appearance, nosed around the point, the beach was bare of human life, the palisade bristling with helmets and scarf-bound heads. The buccaneers accepted the alliance with the easy adaptability of adventurers, the henchmen with the apathy of serfs.

Zarono ground his teeth as a longboat swung leisurely in to the beach, and he sighted the tawny head of his rival in the bow. The boat grounded, and Strom strode toward the fort alone.

Some distance away he halted and shouted in a bull's bellow that carried clearly in the still morning. "Ahoy, the fort! I want to parley!"

"Well, why in hell don't you?" snarled Zarono.

"The last time I approached under a flag of truce an arrow broke on my brisket!" roared the pirate. "I want a promise it won't happen again!"

"You have my promise!" called Zarono sardonically.

"Damn your promise, you Zingaran dog! I want Valenso's word."

A measure of dignity remained to the Count. There was an edge of authority to his voice as he answered: "Advance, but keep your men back. You will not be fired upon."

"That's enough for me," said Strom instantly. "Whatever a Korzetta's sins, once his word is given, you can trust him."

He strode forward and halted under the gate, laughing at the hate-darkened visage Zarono thrust over at him.

"Well, Zarono," he taunted, "you are a ship shorter than you were when last I saw you! But you Zingarans never were sailors."

"How did you save your ship, you Messantian gutter-scum?" snarled the buccaneer.

"There's a cove some miles to the north protected by a high-ridged arm of land that broke the force of the gale," answered Strom. "I was anchored behind it. My anchors dragged, but they held me off the shore."

Zarono scowled blackly. Valenso said nothing. He had not known of that cove. He had done scant exploring of his domain. Fear of the Picts and lack of curiosity had kept him and his men near the fort. The Zingarans were by nature neither explorers nor colonists.

"I come to make a trade," said Strom, easily.

"We've naught to trade with you save sword-strokes," growled Zarono.

"I think otherwise," grinned Strom, thin-lipped. "You tipped your hand when you murdered Galacus, my first

mate, and robbed him. Until this morning I supposed that
Valenso had Tranicos's treasure. But if either of you had
it, you wouldn't have gone to the trouble of following me
and killing my mate to get the map.''

"The map?'' Zarono ejaculated, stiffening.

"Oh, don't dissemble!'' laughed Strom, but anger blazed
blue in his eyes. "I know you have it. Picts don't wear
boots!''

"But—'' began the Count, nonplussed, but fell silent
as Zarono nudged him.

"And if we have the map,'' said Zarono, "what have
you to trade that we might require?''

"Let me come into the fort,'' suggested Strom. "There
we can talk.''

He was not so obvious as to glance at the men peering at
them from along the wall, but his two listeners understood.
And so did the men. Strom had a ship. That fact would
figure in any bargaining, or battle. But it would carry just
so many, regardless of who commanded; whoever sailed
away in it, there would be some left behind. A wave of
tense speculation ran along the silent throng at the palisade.

"Your men will stay where they are,'' warned Zarono,
indicating both the boat drawn up on the beach, and the
ship anchored out in the bay.

"Aye. But don't get the idea that you can seize me and
hold me for a hostage!'' He laughed grimly. "I want
Valenso's word that I'll be allowed to leave the fort alive
and unhurt within the hour, whether we come to terms or
not.''

"You have my pledge,'' answered the Count.

"All right, then. Open that gate and let's talk plainly.''

The gate opened and closed, the leaders vanished from
sight, and the common men of both parties resumed their
silent surveillance of each other: the men on the palisade,
and the men squatting beside their boat, with a broad

stretch of sand between; and beyond a strip of blue water, the carack, with steel caps glinting all along her rail.

On the broad stair, above the great hall, Belesa and Tina crouched, ignored by the men below. These sat about the broad table: Valenso, Galbro, Zarono and Strom. But for them the hall was empty.

Strom gulped wine and set the empty goblet on the table. The frankness suggested by his bluff countenance was belied by the dancing lights of cruelty and treachery in his wide eyes. But he spoke bluntly enough.

"We all want the treasure old Tranicos hid somewhere near this bay," he said abruptly. "Each has something the others need. Valenso has laborers, supplies, and a stockade to shelter us from the Picts. You, Zarono, have my map. I have a ship."

"What I'd like to know," remarked Zarono, "is this: if you've had that map all these years, why haven't you come after the loot sooner?"

"I didn't have it. It was that dog, Zingelito, who knifed the old miser in the dark and stole the map. But he had neither ship nor crew, and it took him more than a year to get them. When he did come after the treasure, the Picts prevented his landing, and his men mutinied and made him sail back to Zingara. One of them stole the map from him, and recently sold it to me."

"That was why Zingelito recognized the bay," muttered Valenso.

"Did that dog lead you here, Count? I might have guessed it. Where is he?"

"Doubtless in hell, since he was once a buccaneer. The Picts slew him, evidently while he was searching in the woods for the treasure."

"Good!" approved Strom heartily. "Well, I don't know how you knew my mate was carrying the map. I trusted him, and the men trusted him more than they did me, so I

let him keep it. But this morning he wandered inland with
some of the others, got separated from them, and we found
him sworded to death near the beach, and the map gone. The
men were ready to accuse me of killing him, but I showed the
fools the tracks left by his slayer, and proved to them that
my feet wouldn't fit them. And I knew it wasn't any one
of the crew, because none of them wear boots that make
that sort of track. And Picts don't wear boots at all. So it
had to be a Zingaran.

"Well, you've got the map, but you haven't got the
treasure. If you had it, you wouldn't have let me inside the
stockade. I've got you penned up in this fort. You can't
get out to look for the loot, and even if you did get it, you
have no ship to get away in.

"Now here's my proposal: Zarono, give me the map.
And you, Valenso, give me fresh meat and other supplies. My men are nigh to scurvy after the long voyage. In
return I'll take you three men, the Lady Belesa and her
girl, and set you ashore within reach of some Zingaran
port—or I'll put Zarono ashore near some buccaneer rendezvous if he prefers, since doubtless a noose awaits him
in Zingara. And to clinch the bargain I'll give each of you
a handsome share in the treasure."

The buccaneer tugged his mustache meditatively. He
knew that Strom would not keep any such pact, if made.
Nor did Zarono even consider agreeing to his proposal.
But to refuse bluntly would be to force the issue into a
clash of arms. He sought his agile brain for a plan to
outwit the pirate. He wanted Strom's ship as avidly as he
desired the lost treasure.

"What's to prevent us from holding you captive and
forcing your men to give us your ship in exchange for
you?" he asked.

Strom laughed at him.

"Do you think I'm a fool? My men have orders to

heave up the anchors and sail hence if I don't reappear within the hour, or if they suspect treachery. They wouldn't give you the ship, if you skinned me alive on the beach. Besides, I have the Count's word."

"My pledge is not straw," said Valenso somberly. "Have done with threats, Zarono."

Zarono did not reply, his mind wholly absorbed in the problem of getting possession of Strom's ship; of continuing the parley without betraying the fact that he did not have the map. He wondered who in Mitra's name *did* have the accursed map.

"Let me take my men away with me on your ship when we sail," he said. "I can not desert my faithful followers—"

Strom snorted.

"Why don't you ask for my cutlass to slit my gullet with? Desert your faithful—bah! You'd desert your brother to the devil if you could gain anything by it. No! You're not going to bring enough men aboard to give you a chance to mutiny and take my ship."

"Give us a day to think it over," urged Zarono, fighting for time.

Strom's heavy fist banged on the table, making the wine dance in the glasses.

"No, by Mitra! Give me my answer now!"

Zarono was on his feet, his black rage submerging his craftiness.

"You Barachan dog! I'll give you your answer—in your guts—"

He tore aside his cloak, caught at his sword-hilt. Strom heaved up with a roar, his chair crashing backward to the floor. Valenso sprang up, spreading his arms between them as they faced one another across the board, jutting jaws close together, blades half drawn, faces convulsed.

"Gentlemen, have done! Zarono, he has my pledge—"

"The foul fiends gnaw your pledge!" snarled Zarono.

"Stand from between us, my Lord," growled the pirate, his voice thick with the killing lust. "Your word was that I should not be treacherously entreated. It shall be considered no violation of your pledge for this dog and me to cross swords in equal play."

"Well spoken, Strom!" It was a deep, powerful voice behind them, vibrant with grim amusement. All wheeled and glared, open-mouthed. Up on the stair Belesa started up with an involuntary exclamation.

A man strode out from the hangings that masked a chamber door, and advanced toward the table without haste or hesitation. Instantly he dominated the group, and all felt the situation subtly charged with a new, dynamic atmosphere.

The stranger was as tall as either of the freebooters, and more powerfully built than either, yet for all his size he moved with pantherish suppleness in his high, flaring-topped boots. His thighs were cased in close-fitting breeches of white silk, his wide-skirted sky-blue coat open to reveal an open-necked white silken shirt beneath, and the scarlet sash that girdled his waist. There were silver acorn-shaped buttons on the coat, and it was adorned with gilt-worked cuffs and pocket-flaps, and a satin collar. A lacquered hat completed a costume obsolete by nearly a hundred years. A heavy cutlass hung at the wearer's hip.

"Conan!" ejaculated both freebooters together, and Valenso and Galbro caught their breath at that name.

"Who else?" The giant strode up to the table, laughing sardonically at their amazement.

"What—what do you here?" stuttered the seneschal. "How come you here, uninvited and unannounced?"

"I climbed the palisade on the east side while you fools were arguing at the gate," Conan answered. "Every man in the fort was craning his neck westward. I entered the manor while Strom was being let in at the gate. I've been in that chamber there ever since, eavesdropping.''

''I thought you were dead,'' said Zarono slowly. ''Three years ago the shattered hull of your ship was sighted off a reefy coast, and you were heard of on the Main no more.''

''I didn't drown with my crew,'' answered Conan. ''It'll take a bigger ocean than that one to drown me.''

Up on the stair Tina was clutching Belesa in her excitement and staring through the balustrades with all her eyes.

''Conan! My Lady, it is Conan! Look! Oh, look!''

Belesa was looking; it was like encountering a legendary character in the flesh. Who of all the sea-folk had not heard the wild, bloody tales told of Conan, the wild rover who had once been a captain of the Barachan pirates, and one of the greatest scourges of the sea? A score of ballads celebrated his ferocious and audacious exploits. The man could not be ignored; irresistibly he had stalked into the scene, to form another, dominant element in the tangled plot. And in the midst of her frightened fascination, Belesa's feminine instinct prompted the speculation as to Conan's attitude toward her—would it be like Strom's brutal indifference, or Zarono's violent desire?

Valenso was recovering from the shock of finding a stranger within his very hall. He knew Conan was a Cimmerian, born and bred in the wastes of the far north, and therefore not amenable to the physical limitations which controlled civilized men. It was not so strange that he had been able to enter the fort undetected, but Valenso flinched at the reflection that other barbarians might duplicate that feat—the dark, silent Picts, for instance.

''What do you want here?'' he demanded. ''Did you come from the sea?''

''I came from the woods.'' The Cimmerian jerked his head toward the east.

"You have been living with the Picts?" Valenso asked coldly.

A momentary anger flickered bluely in the giant's eyes.

"Even a Zingaran ought to know there's never been peace between Picts and Cimmerians, and never will be," he retorted with an oath. "Our feud with them is older than the world. If you'd said that to one of my wilder brothers, you'd have found yourself with a split head. But I've lived among you civilized men long enough to understand your ignorance and lack of common courtesy—the churlishness that demands his business of a man who appears at your door out of a thousand-mile wilderness. Never mind that." He turned to the two freebooters who stood staring glumly at him.

"From what I overhead," quoth he, "I gather there is some dissension over a map!"

"That is none of your affair," growled Strom.

"Is this it?" Conan grinned wickedly and drew from his pocket a crumpled object—a square of parchment, marked with crimson lines.

Strom stared violently, paling.

"My map!" he ejaculated. "Where did you get it?"

"From your mate, Galacus, when I killed him," answered Conan with grim enjoyment.

"You dog!" raved Strom, turning on Zarono. "You never had the map! You lied—"

"I didn't say I had it," snarled Zarono. "You deceived yourself. Don't be a fool. Conan is alone. If he had a crew he'd have already cut our throats. We'll take the map from him—"

"You'll never touch it!" Conan laughed fiercely.

Both men sprang at him, cursing. Stepping back he crumpled the parchment and cast it into the glowing coals of the fireplace. With an incoherent bellow Strom lunged past him, to be met with a buffet under the ear that stretched him half-senseless on the floor. Zarono whipped out his sword but before he could thrust, Conan's cutlass beat it out of his hand.

Zarono staggered against the table, with all hell in his eyes. Strom dragged himself erect, his eyes glazed, blood dripping from his bruised ear. Conan leaned slightly over the table, his outstretched cutlass just touched the breast of Count Valenso.

"Don't call for your soldiers, Count," said the Cimmerian softly. "Not a sound out of you—or from you, either, dog-face!" His name for Galbro, who showed no intention of braving his wrath. "The map's burned to ashes, and it'll do no good to spill blood. Sit down, all of you."

Strom hesitated, made an abortive gesture toward his hilt, then shrugged his shoulders and sank sullenly into a chair. The others followed suit. Conan remained standing, towering over the table, while his enemies watched him with bitter eyes of hate.

"You were bargaining," he said. "That's all I've come to do."

"And what have you to trade?" sneered Zarono.

"The treasure of Tranicos!"

"What?" All four men were on their feet, leaning toward him.

"Sit down!" he roared, banging his broad blade on the table. They sank back, tense and white with excitement.

He grinned in huge enjoyment of the sensation his words had caused.

"Yes! I found it before I got the map. That's why I burned the map. I don't need it. And now nobody will ever find it, unless I show him where it is."

They stared at him with murder in their eyes.

"You're lying," said Zarono without conviction. "You've told us one lie already. You said you came from the woods, yet you say you haven't been living with the Picts.

All men know this country is a wilderness, inhabited only by savages. The nearest outposts of civilization are the Aquilonian settlements on Thunder River, hundreds of miles to eastward.''

"That's where I came from," replied Conan imperturbably. "I believe I'm the first white man to cross the Pictish Wilderness. I crossed Thunder River to follow a raiding party that had been harrying the frontier. I followed them deep into the wilderness, and killed their chief, but was knocked senseless by a stone from a sling during the melee, and the dogs captured me alive. They were Wolfmen, but they traded me to the Eagle clan in return for a chief of theirs the Eagles had captured. The Eagles carried me nearly a hundred miles westward to burn me in their chief village, but I killed their war-chief and three or four others one night, and broke away.

"I couldn't turn back. They were behind me, and kept herding me westward. A few days ago I shook them off, and by Crom, the place where I took refuge turned out to be the treasure trove of old Tranicos! I found it all: chests of garments and weapons—that's where I got these clothes and this blade—heaps of coins and gems and gold ornaments, and in the midst of all, the jewels of Tothmekri gleaming like frozen starlight! And old Tranicos and his eleven captains sitting about an ebon table and staring at the hoard, as they've stared for a hundred years!"

"What?"

"Aye!" he laughed. "Tranicos died in the midst of his treasure, and all with him! Their bodies have not rotted nor shrivelled. They sit there in their high boots and skirted coats and lacquered hats, with their wineglasses in their stiff hands, just as they have sat for a century!"

"That's an unchancy thing!" muttered Strom uneasily, but Zarono snarled: "What boots it? It's the treasure we want. Go on, Conan."

Conan seated himself at the board, filled a goblet and quaffed it before he answered.

"The first wine I've drunk since I left Conawaga, by Crom! Those cursed Eagles hunted me so closely through the forest I had hardly time to munch the nuts and roots I found. Sometimes I caught frogs and ate them raw because I dared not light a fire."

His impatient hearers informed him profanely that they were not interested in his adventures prior to finding the treasure.

He grinned hardly and resumed: "Well, after I stumbled onto the trove I lay up and rested a few days, and made snares to catch rabbits, and let my wounds heal. I saw smoke against the western sky, but thought it some Pictish village on the beach. I lay close, but as it happens, the loot's hidden in a place the Picts shun. If any spied on me, they didn't show themselves.

"Last night I started westward, intending to strike the beach some miles north of the spot where I'd seen the smoke. I wasn't far from the shore when that storm hit. I took shelter under the lee of a rock and waited until it had blown itself out. Then I climbed a tree to look for Picts, and from it I saw your carack at anchor, Strom, and your men coming in to shore. I was making my way toward your camp on the beach when I met Galacus. I shoved a sword through him because there was an old feud between us. I wouldn't have known he had a map, if he hadn't tried to eat it before he died.

"I recognized it for what it was, of course, and was considering what use I could make of it, when the rest of you dogs came up and found the body. I was lying in a thicket not a dozen yards from you while you were arguing with your men over the matter. I judged the time wasn't ripe for me to show myself then!"

He laughed at the rage and chagrin displayed in Strom's face.

"Well, while I lay there, listening to your talk, I got a drift of the situation, and learned, from the things you let fall, that Zarono and Valenso were a few miles south on the beach. So when I heard you say that Zarono must have done the killing and taken the map, and that you meant to go and parley with him, seeking an opportunity to murder him and get it back—"

"Dog!" snarled Zarono. Strom was livid, but he laughed mirthlessly.

"Do you think I'd play fairly with a treacherous dog like you?—Go on, Conan."

The Cimmerian grinned. It was evident that he was deliberately fanning the fires of hate between the two men.

"Nothing much, then. I came straight through the woods while you tacked along the coast, and raised the fort before you did. Your guess that the storm had destroyed Zarono's ship was a good one—but then, you knew the configuration of this bay.

"Well, there's the story. I have the treasure, Strom has a ship, Valenso has supplies. By Crom, Zarono, I don't see where you fit into the scheme, but to avoid strife I'll include you. My proposal is simple enough.

"We'll split the treasure four ways. Strom and I will sail away with our shares aboard *The Red Hand*. You and Valenso take yours and remain lords of the wilderness, or build a ship out of tree trunks, as you wish."

Valenso blenched and Zarono swore, while Strom grinned quietly.

"Are you fool enough to go aboard *The Red Hand* alone with Strom?" snarled Zarono. "He'll cut your throat before you're out of sight of land!"

Conan laughed with genuine enjoyment.

"This is like the problem of the sheep, the wolf and the

cabbage," he admitted. "How to get them across the river without their devouring each other!"

"And that appeals to your Cimmerian sense of humor," complained Zarono.

"I will not stay here!" cried Valenso, a wild gleam in his dark eyes. "Treasure or no treasure, I must go!"

Conan gave him a slit-eyed glance of speculation.

"Well, then," said he, "how about this plan: we divide the loot as I suggested. Then Strom sails away with Zarono, Valenso, and such members of the Count's household as he may select, leaving me in command of the fort and the rest of Valenso's men, and all of Zarono's. I'll build my own ship."

Zarono looked slightly sick.

"I have the choice of remaining here in exile, or abandoning my crew and going alone on *The Red Hand* to have my throat cut?"

Conan's laughter rang gustily through the hall, and he smote Zarono jovially on the back, ignoring the black murder in the buccaneer's glare.

"That's it, Zarono!" quoth he. "Stay here while Strom and I sail away, or sail away with Strom, leaving your men with me."

"I'd rather have Zarono," said Strom frankly. "You'd turn my own men against me, Conan, and cut my throat before I raised the Barachans."

Sweat dripped from Zarono's livid face.

"Neither I, the Count, nor his niece will ever reach the land alive if we ship with that devil," said he. "You are both in my power in this hall. My men surround it. What's to prevent me cutting you both down?"

"Not a thing," Conan admitted cheerfully. "Except the fact that if you do Strom's men will sail away and leave you stranded on this coast where the Picts will presently cut all your throats; and the fact that with me dead you'll never find the treasure; and the fact that I'll split your skull down to your chin if you try to summon your men.''

Conan laughed as he spoke, as if at some whimsical situation, but even Belesa sensed that he meant what he said. His naked cutlass lay across his knees, and Zarono's sword was under the table, out of the buccaneer's reach. Galbro was not a fighting man, and Valenso seemed incapable of decision or action.

"Aye!" said Strom with an oath. "You'd find the two of us no easy prey. I'm agreeable to Conan's proposal. What do you say, Valenso?''

"I must leave this coast!'' whispered Valenso, staring blankly. "I must hasten—I must go—go far—quickly!''

Strom frowned, puzzled at the Count's strange manner, and turned to Zarono, grinning wickedly: "And you, Zarono?''

"What can I say?'' snarled Zarono. "Let me take my three officers and forty men aboard *The Red Hand*, and the bargain's made.''

"The officers and thirty men!''

"Very well.''

"Done!''

There was no shaking of hands, or ceremonial drinking of wine to seal the pact. The two captains glared at each other like hungry wolves. The Count plucked his mustache with a trembling hand, rapt in his own somber thoughts. Conan stretched like a great cat, drank wine, and grinned on the assemblage, but it was the sinister grin of a stalking tiger. Belesa sensed the murderous purposes that reigned there, the treacherous intent that dominated each man's mind. Not one had any intention of keeping his part of the pact, Valenso possibly excluded. Each of the freebooters intended to possess both the ship and the entire treasure. Neither would be satisfied with less. But how? What was going on in each crafty mind? Belesa felt oppressed and stifled by the atmosphere of hatred and treachery. The Cimmerian, for all his ferocious frankness, was no less subtle than the others—and even fiercer. His domination of the situation was not physical alone, though his gigantic shoulders and massive limbs seemed too big even for the great hall. There was an iron vitality about the man that overshadowed even the hard vigor of the other freebooters.

"Lead us to the treasure!" Zarono demanded.

"Wait a bit," answered Conan. "We must keep our power evenly balanced, so one can't take advantage of the others. We'll work it this way: Strom's men will come ashore, all but half a dozen or so, and camp on the beach. Zarono's men will come out of the fort, and likewise camp on the strand, within easy sight of them. Then each crew can keep a check on the other, to see that nobody slips after us who go after the treasure, to ambush either of us. Those left aboard *The Red Hand* will take her out into the bay out of reach of either party. Valenso's men will stay in the fort, but will leave the gate open. Will you come with us, Count?"

"Go into that forest?" Valenso shuddered, and drew his cloak about his shoulders. "Not for all the gold of Tranicos!"

"All right. It'll take about thirty men to carry the loot. We'll take fifteen from each crew and start as soon as possible."

Belesa, keenly alert to every angle of the drama being played out beneath her, saw Zarono and Strom shoot furtive glances at one another, then lower their gaze quickly as they lifted their glasses to hide the murky intent in their eyes. Belesa saw the fatal weakness in Conan's plan, and wondered how he could have overlooked it. Perhaps he was too arrogantly confident in his personal prowess. But she knew that he would never come out of that forest alive. Once the treasure was in their grasp, the others would form a rogues' alliance long enough to rid themselves of the man both hated. She shuddered, staring morbidly at the man she knew was doomed; strange to see that powerful fighting man sitting there, laughing and swilling wine, in full prime and power, and to know that he was already doomed to a bloody death.

The whole situation was pregnant with dark and bloody portents. Zarono would trick and kill Strom if he could, and she knew that Strom had already marked Zarono for death, and doubtless, also, her uncle and herself. If Zarono won the final battle of cruel wits, their lives were safe—but looking at the buccaneer as he sat there chewing his mustache, with all the stark evil of his nature showing naked in his dark face, she could not decide which was more abhorrent—death or Zarono.

"How far is it?" demanded Strom.

"If we start within the hour wc can be back before midnight," answered Conan. He emptied his glass, rose, adjusted his girdle, and glanced at the Count.

"Valenso," he said, "are you mad, to kill a Pict in his hunting paint?"

Valenso started.

"What do you mean?"

"Do you mean to say you don't know that your men killed a Pict hunter in the woods last night?"

The Count shook his head.

"None of my men was in the woods last night."

"Well, somebody was," grunted the Cimmerian, fumbling in a pocket. "I saw his head nailed to a tree near the edge of the forest. He wasn't painted for war. I didn't find any boot-tracks, from which I judged that it had been nailed up there before the storm. But there were plenty of other signs—moccasin tracks on the wet ground. Picts have been there and seen that head. They were men of some other clan, or they'd have taken it down. If they happen to be at peace with the clan the dead man belonged to, they'll make tracks to his village to tell his tribe."

"Perhaps they killed him," suggested Valenso.

"No, they didn't. But they know who did, for the same reason that I know. This chain was knotted about the stump of the severed neck. You must have been utterly mad, to identify your handiwork like that."

He drew forth something and tossed it on the table before the Count, who lurched up, choking, as his hand flew to his throat. It was the gold seal-chain he habitually wore about his neck.

"I recognized the Korzetta seal," said Conan. "The presence of that chain would tell any Pict it was the work of a foreigner."

Valenso did not reply. He sat staring at the chain as if at a venomous serpent.

Conan scowled at him, and glanced questioningly at the others. Zarono made a quick gesture to indicate the Count was not quite right in the head.

Conan sheathed his cutlass and donned his lacquered hat.

"All right; let's go."

The captains gulped down their wine and rose, hitching at their sword-belts. Zarono laid a hand on Valenso's arm and shook him slightly. The Count started and stared about him, then followed the others out, like a man in a daze, the chain dangling from his fingers. But not all left the hall.

Belesa and Tina, forgotten on the stair, peeping between the balusters, saw Galbro fall behind the others, loitering until the heavy door closed after them. Then he hurried to the fireplace and raked carefully at the smoldering coals. He sank to his knees and peered closely at something for a long space. Then he straightened, and with a furtive air stole out of the hall by another door.

"What did Galbro find in the fire?" whispered Tina. Belesa shook her head, then, obeying the promptings of her curiosity, rose and went down to the empty hall. An instant later she was kneeling where the seneschal had knelt, and she saw what he had seen.

It was the charred remnant of the map Conan had thrown into the fire. It was ready to crumble at a touch, but faint lines and bits of writing were still discernible upon it. She could not read the writing, but she could trace the outlines of what seemed to be the picture of a hill or crag, surrounded by marks evidently representing dense trees. She could make nothing of it, but from Galbro's actions, she believed he recognized it as portraying some scene or topographical feature familiar to him. She knew the seneschal had penetrated inland further than any other man of the settlement.

Chapter 6
The Plunder of the Dead

Belesa came down the stair and paused at the sight of Count Valenso seated at the table, turning the broken chain about in his hands. She looked at him without love, and with more than a little fear. The change that had come over him was appalling; he seemed to be locked up in a grim world all his own, with a fear that flogged all human characteristics out of him.

The fortress stood strangely quiet in the noonday heat that had followed the storm of the dawn. Voices of people within the stockade sounded subdued, muffled. The same drowsy stillness reigned on the beach outside where the rival crews lay in armed suspicion, separated by a few hundred yards of bare sand. Far out in the bay *The Red Hand* lay at anchor with a handful of men aboard her, ready to snatch her out of reach at the slightest indication of treachery. The carack was Strom's trump card, his best guarantee against the trickery of his associates.

Conan had plotted shrewdly to eliminate the chances of an ambush in the forest by either party. But as far as Belesa could see, he had failed utterly to safeguard himself against the treachery of his companions. He had disappeared into the woods, leading the two captains and their thirty men, and the Zingaran girl was positive that she would never see him alive again.

Presently she spoke, and her voice was strained and harsh to her own ear.

"The barbarian has led the captains into the forest. When they have the gold in their hands, they'll kill him. But when they return with the treasure, what then? Are we to go aboard the ship? Can we trust Strom?"

Valenso shook his head absently.

"Strom would murder us all for our shares of the loot. But Zarono whispered his intentions to me secretly. We will not go aboard *The Red Hand* save as her masters. Zarono will see that night overtakes the treasure-party, so they are forced to camp in the forest. He will find a way to kill Strom and his men in their sleep. Then the buccaneers will come on stealthily to the beach. Just before dawn I will send some of my fishermen secretly from the fort to swim out to the ship and seize her. Strom never thought of that, neither did Conan. Zarono and his men will come out of the forest and with the buccaneers encamped on the beach, fall upon the pirates in the dark, while I lead my men-at-arms from the fort to complete the rout. Without their captain they will be demoralized, and outnumbered, fall easy prey to Zarono and me. Then we will sail in Strom's ship with all the treasure."

"And what of me?" she asked with dry lips.

"I have promised you to Zarono," he answered harshly. "But for my promise he would not take us off."

"I will never marry him," she said helplessly.

"You will," he responded gloomily, and without the slightest touch of sympathy. He lifted the chain so it caught the gleam of the sun, slanting through a window. "I must have dropped it on the sand," he muttered. "*He* has been that near—on the beach—"

"You did not drop it on the strand," said Belesa, in a voice as devoid of mercy as his own; her soul seemed turned to stone. "You tore it from your throat, by accident, last night in this hall, when you flogged Tina. I saw it gleaming on the floor before I left the hall."

He looked up, his face grey with a terrible fear.

She laughed bitterly, sensing the mute question in his dilated eyes.

"Yes! The black man! He was here! In this hall! He must have found the chain on the floor. The guardsmen did not see him. But he was at your door last night. I saw him, padding along the upper hallway."

For an instant she thought he would drop dead of sheer terror. He sank back in his chair, the chain slipping from his nerveless fingers and clinking on the table.

"In the manor!" he whispered. "I thought bolts and bars and armed guards could keep him out, fool that I was! I can no more guard against him than I can escape him! At my door! At my door!" The thought overwhelmed him with horror. "Why did he not enter?" he shrieked, tearing at the lace upon his collar as though it strangled him. "Why did he not end it? I have dreamed of waking in my darkened chamber to see him squatting above me and the blue hell-fire playing about his horned head! Why—"

The paroxysm passed, leaving him faint and trembling.

"I understand!" he panted. "He is playing with me, as

a cat with a mouse. To have slain me last night in my chamber were too easy, too merciful. So he destroyed the ship in which I might have escaped him, and he slew that wretched Pict and left my chain upon him, so that the savages might believe I had slain him—they have seen that chain upon my neck many a time.

"But why? What subtle deviltry has he in mind, what devious purpose no human mind can grasp or understand?"

"Who is this black man?" asked Belesa, chill fear crawling along her spine.

"A demon loosed by my greed and lust to plague me throughout eternity!" he whispered. He spread his long thin fingers on the table before him, and stared at her with hollow, weirdly-luminous eyes that seemed to see her not at all, but to look through her and far beyond to some dim doom.

"In my youth I had an enemy at court," he said, as if speaking more to himself than to her. "A powerful man who stood between me and my ambition. In my lust for wealth and power I sought aid from the people of the black arts—a black magician, who, at my desire, raised up a fiend from the outer gulfs of existence and clothed it in the form of a man. It crushed and slew my enemy; I grew great and wealthy and none could stand before me. But I thought to cheat my fiend of the price a mortal must pay who calls *the black folk* to do his bidding.

"By his grim arts the magician tricked the soulless waif of darkness and bound him in hell where he howled in vain—I supposed for eternity. But because the sorcerer had given the fiend the form of a man, he could never break the link that bound it to the material world; never completely close the cosmic corridors by which it had gained access to this planet.

"A year ago in Kordava word came to me that the magician, now an ancient man, had been slain in his castle, with marks of demon fingers on his throat. Then I knew that the black one had escaped from the hell where the magician had bound him, and that he would seek vengeance upon me. One night I saw his demon face leering at me from the shadows in my castle hall—

"It was not his material body, but his spirit sent to plague me—his spirit which could not follow me over the windy waters. Before he could reach Kordava in the flesh, I sailed to put broad seas between me and him. He has his limitations. To follow me across the seas he must remain in his man-like body of flesh. But that flesh is not human flesh. He can be slain, I think, by fire, though the magician, having raised him up, was powerless to slay him— such are the limits set upon the powers of sorcerers.

"But the black one is too crafty to be trapped or slain. When he hides himself no man can find him. He steals like a shadow through the night, making naught of bolts and bars. He blinds the eyes of guardsmen with sleep. He can raise storms and command the serpents of the deep, and the fiends of the night. I hoped to drown my trail in the blue rolling wastes—but he has tracked me down to claim his grim forfeit."

The weird eyes lit palely as he gazed beyond the tapestried walls to far, invisible horizons.

"I'll trick him yet," he whispered. "Let him delay to strike this night—dawn will find me with a ship under my heels and again I will cast an ocean between me and his vengeance."

"Hell's fire!"

Conan stopped short, glaring upward. Behind him the seamen halted—two compact clumps of them, bows in their hands, and suspicion in their attitude. They were following an old path made by Pictish hunters which led due east, and though they had progressed only some thirty yards, the beach was no longer visible.

"What is it?" demanded Strom suspiciously. "What are you stopping for?"

"Are you blind? Look there!"

From the thick limb of a tree that overhung the trail a head grinned down at them—a dark painted face, framed in thick black hair, in which a toucan feather drooped over the left ear.

"I took that head down and hid it in the bushes," growled Conan, scanning the woods about them narrowly. "What fool could have stuck it back up there? It looks as if somebody was trying his damndest to bring the Picts down on the settlement."

Men glanced at each other darkly, a new element of suspicion added to the already seething caldron.

Conan climbed the tree, secured the head and carried it into the bushes, where he tossed it into a stream and saw it sink.

"The Picts whose tracks are about this tree weren't Toucans," he growled, returning through the thicket. "I've sailed these coasts enough to know something about the sea-land tribes. If I read the prints of their moccasins right, they were Cormorants. I hope they're having a war with the Toucans. If they're at peace, they'll head straight for the Toucan village, and there'll be hell to pay. I don't know how far away that village is—but as soon as they learn of this murder, they'll come through the forest like starving wolves. That's the worst insult possible to a Pict—kill a man not in war-paint and stick his head up in a tree for the vultures to eat. Damn' peculiar things going on along this coast. But that's always the way when civilized men come into the wilderness. They're all crazy as hell. Come on."

Men loosened blades in their scabbards and shafts in their quivers as they strode deeper into the forest. Men of the sea, accustomed to the rolling expanses of grey water, they were ill at ease with the green mysterious walls of trees and vines hemming them in. The path wound and twisted until most of them quickly lost their sense of direction, and did not even know in which direction the beach lay.

Conan was uneasy for another reason. He kept scanning the trail, and finally grunted: "Somebody's passed along here recently—not more than an hour ahead of us. Some-body in boots, with no woods-craft. Was he the fool who found that Pict's head and stuck it back up in that tree? No, it couldn't have been him. I didn't find his tracks under the tree. But who was it? I didn't find any tracks there, except those of the Picts I'd seen already. And who's this fellow hurrying ahead of us? Did either of you bastards send a man ahead of us for any reason?"

Both Strom and Zarono loudly disclaimed any such act, glaring at each other with mutual disbelief. Neither man could see the signs Conan pointed out; the faint prints which he saw on the grassless, hard-beaten trail were invisible to their untrained eyes.

Conan quickened his pace and they hurried after him, fresh coals of suspicion added to the smoldering fire of distrust. Presently the path veered northward, and Conan left it, and began threading his way through the dense trees in a southeasterly direction. Strom stole an uneasy glance at Zarono. This might force a change in their plans. Within a few hundred feet from the trail both were hopelessly lost, and convinced of their inability to find their way back to the path. They were shaken by the fear that, after all, the Cimmerian had a force at his command, and was leading them into an ambush.

This suspicion grew as they advanced, and had almost reached panic-proportions when they emerged from the thick woods and saw just ahead of them a gaunt crag that jutted up from the forest floor. A dim path leading out of the woods from the east ran among a cluster of boulders and wound up the crag on a ladder of stony shelves to a flat ledge near the summit.

Conan halted, a bizarre figure in his piratical finery.

"That trail is the one I followed, running from the Eagle-Picts," he said. "It leads up to a cave behind that ledge. In that cave are the bodies of Tranicos and his captains, and the treasure he plundered from Tothmekri. But a word before we go up after it: if you kill me here, you'll never find your way back to the trail we followed from the beach. I know you sea-faring men. You're helpless in the deep woods. Of course the beach lies due west, but if you have to make your way through the tangled woods, burdened with the plunder, it'll take you not hours, but days. And I don't think these woods will be very safe for white men, when the Toucans learn about their hunter." He laughed at the ghastly, mirthless smiles with which they greeted his recognition of their intentions regarding him. And he also comprehended the thought that sprang in the mind of each: let the barbarian secure the loot for them, and lead them back to the beach-trail before they killed him.

"All of you stay here except Strom and Zarono," said Conan. "We three are enough to pack the treasure down from the cave."

Strom grinned mirthlessly.

"Go up there alone with you and Zarono? Do you take me for a fool? One man at least comes with me!" And he designated his boatswain, a brawny, hard-faced giant, naked to his broad leather belt, with gold hoops in his ears, and a crimson scarf knotted about his head.

"And my executioner comes with me!" growled Zarono. He beckoned to a lean sea-thief with a face like a parchment-

covered skull, who carried a two-handed scimitar naked
over his bony shoulder.

Conan shrugged his shoulders. "Very well. Follow me."

They were close on his heels as he strode up the winding path and mounted the ledge. They crowded him close
as he passed through the cleft in the wall behind it, and
their breath sucked greedily between their teeth as he
called their attention to the iron-bound chests on either side
of the short tunnel-like cavern.

"A rich cargo there," he said carelessly. "Silks, laces,
garments, ornaments, weapons—the loot of the southern
seas. But the real treasure lies beyond that door."

The massive door stood partly open. Conan frowned.
He remembered closing that door before he left the cavern.
But he said nothing of the matter to his eager companions
as he drew aside to let them look through.

They looked into a wide cavern, lit by a strange blue
glow that glimmered through a smoky mist-like haze. A
great ebon table stood in the midst of the cavern, and in a
carved chair with a high back and broad arms, that might
once have stood in the castle of some Zingaran baron, sat a
giant figure, fabulous and fantastic—there sat Bloody
Tranicos, his great head sunk on his bosom, one brawny
hand still gripping a jeweled goblet in which wine still
sparkled; Tranicos, in his lacquered hat, his gilt-embroidered
coat with jeweled buttons that winked in the blue flame,
his flaring boots and gold-worked baldric that upheld a
jewel-hilted sword in a golden sheath.

And ranging the board, each with his chin resting on his
lace-bedecked crest, sat the eleven captains. The blue fire
played weirdly on them and on their giant admiral, as it
flowed from the enormous jewel on the tiny ivory pedestal, striking glints of frozen fire from the heaps of fantastically cut gems which shone before the place of Tranicos—the
plunder of Khemi, the jewels of Tothmekri! The stones

whose value was greater than the value of all the rest of the known jewels in the world put together!

The faces of Zarono and Strom showed pallid in the blue glow; over their shoulders their men gaped stupidly.

"Go in and take them," invited Conan, drawing aside, and Zarono and Strom crowded avidly past him, jostling one another in their haste. Their followers were treading on their heels. Zarono kicked the door wide open—and halted with one foot on the threshold at the sight of a figure on the floor, previously hidden from view by the partly-closed door. It was a man, prone and contorted, head drawn back between his shoulders, white face twisted in a grin of mortal agony, gripping his own throat with clawed fingers.

"Galbro!" ejaculated Zarono. "Dead! What—" With sudden suspicion he thrust his head over the threshold, into the bluish mist that filled the inner cavern. And he screamed, chokingly: "There is death in the smoke!"

Even as he screamed, Conan hurled his weight against the four men bunched in the doorway, sending them staggering—but not headlong into the mist-filled cavern as he had planned. They were recoiling at the sight of the dead man and the realization of the trap, and his violent push, while it threw them off their feet, yet failed of the result he desired. Strom and Zarono sprawled half over the threshold on their knees, the boatswain tumbling over their legs, and the executioner caromed against the wall. Before Conan could follow up his ruthless intention of kicking the fallen men into the cavern and holding the door against them until the poisonous mist did its deadly work, he had to turn and defend himself against the frothing onslaught of the executioner who was the first to regain his balance and his wits.

The buccaneer missed a tremendous swipe with his headsman's sword as the Cimmerian ducked, and the great blade banged against the stone wall, spattering blue sparks. The next instant his skull-faced head rolled on the cavern-floor under the bite of Conan's cutlass.

In the split seconds this swift action consumed, the boatswain regained his feet and fell on the Cimmerian, raining blows with a cutlass that would have overwhelmed a lesser man. Cutlass met cutlass with a ring of steel that was deafening in the narrow cavern. The two captains rolled back across the threshold, gagging and gasping, purple in the face and too near strangled to shout, and Conan redoubled his efforts, in an endeavor to dispose of his antagonist and cut down his rivals before they could recover from the effects of the poison. The boatswain dripped blood at each step, as he was driven back before the ferocious onslaught, and he began desperately to bellow for his companions. But before Conan could deal the finishing stroke, the two chiefs, gasping but murderous, came at him with swords in their hands, croaking for their men.

The Cimmerian bounded back and leaped out onto the ledge. He felt himself a match for all three men, though each was a famed swordsman, but he did not wish to be trapped by the crews which would come charging up the path at the sound of the battle.

These were not coming with as much celerity as he expected, however. They were bewildered at the sounds and muffled shouts issuing from the cavern above them, but no man dared start up the path for fear of a sword in the back. Each band faced the other tensely, grasping their weapons but incapable of decision, and when they saw the Cimmerian bound out on the ledge, they still hesitated. While they stood with their arrows nocked he ran up the ladder of handholds niched in the rock near the cleft, and threw himself prone on the summit of the crag, out of their sight.

The captains stormed out on the ledge, raving and brandishing their swords, and their men, seeing their leaders were not at sword-strokes, ceased menacing each other, and gaped bewilderedly.

"Dog!" screamed Zarono. "You planned to poison us! Traitor!"

Conan mocked them from above.

"Well, what did you expect? You two were planning to cut my throat as soon as I got the plunder for you. If it hadn't been for that fool Galbro I'd have trapped the four of you, and explained to your men how you rushed in heedless to your doom."

"And with us both dead, you'd have taken my ship, and all the loot too!" frothed Strom.

"Aye! And the pick of each crew! I've been wanting to get back on the Main for months, and this was a good opportunity!

"It was Galbro's foot-prints I saw on the trail. I wonder how the fool learned of this cave, or how he expected to lug away the loot by himself."

"But for the sight of his body we'd have walked into that death-trap," muttered Zarono, his swarthy face still ashy. "That blue smoke was like unseen fingers crushing my throat."

"Well, what are you going to do?" their unseen tormentor yelled sardonically.

"What *are* we to do?" Zarono asked of Strom. "The treasure-cavern is filled with that poisonous mist, though for some reason it does not flow across the threshold."

"You can't get the treasure," Conan assured them with satisfaction from his aerie. "That smoke will strangle you. It nearly got me, when I stepped in there. Listen, and I'll tell you a tale the Picts tell in their huts when the fires burn low! Once, long ago, twelve strange men came out of the sea, and found a cave and heaped it with gold and jewels; but a Pictish *shaman* made magic and the earth shook, and smoke came out of the earth and strangled them where they sat at wine. The smoke, which was the smoke of hell's fire, was confined within the cavern by the magic of the wizard. The tale was told from tribe to tribe, and all the clans shun the accursed spot.

"When I crawled in there to escape the Eagle-Picts, I realized that the old legend was true, and referred to old Tranicos and his men. An earthquake cracked the rock floor of the cavern while he and his captains sat at wine, and let the mist out of the depths of the earth—doubtless out of hell, as the Picts say. Death guards old Tranicos's treasure!"

"Bring up the men!" frothed Strom. "We'll climb up and hew him down!"

"Don't be a fool," snarled Zarono. "Do you think any man on earth could climb those hand-holds in the teeth of his sword? We'll have the men up here, right enough, to feather him with shafts if he dares show himself. But we'll get those gems yet. He had some plan of obtaining the loot, or he wouldn't have brought thirty men to bear it back. If he could get it, so can we. We'll bend a cutlass-blade to make a hook, tie it to a rope and cast it about the leg of that table, then drag it to the door."

"Well thought, Zarono!" came down Conan's mocking voice. "Exactly what I had in mind. But how will you find your way back to the beach-path? It'll be dark long before you reach the beach, if you have to feel your way through the woods, and I'll follow you and kill you one by one in the dark."

"It's no empty boast," muttered Strom. "He can move and strike in the dark as subtly and silently as a ghost. If he hunts us back through the forest, few of us will live to see the beach."

"Then we'll kill him here," gritted Zarono. "Some of

us will shoot at him while the rest climb the crag. If he is not struck by arrows, some of us will reach him with our swords. Listen! Why does he laugh?''

"To hear dead men making plots," came Conan's grimly amused voice.

"Heed him not," scowled Zarono, and lifting his voice, shouted for the men below to join him and Strom on the ledge.

The sailors started up the slanting trail, and one started to shout a question. Simultaneously there sounded a hum like that of an angry bee, ending in a sharp thud. The buccaneer gasped and blood gushed from his open mouth. He sank to his knees, clutching the black shaft that quivered in his breast. A yell of alarm went up from his companions.

"What's the matter?" shouted Strom.

"*Picts!*" bawled a pirate, lifting his bow and loosing blindly. At his side a man moaned and went down with an arrow through his throat.

"Take cover, you fools!" shrieked Zarono. From his vantage-point he glimpsed painted figures moving in the bushes. One of the men on the winding path fell back dying. The rest scrambled hastily down among the rocks about the foot of the crag. They took cover clumsily, not used to this kind of fighting. Arrows flickered from the bushes, splintering on the boulders. The men on the ledge lay prone at full length.

"We're trapped!" Strom's face was pale. Bold enough with a deck under his feet, this silent, savage warfare shook his ruthless nerves.

"Conan said they feared this crag," said Zarono. "When night falls the men must climb up here. We'll hold the crag. The Picts won't rush us."

"Aye!" mocked Conan above them. "They won't climb the crag to get at you, that's true. They'll merely surround it and keep you here until you all die of thirst and starvation.''

"He speaks truth," said Zarono helplessly. "What shall we do?"

"Make a truce with him," muttered Strom. "If any man can get us out of this jam, he can. Time enough to cut his throat later." Lifting his voice he called: "Conan, let's forget our feud for the time being. You're in this fix as much as we are. Come down and help us out of it."

"How do you figure that?" retorted the Cimmerian. "I have but to wait until dark, climb down the other side of this crag and melt into the forest. I can crawl through the line the Picts have thrown around this hill, and return to the fort to report you all slain by the savages—which will shortly be truth!"

Zarono and Strom stared at each other in pallid silence.

"But I'm not going to do that!" Conan roared. "Not because I have any love for you dogs, but because a white man doesn't leave white men, even his enemies, to be butchered by Picts."

The Cimmerian's tousled black head appeared over the crest of the crag.

"Now listen closely: that's only a small band down there. I saw them sneaking through the brush when I laughed, a while ago. Anyway, if there had been many of them, every man at the foot of the crag would be dead already. I think that's a band of fleet-footed young men sent ahead of the main war-party to cut us off from the beach. I'm certain a big war-band is heading in our direction from somewhere.

"They've thrown a cordon around the west side of the crag, but I don't think there are any on the east side. I'm going down on that side and get in the forest and work around behind them. Meanwhile, you crawl down the path and join your men among the rocks. Tell them to sling their bows and draw their swords. When you hear me yell, rush the trees on the west side of the clearing.''

"What of the treasure?"

"To hell with the treasure! We'll be lucky if we get out of here with our heads on our shoulders."

The black-maned head vanished. They listened for sounds to indicate that Conan had crawled to the almost sheer eastern wall and was working his way down, but they heard nothing. Nor was there any sound in the forest. No more arrows broke against the rocks where the sailors were hidden. But all knew that fierce black eyes were watching with murderous patience. Gingerly Strom, Zarono and the boatswain started down the winding path. They were halfway down when the black shafts began to whisper around them. The boatswain groaned and toppled limply down the slope, shot through the heart. Arrows shivered on the helmets and breastplates of the chiefs as they tumbled in frantic haste down the steep trail. They reached the foot in a scrambling rush and lay panting among the boulders, swearing breathlessly.

"Is this more of Conan's trickery?" wondered Zarono profanely.

"We can trust him in this matter," asserted Strom. "These barbarians live by their own particular code of honor, and Conan would never desert men of his own complexion to be slaughtered by people of another race. He'll help us against the Picts, even though he plans to murder us himself—*hark!*"

A blood-freezing yell knifed the silence. It came from the woods to the west, and simultaneously an object arched out of the trees, struck the ground and rolled bouncingly toward the rocks—a severed human head, the hideously painted face frozen in a snarl of death.

"Conan's signal!" roared Strom, and the desperate free-

booters rose like a wave from the rocks and rushed headlong toward the woods.

Arrows whirred out of the bushes, but their flight was
hurried and erratic, only three men fell. Then the wild men
of the sea plunged through the fringe of foliage and fell on
the naked painted figures that rose out of the gloom before
them. There was a murderous instant of panting, ferocious
effort, hand-to-hand, cutlasses beating down war-axes,
booted feet trampling naked bodies, and then bare feet
were rattling through the bushes in headlong flight as
the survivors of that brief carnage quit the fray, leaving
seven still, painted figures stretched on the blood-stained
leaves that littered the earth. Further back in the thickets
sounded a thrashing and heaving, and then it ceased and
Conan strode into view, his lacquered hat gone, his coat
torn, his cutlass dripping in his hand.

"What now?" panted Zarono. He knew the charge had
succeeded only because Conan's unexpected attack on the
rear of the Picts had demoralized the painted men, and
prevented them from falling back before the rush. But he
exploded into curses as Conan passed his cutlass through a
buccaneer who writhed on the ground with a shattered hip.

"We can't carry him with us," grunted Conan. "It
wouldn't be any kindness to leave him to be taken alive by
the Picts. Come on!"

They crowded close at his heels as he trotted through the
trees. Alone they would have sweated and blundered among
the thickets for hours before they found the beach-trail—
if they had ever found it. The Cimmerian led them as
unerringly as if he had been following a blazed path, and
the rovers shouted with hysterical relief as they burst
suddenly upon the trail that ran westward.

"Fool!" Conan clapped a hand on the shoulder of a pirate
who started to break into a run, and hurled him back
among his companions. "You'll burst your heart and fall

within a thousand yards. We're miles from the beach. Take an easy gait. We may have to sprint the last mile. Save some of your wind for it. Come on, now.''

He set off down the trail at a steady jog-trot; the seamen followed him, suiting their pace to his.

The sun was touching the waves of the western ocean. Tina stood at the window from which Belesa had watched the storm.

''The setting sun turns the ocean to blood,'' she said. ''The carack's sail is a white fleck on the crimson waters. The woods are already darkened with clustering shadows.''

''What of the seamen on the beach?'' asked Belesa languidly. She reclined on a couch, her eyes closed, her hands clasped behind her head.

''Both camps are preparing their supper,'' said Tina. ''They gather driftwood and build fires. I can hear them shouting to one another—*what is that?*''

The sudden tenseness in the girl's tone brought Belesa upright on the couch. Tina grasped the window-sill, her face white.

''Listen! A howling, far off, like many wolves!''

''Wolves?'' Belesa sprang up, fear clutching her heart. ''Wolves do not hunt in packs at this time of the year—''

''Oh, look!'' shrilled the girl, pointing. ''Men are running out of the forest!''

In an instant Belesa was beside her, staring wide-eyed at the figures, small in the distance, streaming out of the woods.

''The sailors!'' she gasped. ''Empty-handed! I see Zarono—Strom—''

''Where is Conan?'' whispered the girl.

Belesa shook her head.

''Listen! Oh, listen!'' whimpered the child, clinging to her. ''The Picts!''

All in the fort could hear it now—a vast ululation of mad exultation and blood-lust, from the depths of the dark forest.

That sound spurred on the panting men reeling toward the palisade.

"Hasten!" gasped Strom, his face a drawn mask of exhausted effort. "They are almost at our heels. My ship—"

"She is too far out for us to reach," panted Zarono. "Make for the stockade. See, the men camped on the beach have seen us!" He waved his arms in breathless pantomime, but the men on the strand understood, and they recognized the significance of that wild howling, rising to a triumphant crescendo. The sailors abandoned their fires and cooking-pots and fled for the stockade gate. They were pouring through it as the fugitives from the forest rounded the south angle and reeled into the gate, a heaving, frantic mob, half-dead from exhaustion. The gate was slammed with frenzied haste, and sailors began to climb the firing-ledge, to join the men-at-arms already there.

Belesa confronted Zarono.

"Where is Conan?"

The buccaneer jerked a thumb toward the blackening woods; his chest heaved; sweat poured down his face. "Their scouts were at our heels before we gained the beach. He paused to slay a few and give us time to get away."

He staggered away to take his place on the firing-ledge, whither Strom had already mounted. Valenso stood there, a somber, cloak-wrapped figure, strangely silent and aloof. He was like a man bewitched.

"Look!" yelped a pirate, above the deafening howling of the yet unseen horde.

A man emerged from the forest and raced fleetly across the open belt.

"Conan!"

Zarono grinned wolfishly.

"We're safe in the stockade; we know where the treasure is. No reason why we shouldn't feather him with arrows now."

"Nay!" Strom caught his arm. "We'll need his sword! Look!"

Behind the fleet-footed Cimmerian a wild horde burst from the forest, howling as they ran—naked Picts, hundreds and hundreds of them. Their arrows rained about the Cimmerian. A few strides more and Conan reached the eastern wall of the stockade, bounded high, seized the points of the logs and heaved himself up and over, his cutlass in his teeth. Arrows thudded venomously into the logs where his body had just been. His resplendent coat was gone, his white silk shirt torn and blood-stained.

"Stop them!" he roared as his feet hit the ground inside. "If they get on the wall, we're done for!"

Pirates, buccaneers and men-at-arms responded instantly, and a storm of arrows and quarrels tore into the oncoming horde.

Conan saw Belesa, with Tina clinging to her hand, and his language was picturesque.

"Get into the manor," he commanded in conclusion. "Their shafts will arch over the wall—what did I tell you?" As a black shaft cut into the earth at Belesa's feet and quivered like a serpent-head, Conan caught up a longbow and leaped to the firing-ledge. "Some of you fellows prepare torches!" he roared, above the rising clamor of battle. "We can't fight them in the dark!"

The sun had sunk in a welter of blood; out in the bay the men aboard the carack had cut the anchor chain and *The Red Hand* was rapidly receding on the crimson horizon.

Chapter 7
Men of the Woods

Night had fallen, but torches streamed across the strand, casting the mad scene into lurid revealment. Naked men in paint swarmed the beach; like waves they came against the palisade, bared teeth and blazing eyes gleaming in the glare of the torches thrust over the wall. Toucan feathers waved in black manes, and the feathers of the cormorant and the sea-falcon. A few warriors, the wildest and most barbaric of them all, wore shark's teeth woven in their tangled locks. The sea-land tribes had gathered from up and down the coast in all directions to rid their country of the white-skinned invaders.

They surged against the palisade, driving a storm of arrows before them, fighting into the teeth of the shafts and bolts that tore into their masses from the stockade. Sometimes they came so close to the wall they were hewing at the gate with their war-axes and thrusting their spears through the loop-holes. But each time the tide ebbed back without flowing over the palisade, leaving its drift of dead. At this kind of fighting the freebooters of the sea were at their stoutest; their arrows and bolts tore holes in the charging horde, their cutlasses hewed the wild men from the palisades they strove to scale.

Yet again and again the men of the woods returned to the onslaught with all the stubborn ferocity that had been roused in their fierce hearts.

"They are like mad dogs!" gasped Zarono, hacking downward at the dark hands that grasped at the palisade points, the dark faces that snarled up at him.

"If we can hold the fort until dawn they'll lose heart," grunted Conan, splitting a feathered skull with professional precision. "They won't maintain a long siege. Look, they're falling back."

The charge rolled back and the men on the wall shook the sweat out of their eyes, counted their dead and took a fresh grasp on the blood-slippery hilts of their swords. Like blood-hungry wolves, grudgingly driven from a cornered prey, the Picts skulked back beyond the ring of torches. Only the bodies of the slain lay before the palisade.

"Have they gone?" Strom shook back his wet, tawny locks. The cutlass in his fist was notched and red, his brawny bare arm was splashed with blood.

"They're still out there," Conan nodded toward the outer darkness which ringed the circle of torches, made more intense by their light. He glimpsed movements in the shadows; glitter of eyes and the dull sheen of steel.

"They've drawn off for a bit, though," he said. "Put sentries on the wall, and let the rest drink and eat. It's past midnight. We've been fighting for hours without much interval."

The chiefs clambered down from the ledges, calling their men from the walls. A sentry was posted in the middle of each wall, east, west, north and south, and a clump of men-at-arms were left at the gate. The Picts, to reach the wall, would have to charge across a wide, torch-lit space, and the defenders could resume their places long before the attackers could reach the palisade.

"Where's Valenso?" demanded Conan, gnawing a huge beef-bone as he stood beside the fire the men had built in the center of the compound. Pirates, buccaneers and henchmen mingled with each other, wolfing the meat and ale the women brought them, and allowing their wounds to be bandaged.

"He disappeared an hour ago," grunted Strom. "He was fighting on the wall beside me, when suddenly he stopped short and glared out into the darkness as if he saw a ghost. 'Look!' he croaked. 'The black devil! I see him! Out there in the night!' Well, I could swear I saw a figure moving among the shadows that was too tall for a Pict. But it was just a glimpse and it was gone. But Valenso jumped down from the firing-ledge and staggered into the manor like a man with a mortal wound. I haven't seen him since.''

"He probably saw a forest-devil," said Conan tranquilly. "The Picts say this coast is lousy with them. What I'm more afraid of is fire-arrows. The Picts are likely to start shooting them at any time. What's that? It sounded like a cry for help?"

When the lull came in the fighting, Belesa and Tina had crept to their window, from which they had been driven by the danger of flying arrows. Silently they watched the men gather about the fire.

"There are not enough men on the stockade," said Tina.

In spite of her nausea at the sight of the corpses sprawled about the palisade, Belesa was forced to laugh.

"Do you think you know more about wars and sieges than the freebooters?" she chided gently.

"There should be more men on the walls," insisted the child, shivering. "Suppose the black man came back?"

Belesa shuddered at the thought.

"I am afraid," murmured Tina. "I hope Strom and Zarono are killed."

"And not Conan?" asked Belesa curiously.

"Conan would not harm us," said the child, confidently. "He lives up to his barbaric code of honor, but they are men who have lost all honor."

"You are wise beyond your years, Tina," said Belesa, with the vague uneasiness the precocity of the girl frequently roused in her.

"Look!" Tina stiffened. "The sentry is gone from the south wall! I saw him on the ledge a moment ago; now he has vanished."

From their window the palisade points of the south wall were just visible over the slanting roofs of a row of huts which paralleled that wall almost its entire length. A sort of open-topped corridor, three or four yards wide, was formed by the stockade and the back of the huts, which were built in a solid row. These huts were occupied by the serfs.

"Where could the sentry have gone?" whispered Tina uneasily.

Belesa was watching one end of the hut-row which was not far from a side door of the manor. She could have sworn she saw a shadowy figure glide from behind the huts and disappear at the door. Was that the vanished sentry? Why had he left the wall, and why should he steal so subtly into the manor? She did not believe it was the sentry she had seen, and a nameless fear congealed her blood.

"Where is the Count, Tina?" she asked.

"In the great hall, my Lady. He sits alone at the table, wrapped in his cloak and drinking wine, with a face grey as death."

"Go and tell him what we have seen. I will keep watch from this window, lest the Picts steal to the unguarded wall."

Tina scampered away. Belesa heard her slippered feet pattering along the corridor, receding down the stair. Then abruptly, terribly, there rang out a scream of such poignant fear that Belesa's heart almost stopped with the shock of it. She was out of the chamber and flying down the corridor before she was aware that her limbs were in motion. She ran down the stair—and halted as if turned to stone.

She did not scream as Tina had screamed. She was incapable of sound or motion. She saw Tina, was aware of the reality of small hands grasping her frantically. But these were the only sane realities in a scene of black nightmare and lunacy and death, dominated by the monstrous, anthropomorphic shadow which spread awful arms against a lurid, hell-fire glare.

Out in the stockade Strom shook his head at Conan's question.

"I heard nothing."

"I did!" Conan's wild instincts were roused; he was tensed, his eyes blazing. "It came from the south wall, behind those huts!"

Drawing his cutlass he strode toward the palisade. From the compound the wall on the south and the sentry posted there were not visible, being hidden behind the huts. Strom followed, impressed by the Cimmerian's manner.

At the mouth of the open space between the huts and wall Conan halted, warily. The space was dimly lighted by torches flaring at either corner of the stockade. And about mid-way of that natural corridor a crumpled shape sprawled on the ground.

"Bracus!" swore Strom, running forward and dropping on one knee beside the figure. "By Mitra, his throat's been cut from ear to ear!"

Conan swept the space with a quick glance, finding it empty save for himself, Strom and the dead man. He peered through a loop-hole. No living man moved within the ring of torch-light outside the fort.

"Who could have done this?" he wondered.

"Zarono!" Strom sprang up, spitting fury like a wildcat, his hair bristling, his face convulsed. "He has set his thieves to stabbing my men in the back! He plans to wipe me out by treachery! Devils! I am leagued within and without!"

"Wait!" Conan reached a restraining hand. "I don't believe Zarono—"

But the maddened pirate jerked away and rushed around the end of the hut-row, breathing blasphemies. Conan ran after him, swearing. Strom made straight toward the fire by which Zarono's tall lean form was visible as the buccaneer chief quaffed a jack of ale.

His amazement was supreme when the jack was dashed violently from his hand, spattering his breastplate with foam, and he was jerked around to confront the passion-distorted face of the pirate captain.

"You murdering dog!" roared Strom. "Will you slay my men behind my back while they fight for your filthy hide as well as for mine?"

Conan was hurrying toward them and on all sides men ceased eating and drinking to stare in amazement.

"What do you mean?" sputtered Zarono.

"You've set your men to stabbing mine at their posts!" screamed the maddened Barachan.

"You lie!" Smoldering hate burst into sudden flame.

With an incoherent howl Strom heaved up his cutlass and cut at the buccaneer's head. Zarono caught the blow on his armored left arm and sparks flew as he staggered back, ripping out his own sword.

In an instant the captains were fighting like madmen, their blades flaming and flashing in the firelight. Their crews reacted instantly and blindly. A deep roar went up as pirates and buccaneers drew their swords and fell upon each other. The men left on the walls abandoned their posts and leaped down into the stockade, blades in hand. In an instant the compound was a battle-ground, where knotting, writhing groups of men smote and slew in a blind frenzy. Some of the men-at-arms and serfs were drawn into the melee, and the soldiers at the gate turned and stared down in amazement, forgetting the enemy which lurked outside.

It had all happened so quickly—smoldering passions exploding into sudden battle—that men were fighting all over the compound before Conan could reach the maddened chiefs. Ignoring their swords he tore them apart with such violence that they staggered backward, and Zarono tripped and fell headlong.

"You cursed fools, will you throw away all our lives?" Strom was frothing mad and Zarono was bawling for assistance. A buccaneer ran at Conan from behind and cut at his head. The Cimmerian half turned and caught his arm, checking the stroke in mid-air.

"Look, you fools!" he roared, pointing with his sword. Something in his tone caught the attention of the battle-crazed mob; men froze in their places, with lifted swords, Zarono on one knee, and twisted their heads to stare. Conan was pointing at a soldier on the firing-ledge. The man was reeling, arms clawing the air, choking as he tried to shout. Suddenly he pitched headlong to the ground and all saw the black arrow standing up between his shoulders.

A cry of alarm rose from the compound. On the heels of the shout came a clamor of blood-freezing screams, the shattering impact of axes on the gate. Flaming arrows arched over the wall and stuck in logs, and thin wisps of blue smoke curled upward. Then from behind the huts that ranged the south wall came swift and furtive figures racing across the compound.

"The Picts are in!" roared Conan.

Bedlam followed his shout. The freebooters ceased their feud, some turned to meet the savages, some to spring to the wall. Savages were pouring from behind the huts and they streamed over the compound; their axes flashed against the cutlasses of the sailors.

Zarono was struggling to his feet when a painted savage

rushed upon him from behind and brained him with a war-axe.

Conan with a clump of sailors behind him was battling with the Picts inside the stockade, and Strom, with most of his men, was climbing up on the firing-ledges, slashing at the dark figures already swarming over the wall. The Picts, who had crept up unobserved and surrounded the fort while the defenders were fighting among themselves, were attacking from all sides. Valenso's soldiers were clustered at the gate, trying to hold it against a howling swarm of exultant demons.

More and more savages streamed from behind the huts, having scaled the undefended south wall. Strom and his pirates were beaten back from the other sides of the palisade and in an instant the compound was swarming with naked warriors. They dragged down the defenders like wolves; the battle revolved into swirling whirlpools of painted figures surging about small groups of desperate white men. Picts, sailors and henchmen littered the earth, stamped underfoot by the heedless feet. Blood-smeared braves dived howling into huts and the shrieks that rose from the interiors where women and children died beneath the red axes rose above the din of the battle. The men-at-arms abandoned the gate when they heard those pitiful cries, and in an instant the Picts had burst it and were pouring into the palisade at that point also. Huts began to go up in flames.

"Make for the manor!" roared Conan, and a dozen men surged in behind him as he hewed an inexorable way through the snarling pack.

Strom was at his side, wielding his red cutlass like a flail.

"We can't hold the manor," grunted the pirate.

"Why not?" Conan was too busy with his crimson work to spare a glance.

"Because—uh!" A knife in a dark hand sank deep in the Barachan's back. "Devil eat you, bastard!" Strom turned staggeringly and split the savage's head to his teeth. The pirate reeled and fell to his knees, blood starting from his lips.

"The manor's burning!" he croaked, and slumped over in the dust.

Conan cast a swift look about him. The men who had followed him were all down in their blood. The Pict gasping out his life under the Cimmerian's feet was the last of the group which had barred his way. All about him battle was swirling and surging, but for the moment he stood alone. He was not far from the south wall. A few strides and he could leap to the ledge, swing over and be gone through the night. But he remembered the helpless girls in the manor—from which, now, smoke was rolling in billowing masses. He ran toward the manor.

A feathered chief wheeled from the door, lifting a war-axe, and behind the racing Cimmerian lines of fleet-footed braves were converging upon him. He did not check his stride. His downward sweeping cutlass met and deflected the axe and split the skull of the wielder. An instant later Conan was through the door and had slammed and bolted it against the axes that splintered into the wood.

The great hall was full of drifting wisps of smoke through which he groped, half-blinded. Somewhere a woman was whimpering, little, catchy, hysterical sobs of nerve-shattering horror. He emerged from a whorl of smoke and stopped dead in his tracks, glaring down the hall.

The hall was dim and shadowy with drifting smoke; the silver candelabrum was overturned, the candles extinguished; the only illumination was a lurid glow from the great fireplace and the wall in which it was set, where the flames licked from burning floor to smoking roof-beams. And limned against that lurid glare Conan saw a human form swinging slowly at the end of a rope. The dead face turned toward him as the body swung, and it was distorted beyond recognition. But Conan knew it was Count Valenso, hanged to his own roof-beam.

But there was something else in the hall. Conan saw it through the drifting smoke—a monstrous black figure, outlined against the hell-fire glare. That outline was vaguely human; but the shadow thrown on the burning wall was not human at all.

"Crom!" muttered Conan aghast, paralyzed by the realization that he was confronted with a being against which his sword was helpless. He saw Belesa and Tina, clutched in each other's arms, crouching at the bottom of the stair.

The black monster reared up, looming gigantic against the flame, great arms spread wide; a dim face leered through the drifting smoke, semi-human, demonic, altogether terrible—Conan glimpsed the close-set horns, the gaping mouth, the peaked ears—it was lumbering toward him through the smoke, and an old memory woke with desperation.

Near the Cimmerian stood a massive silver bench, ornately carven, once part of the splendor of Korzetta castle. Conan grasped it, heaved it high above his head.

"Silver and fire!" he roared in a voice like a clap of wind, and hurled the bench with all the power of his iron muscles. Full on the great black breast it crashed, a hundred pounds of silver winged with terrific velocity. Not even the black one could stand before such a missile. He was carried off his feet—hurtled backward headlong into the open fireplace which was a roaring mouth of flame. A horrible scream shook the hall, the cry of an unearthly thing gripped suddenly by earthly death. The mantel cracked and stones fell from the great chimney; half-hiding the black writhing limbs at which the flames were eating in elemental fury. Burning beams crashed down from the roof and thundered on the stones, and the whole heap was enveloped by a roaring burst of fire.

Flames were racing down the stair when Conan reached it. He caught up the fainting child under one arm and dragged Belesa to her feet. Through the crackle and snap of the fire sounded the splintering of the door under the war-axes.

He glared about, sighted a door opposite the stair-landing, and hurried through it, carrying Tina and half-dragging Belesa, who seemed dazed. As they came into the chamber beyond, a reverberation behind them announced that the roof was falling in the hall. Through a strangling wall of smoke Conan saw an open, outer door on the other side of the chamber. As he lugged his charges through it, he saw it sagged on broken hinges, lock and bolt snapped and splintered as if by some terrific force.

"The black man came in by this door!" Belesa sobbed hysterically. "I saw him—but I did not know—"

They emerged into the fire-lit compound, a few feet from the hut-row that lined the south wall. A Pict was skulking toward the door, eyes red in the firelight, axe lifted. Turning the girl on his arm away from the blow, Conan drove his cutlass through the savage's breast, and then, sweeping Belesa off her feet, ran toward the south wall, carrying both girls.

The compound was full of billowing smoke clouds that hid half the red work going on there; but the fugitives had been seen. Naked figures, black against the dull glare, pranced out of the smoke, brandishing gleaming axes. They were still yards behind him when Conan ducked into the space between the huts and the wall. At the other end of the corridor he saw other howling shapes, running to cut him off. Halting short he tossed Belesa bodily to the firing-ledge and leaped after her. Swinging her over the palisade he dropped her into the sand outside, and dropped

Tina after her. A thrown axe crashed into a log by his shoulder, and then he too was over the wall and gathering up his dazed and helpless charges. When the Picts reached the wall the space before the palisade was empty of all except the dead.

Chapter 8
A Pirate Returns to the Sea

Dawn was tinging the dim waters with an old rose hue. Far out across the tinted waters a fleck of white grew out of the mist—a sail that seemed to hang suspended in the pearly sky. On a bushy headland Conan the Cimmerian held a ragged cloak over a fire of green wood. As he manipulated the cloak, puffs of smoke rose upward, quivered against the dawn and vanished.

Belesa crouched near him, one arm about Tina.

"Do you think they'll see it and understand?"

"They'll see it, right enough," he assured her. "They've been hanging off and on this coast all night, hoping to sight some survivors. They're scared stiff. There's only half a dozen of them, and not one can navigate well enough to sail from here to the Barachan Isles. They'll understand my signals; it's the pirate code. I'm telling them that the captains are dead and all the sailors, and for them to come inshore and take us aboard. They know I can navigate, and they'll be glad to ship under me; they'll have to. I'm the only captain left."

"But suppose the Picts see the smoke?" She shuddered, glancing back over the misty sands and bushes to where, miles to the north, a column of smoke stood up in the still air.

"They're not likely to see it. After I hid you in the woods I crept back and saw them dragging barrels of wine and ale out of the storehouses. Already most of them were reeling. They'll all be lying around too drunk to move by this time. If I had a hundred men I could wipe out the whole horde. Look! There goes a rocket from *The Red Hand*! That means they're coming to take us off!"

Conan stamped out the fire, handed the cloak back to Belesa and stretched like a great lazy cat. Belesa watched him in wonder. His unperturbed manner was not assumed; the night of fire and blood and slaughter, and the flight through the black woods afterward, had left his nerves untouched. He was as calm as if he had spent the night in feast and revel. Belesa did not fear him; she felt safer than she had felt since she landed on that wild coast. He was not like the freebooters, civilized men who had repudiated all standards of honor, and lived without any. Conan, on the other hand, lived according to the code of his people, which was barbaric and bloody, but at least upheld its own peculiar standards of honor.

"Do you think he is dead?" she asked, with seeming irrelevancy.

He did not ask her to whom she referred.

"I believe so. Silver and fire are both deadly to evil spirits, and he got a belly-full of both."

Neither spoke of that subject again; Belesa's mind shrank from the task of conjuring up the scene when a black figure skulked into the great hall and a long-delayed vengeance was horribly consummated.

"What will you do when you get back to Zingara?" Conan asked.

She shook her head helplessly. "I do not know. I have neither money nor friends. I am not trained to earn my living. Perhaps it would have been better had one of those arrows struck my heart."

"Do not say that, my Lady!" begged Tina. "I will work for us both!"

Conan drew a small leather bag from inside his girdle.

"I didn't get Tothmekri's jewels," he rumbled. "But here are some baubles I found in the chest where I got the clothes I'm wearing." He spilled a handful of flaming rubies into his palm. "They're worth a fortune, themselves." He dumped them back into the bag and handed it to her.

"But I can't take these—" she began.

"Of course you'll take them. I might as well leave you for the Picts to scalp as to take you back to Zingara to starve," said he. "I know what it is to be penniless in a Hyborian land. Now in my country sometimes there are famines; but people are hungry only when there's no food in the land at all. But in civilized countries I've seen people sick of gluttony while others were starving. Aye, I've seen men fall and die of hunger against the walls of shops and storehouses crammed with food.

"Sometimes I was hungry, too, but then I took what I wanted at sword's-point. But you can't do that. So you take these rubies. You can sell them and buy a castle, and slaves and fine clothes, and with them it won't be hard to get a husband, because civilized men all desire wives with these possessions."

"But what of you?"

Conan grinned and indicated *The Red Hand* drawing swiftly inshore.

"A ship and a crew are all I want. As soon as I set foot on that deck, I'll have a ship, and as soon as I can raise the Barachans I'll have a crew. The lads of the Red Brotherhood are eager to ship with me, because I always lead them to rare loot. And as soon as I've set you and the girl ashore on the Zingaran coast, I'll show the dogs some looting! Nay, nay, no thanks! What are a handful of gems to me, when all the loot of the southern seas will be mine for the grasping?"

Editor's Introduction to

"Adept's Gambit"

*F*ritz Leiber is one of the diminishing group of authors from the Golden Age of the pulp magazines who are still actively writing today. Generally considered the dean of fantasy writers, Leiber's numerous awards from both the science fiction and the fantasy communities establish him as the most honored author ever to cross these frequently antipathetic genres. Born in Chicago on December 24, 1910, Leiber has for many years resided in San Francisco. Both cities have frequently furnished settings for the tales of modern urban horrors that Leiber was among the first to define—ranging from his early short story, "Smoke Ghost" (Unknown Worlds, October 1941), to his World Fantasy Award–winning novel, Our Lady of Darkness (1977).

This theme of urban terrors extends to Leiber's most popular work, a series of tales concerning the Gray Mouser and Fafherd. Despite Fafhrd's ostensible typecasting as the familiar hulking barbarian from northern climes, the pair are obviously civilized and sophisticated ("street wise" in the current idiom), and between forays into distant realms they return to their preferred base of operations in the mythical city of Lankhmar—itself the setting of many by-no-means-prosaic adventures.

*The series originated about 1934 in the course of a
letter from Leiber's friend, Harry Fischer, which described
the two adventurers. Leiber responded with some ideas as
to their possible exploits, and through subsequent corre-
spondence the saga of the Gray Mouser and Fafhrd was
born. Early episodes, written primarily for their private
amusement, included such as* "Conquest Among the Baldest
Rats," "The Seventh Eye of Ningauble," *and* "The Adventure of the Grain Ships." *These early manuscripts were
circulated among other correspondents, one of whom was
H. P. Lovecraft, who wrote back:* "Some day I hope the
Fafhrd cycle will get into print, leading off with Adept's
Gambit."

*Getting into print wouldn't prove easy. Weird Tales was
the obvious market for the stories, particularly after Robert E. Howard's death. However, editor Farnsworth Wright,
committing one of his more resounding lapses of judgment,
rejected the series. Success came when* "Two Sought Adventure" *finally appeared in the August 1939 issue of*
Unknown. *Editor John Campbell complained to Leiber
that the series really belonged in* Weird Tales, *but that
didn't keep him from publishing five of the stories before
the magazine was discontinued in 1943. Perhaps Wright's
hesitance derived from the fact that Leiber's creation owed
nothing to the stories of Robert E. Howard. Instead one
sees traces of Lord Dunsany and particularly of James
Branch Cabell in the sardonic elegance of Leiber's writing.*

"Adept's Gambit," *the earliest circulated work in the
series, despite Lovecraft's high regard for it, would not
see print until 1947 in Leiber's Arkham House collection,*
Night's Black Agents. *This would soon become a rare
book, and* "Adept's Gambit" *would not become readily
accessible to readers until its inclusion in* Swords in the
Mist *(1968), one of several paperback volumes from Ace
Books that collected all the stories in the series written up*

*until that time. Since Leiber is still writing new episodes in
the saga of the Gray Mouser and Fafhrd, one hopes that
the definitive "complete collection" is to be many years in
the future. Indeed, the half-century of imagination devoted
to the two adventurers is one of the reasons why the
Gray Mouser and Fafhrd are unique in a genre whose
heroes as a rule are hastily conceived and short-lived
products of the adolescent mind.*

*The world of Lankhmar, wherein most of the stories take
place, is that of a parallel universe. "Adept's Gambit,"
however, is set in a world of the historical past—a circum-
stance that required a little rearranging when this short
novel was incorporated into the later body of work. This
version is that of the original 1947 publication, and it is
the version Fritz Leiber considers to be the definitive one.*

Adept's Gambit

Fritz Leiber

1
Tyre

It happened that while Fafhrd and the Gray Mouser
were dallying in a wine shop near the Sidonian Harbor of
Tyre, where all wine shops are of doubtful repute, a long-
limbed yellow-haired Galatian girl lolling in Fafhrd's lap
turned suddenly into a wallopingly large sow. It was a

singular occurrence, even in Tyre. The Mouser's eyebrows
arched as the Galatian's breasts, exposed by the Cretan
dress that was the style revival of the hour, became the
uppermost pair of slack white dugs, and he watched the
whole proceeding with unfeigned interest.

The next day four camel traders, who drank only water
disinfected with sour wine, and two purple-armed dyers,
who were cousins of the host, swore that no transformation
took place and that they saw nothing, or very little out of
the ordinary. But three drunken soldiers of King Antiochus
and the four women with them, as well as a completely
sober Armenian juggler, attested the event in all its details.
An Egyptian mummy-smuggler won brief attention with
the claim that the oddly garbed sow was only a semblance,
or phantom, and made dark references to visions vouchsafed men by the animal gods of his native land, but since
it was hardly a year since the Seluicids had beaten the
Ptolomies out of Tyre, he was quickly shouted down. An
impecunious travelling lecturer from Jerusalem took up an
even more attenuated position, the semblance of a semblance of a sow.

Fafhrd, however, had no time for such metaphysical
niceties. When, maintaining that the sow was not a sow,
or even a semblance, but only with a roar of disgust not
unmingled with terror, he had shoved the squealing mon-
strosity halfway across the room so that it fell with a great
splash into the water tank, it turned back again into a
long-limbed Galatian girl and a very angry one, for the
stale water in which the sow had floundered drenched her
garments and plastered down her yellow hair (the Mouser
murmured, "Aphrodite!") and the sow's uncorsettable bulk
had split the tight Cretan waist. The stars of midnight were
peeping through the skylight above the tank, and the wine
cups had been many times refilled, before her anger was
dissipated. Then, just as Fafhrd was impressing a re-

introductory kiss upon her melting lips, he felt them once again become slobbering and tusky. This time she picked herself up from between two wine casks and, ignoring the shrieks, excited comments, and befuddled stares as merely part of a rude mystification that had been carried much too far, she walked with Amazonian dignity from the room. She paused only once, on the dark and deep-worn threshold, and then but to hurl at Fafhrd a small dagger, which he absentmindedly deflected upward with his copper goblet, so that it struck full in the mouth a wooden satyr on the wall, giving that deity the appearance of introspectively picking his teeth.

Fafhrd's sea-green eyes became likewise thoughtful. He slowly scanned the wine-shop patrons, face by sly-eyed face, pausing doubtfully when he came to a tall, dark-haired girl beyond the water tank, finally returning to the Mouser. There he stopped, and a certain suspiciousness became apparent in his gaze.

The Mouser folded his arms, flared his snub nose, and returned the stare with all the sneering suavity of a Parthian ambassador. Abruptly he turned, embraced and kissed the cross-eyed Greek girl sitting beside him, grinned wordlessly at Fafhrd, dusted from his coarse-woven gray silk robe the antimony that had fallen from her eyelids, and folded his arms again.

Fafhrd began softly to beat the base of his goblet against the butt of his palm. His wide, tight-laced leather belt, wet with the sweat that stained his white linen tunic, creaked faintly.

Meanwhile murmured speculation as to the person responsible for casting a spell on Fafhrd's Galatian eddied around the tables and settled uncertainly on the tall, dark-haired girl, probably because she was sitting alone and therefore could not join the suspicious whispering.

"She's an odd one," Chloe, the cross-eyed Greek,

confided to the Mouser. "Silent Salmacis they call her, but I happen to know that her real name is Ahura."

"A Persian?" asked the Mouser.

Chloe shrugged. "She's been around for years, though no one knows exactly where she lives or what she does. She used to be a gay, gossipy little thing, though she never would go with men. Once she gave me an amulet, to protect me from someone, she said—I still wear it. But then she was away for a while," Chloe continued garrulously, "and when she came back she was just like you see her now—shy, and tight-mouthed as a clam, with a look in her eyes of someone peering through a crack in a brothel wall."

"Ah," said the Mouser. He looked at the dark-haired girl, and continued to look, appreciatively, even when Chloe tugged at his sleeve. Chloe gave herself a mental bastinado for having been so foolish as to call a man's attention to another girl.

Fafhrd was not distracted by this byplay. He continued to stare at the Mouser with the stony intentness of a whole avenue of Egyptian colossi. The cauldron of his anger came to a boil.

"Scum of wit-weighted culture," he said, "I consider it the nadir of base perfidy that you should try out on me your puking sorcery."

"Softly, man of strange loves," purred the Mouser. "This unfortunate mishap has befallen several others besides yourself, among them an ardent Assyrian warlord whose paramour was changed into a spider between the sheets, and an impetuous Ethiope who found himself hoisted several yards into the air and kissing a giraffe. Truly, to one who knows the literature, there is nothing new in the annals of magic and thaumaturgy."

"Moreover," continued Fafhrd, his low-pitched voice loud in the silence, "I regard it an additional treachery that you should practice your pig-trickery on me in an unsuspecting moment of pleasure.''

"And even if I should choose sorcerously to discommode your lechery," hypothesized the Mouser, "I do not think it would be the woman that I would metamorphose."

"Furthermore," pursued Fafhrd, leaning forward and laying his hand on the large sheathed dirk beside him on the bench, "I judge it an intolerable and direct affront to myself that you should pick a Galatian girl, member of a race that is cousin to my own."

"It would not be the first time," observed the Mouser portentously, slipping his fingers inside his robe, "that I have had to fight you over a woman."

"But it would be the first time," asserted Fafhrd, with an even greater portentousness, "that you had to fight me over a pig!"

For a moment he maintained his belligerent posture, head lowered, jaw outthrust, eyes slitted. Then he began to laugh.

It was something, Fahrd's laughter. It began with windy snickers through the nostrils, next spewed out between clenched teeth, then became a series of jolting chortles, swiftly grew into a roar against which the barbarian had to brace himself, legs spread wide, head thrown back, as if against a gale. It was a laughter of the storm-lashed forest or the sea, a laughter that conjured up wide visions, that seemed to blow from a more primeval, heartier, lusher time. It was the laughter of the Elder Gods observing their creature man and noting their omissions, miscalculations, and mistakes.

The Mouser's lips began to twitch. He grimaced wryly, seeking to avoid the infection. Then he joined in.

Fafhrd paused, panted, snatched up the wine pitcher, drained it.

"Pig-trickery!" he bellowed, and began to laugh all over again.

The Tyrian riff-raff gawked at them in wonder—astounded, awestruck, their imaginations cloudily stirred.

Among them, however, was one whose response was noteworthy. The dark-haired girl was staring at Fafhrd avidly, drinking in the sound, the oddest sort of hunger and baffled curiosity—and calculation—in her eyes.

Mouser noticed her and stopped his laughter to watch. Mentally Chloe gave herself an especially heavy swipe on the soles of her bound, naked feet.

Fafhrd's laughter trailed off. He blew out the last of it soundlessly, sucked in a normal breath, hooked his thumbs in his belt.

"The dawn stars are peeping," he commented to the Mouser, ducking his head for a look through the skylight. "It's time we were about the business."

And without more ado he and the Mouser left the shop, pushing out of their way a newly arrived and very drunken merchant of Perganum, who looked after them bewilderedly, as if he were trying to decide whether they were a tall god and his dwarfish servitor, or a small sorcerer and the great-thewed automaton who did his bidding.

Had it ended there, two weeks would have seen Fafhrd claiming that the incident of the wine shop was merely a drunken dream that had been dreamed by more than one—a kind of coincidence with which he was by no means unfamiliar. But it did not. After "the business" (which turned out to be much more complicated than had been anticipated, evolving from a fairly simple affair of Sidonian smugglers into a glittering intrigue studded with Cilician pirates, a kidnapped Cappadocian princess, a forged letter of credit on a Syracusian financier, a bargain with a female Cyprian slave-dealer, a rendezvous that turned into an ambush, some priceless tomb-filched Egyptian jewels that no one ever saw, and a band of Idumean brigands who came galloping out of the desert to upset everyone's calculations) and after Fafhrd and the Gray Mouser had returned to the soft embraces and sweet polyglot of the seaport ladies, pig-trickery befell Fafhrd once more, this time ending in a dagger brawl with some men who thought they were rescuing a pretty Bithynian girl from death by salty and odorous drowning at the hands of a murderous red-haired giant—Fafhrd had insisted on dipping the girl, while still metamorphosed, into a hogshead of brine remaining from pickled pork. This incident suggested to the Mouser a scheme he never told Fafhrd: namely, to engage an amiable girl, have Fafhrd turn her into a pig, immediately sell her to a butcher, next sell her to an amorous merchant when she had escaped the bewildered butcher as a furious girl, have Fafhrd sneak after the merchant and turn her back into a pig (by this time he ought to be able to do it merely by making eyes at her), then sell her to another butcher and begin all over again. Low prices, quick profits.

For a while Fafhrd stubbornly continued to suspect the Mouser, who was forever dabbling in black magic and carried a gray leather case of bizarre instruments picked from the pockets of wizards and recondite books looted from Chaldean libraries—even though long experience had taught Fafhrd that the Mouser seldom read systematically beyond the prefaces in the majority of his books (though he often unrolled the later portions to the accompaniment of penetrating glances and trenchant criticisms) and that he was never able to evoke the same results two times running with his enchantments. That he could manage to transform two of Fafhrd's lights of love was barely possible; that he should get a sow each time was unthinkable. Besides the thing happened more than twice; in fact, there was never a time when it did not happen. Moreover, Fafhrd did not really believe in magic, least of all the Mouser's. And if

there was any doubt left in his mind, it was dispelled when
a dark and satiny-skinned Egyptian beauty in the Mouser's
close embrace was transformed into a giant snail. The
Gray One's disgust at the slimy tracks on his silken garments was not to be mistaken, and was not lessened when
two witnesses, traveling horse doctors, claimed that they
had seen no snail, giant or ordinary, and agreed that the
Mouser was suffering from an obscure kind of wet rot that
induced hallucinations of animals in its victim, and for
which they were prepared to offer a rare Median remedy at
the bargain price of nineteen drachmas a jar.

Fafhrd's glee at his friend's discomfiture was short-
lived, for after a night of desperate and far-flung experi-
mentation, which, some said, blazed from the Sidonian
harbor to the Temple of Melkarth a trail of snail tracks that
next morning baffled all the madams and half the husbands
in Tyre, the Mouser discovered something he had suspected all the time, but had hoped was not the whole truth:
namely, that Chloe alone was immune to the strange plague
his kisses carried.

Needless to say, this pleased Chloe immensely. An
arrogant self-esteem gleamed like two clashing swords
from her crossed eyes and she applied nothing but costly
scented oil to her poor, mentally bruised feet—and not
only mental oil, for she quickly made capital of her position by extorting enough gold from the Mouser to buy a
slave whose duty it was to do very little else. She no
longer sought to avoid calling the Mouser's attention to
other women, in fact she rather enjoyed doing so, and the
next time they encountered the dark-haired girl variously
called Ahura and Silent Salmacis, as they were entering a
tavern known as the Murex Shell, she volunteered more
information.

"Ahura's not so innocent, you know, in spite of the
way she sticks to herself. Once she went off with some old

man—that was before she gave me the charm—and once I heard a primped-up Persian lady scream at her, 'What have you done with your brother?' Ahura didn't answer, just looked at the woman coldly as a snake, and after a while the woman ran out. Brr! You should have seen her eyes!''

But the Mouser pretended not to be interested.

Fafhrd could undoubtedly have had Chloe for the polite asking, and Chloe was more than eager to extend and cement in this fashion her control over the twain. But Fafhrd's pride would not allow him to accept such a favor from his friend, and he had frequently in past days, more-over, railed against Chloe as a decadent and unappetizing contemplater of her own nose.

So he perforce led a monastic life and endured contemp-tuous feminine glares across the drinking table and fended off painted boys who misinterpreted his misogyny and was much irritated by a growing rumor to the effect that he had become a secret eunuch priest of Cybele. Gossip and speculation had already fantastically distorted the truer accounts of what had happened, and it did not help when the girls who had been transformed denied it for fear of hurting their business. Some people got the idea that Fafhrd had committed the nasty sin of bestiality and they urged his prosecution in the public courts. Others accounted him a fortunate man who had been visited by an amorous goddess in the guise of a swine, and who thereafter scorned all earthly girls. While still others whispered that he was a brother of Circe and that he customarily dwelt on a float-ing island in the Tyrrhenian Sea, where he kept cruelly transformed into pigs a whole herd of beautiful shipwrecked maidens. His laughter was heard no more and dark circles appeared in the white skin around his eyes and he began to make guarded inquiries among magicians in hopes of find-ing some remedial charm.

"I think I've hit on a cure for your embarrassing ailment," said the Mouser carelessly one night, laying aside a raggedy brown papyrus. "Came across it in this obscure treatise, 'The Demonology of Isaiah ben Elshaz.' It seems that whatever change takes place in the form of the woman you love, you should continue to make love to her, trusting to the power of your passion to transform her back to her original shape."

Fafhrd left off honing his great sword and asked, "Then why don't you try kissing snails?"

"It would be disagreeable and, for one free of barbarian prejudices, there is always Chloe."

"Pah! You're just going with her to keep your self-respect. I know you. For seven days now you'd had thoughts for no one but that Ahura wench."

"A pretty chit, but not to my liking," said the Mouser icily. "It must be your eye she's the apple of. However, you really should try my remedy; I'm sure you'd prove so good at it that the shes of all the swine in the world would come squealing after you."

Whereupon Fafhrd smote at the Mouser and a scuffle ensued which did not end until the Gray One was half strangled and one of Fafhrd's arms dislocated by a method generally known only to men from beyond the Indus.

However, Fafhrd did go so far as to hold firmly at arm's length the next sow his pent passion created, and feed it slops in the hope of accomplishing something by kindness. But in the end he had once again to admit defeat and assuage with owl-stamped Athenian silver didrachmas a hysterically angry Scythian girl who was sick at the stomach. It was then that an ill-advised curious young Greek philosopher suggested to the Northman that the soul or inward form of the thing loved is alone of importance, the outward form having no ultimate significance.

"You belong to the Socratic school?" Fafhrd questioned gently.

The Greek nodded.

"Socrates was the philosopher who was able to drink unlimited quantities of wine without blinking?"

Again the quick nod.

"That was because his rational soul dominated his animal soul?"

"You are learned," replied the Greek, with a more respectful but equally quick nod.

"I am not through. Do you consider yourself in all ways a true follower of your master?"

This time the Greek's quickness undid him. He nodded, and two days later he was carried out of the wine shop by friends, who found him cradled in a broken wine barrel, as if new born in no common manner. For days he remained drunk, time enough for a small sect to spring up who believed him a reincarnation of Dionysos and as such worshipped him. The sect was dissolved when he became half sober and delivered his first oracular address, which had as its subject the evils of drunkenness.

The morning after the deification of the rash philosopher, Fafhrd awoke when the first hot sunbeams struck the flat roof on which he and the Mouser had chosen to pass the night. Without sound or movement, suppressing the urge to groan out for someone to buy him a bag of snow from the white-capped Lebanons (over which the sun was even now peeping) to cool his aching head, he opened an eye on the sight that he in his wisdom had expected: the Mouser sitting on his heels and looking at the sea.

"Son of a wizard and a witch," he said, "it seems that once again we must fall back upon our last resource."

The Mouser did not turn his head, but he nodded it once, deliberately.

"The first time we did not come away with our lives," Fafhrd went on.

"The second time we lost our souls to the Other Creatures," the Mouser chimed in, as if they were singing a dawn chant to Isis.

"And the last time we fell through the Hole in the World."

"He may trick us into drinking the drink, and we not awake for another five hundred years."

"He may send us to our deaths and we not to be reincarnated for another two thousand," Fafhrd continued.

"He may show us Pan, or offer us to the Elder gods, or send us back to Lankhmar," the Mouser concluded.

There was a pause of several moments.

Then the Gray Mouser whispered, "Nevertheless, we must visit Ningauble of the Seven Eyes."

And he spoke truly, for as Fafhrd had guessed, his soul was hovering over the sea dreaming of dark-haired Ahura.

2
Ningauble

So they crossed the snowy Lebanons and stole three camels, virtuously choosing to rob a rich landlord who made his tenants milk rocks and sow the shores of the Dead Sea, for it was unwise to approach the Gossiper of the Gods with an overly dirty conscience. After seven days of pitching and tossing across the desert, furnace days that made Fafhrd curse Musphelheim's fire gods, in whom he did not believe, they reached the Sand Combers and the Great Sand Whirlpools, and warily slipping past them while they were only lazily twirling, climbed the Rocky

Islet. The city-loving Mouser ranted at Ningauble's prefer-
ence for "a godforsaken hole in the desert," although he
suspected that the Newsmonger and his agents came and
went by a more hospitable road than the one provided for
visitors, and although he knew as well as Fafhrd that the
Snarer of Rumors (especially the false, which are the more
valuable) must live as close to India and the infinite garden
lands of the Yellow Men as to barbaric Britain and
marching Rome, as close to the heaven-steaming trans-
Ethiopian jungle as to the mystery of lonely tablelands and
star-scraping mountains beyond the Caspian Sea.

With high expectations they tethered their camels, took
torches, and fearlessly entered the Bottomless Caves, for it
was not so much in the visiting of Ningauble that danger
lay as in the tantalizing charm of his advice, which was so
great that one had to follow wherever it led.

Nevertheless Fafhrd said, "An earthquake swallowed
Ningauble's house and it stuck in his throat. May he not
hiccup."

As they were passing over the Trembling Bridge span-
ning the Pit of Ultimate Truth, which could have devoured
the light of ten thousand torches without becoming any
less black, they met and edged wordlessly past a helmeted,
impassive fellow whom they recognized as a far-journeying
Mongol. Safely across, they speculated as to whether he too
were a visitor of the Gossiper, or a spy—Fafhrd had no
faith in the clairvoyant powers of the seven eyes, averring
that they were merely a sham to awe fools and that
Ningauble's information was gathered by a corps of ped-
lars, panderers, slaves, urchins, eunuchs, and midwives,
which outnumbered the grand armies of a dozen kings.

Presently they saw a faint light flickering on the stalactited
roof, reflected from a level above them. Soon they were
struggling toward it up the Staircase of Error, an agglom-
eration of great rough rocks. Fafhrd stretched his long

legs; the Mouser leapt catlike. The little creatures that
scurried about their feet, brushed their shoulders in slow
flight, or merely showed their yellow, insatiably curious
eyes from crevice and rocky perch, multiplied in number;
for they were nearing the Arch-eavesdropper.

A little later, having wasted no time in reconnoitering,
they stood before the Great Gate, whose iron-studded upper
reaches disdained the illumination of the tiny fire. It was
not the gate, however, that interested them, but its keeper,
a monstrously paunched creature sitting on the floor beside
a vast heap of potsherds, and whose only movement was a
rubbing of what seemed to be his hands. He kept them
under the shabby but voluminous cloak which also completely hooded his head. A third of the way down the
cloak, two large bats clung.

Fafhrd cleared his throat.

The movement ceased under the cloak.

Then out of the top of it sinuously writhed something
that seemed to be a serpent, only in place of a head it bore
an opalescent jewel with a dark central speck. Nevertheless, one might finally have judged it a serpent, were it
not that it also resembled a thick-stalked exotic bloom idly
waved by an exquisite. It restlessly turned this way and that
until it pointed at the two strangers. Then it went rigid and
the bulbous extremity seemed to glow more brightly. There
came a low purring and five similar stalks twisted rapidly
from under the hood and aligned themselves with their
companion. Then the black pupils dilated.

"Fat-bellied rumor monger!" hailed the Mouser nervously. "Must you forever play at peep show?"

For one could never quite get over the faint initial
uneasiness that came with meeting Ningauble of the Seven
Eyes.

"Is it not time," a voice from under the hood thinly
quavered, "that you ceased to impose on me, because you

once got me an unborn ghoul that I might question it of its parentage? The service to me was slight, accepted only to humor you; and I, by the name of the Spoorless God, have repaid it twenty times over."

"Nonsense, Midwife of Secrets," retorted the Mouser, stepping forward familiarly, his gay impudence almost restored. "You know as well as I that deep in your great paunch you are trembling with delight at having a chance to mouth your knowledge to two such appreciative listeners as we."

"That is as far from the truth as I am from the Secret of the Sphinx," commented Ningauble, four of his eyes following the Mouser's advance, one keeping watch on Fafhrd, while the sixth looped back around the hood to reappear on the other side and gaze suspiciously behind them.

"But, Ancient Talebearer, I am sure you have been closer to the Sphinx than any of her stony lovers. Very likely she first received her paltry riddle from your great store."

Ningauble quivered like jelly at this tickling flattery.

"Nevertheless," he piped, "today I am in a merry humor and will give ear to your question. But remember that it will almost certainly be too difficult for me."

"We know your great ingenuity in the face of insurmountable obstacles," rejoined the Mouser in the properly soothing tones.

"Why doesn't your friend come forward?" asked Ningauble, suddenly querulous again.

Fafhrd had been waiting for that question. It always went against his grain to have to behave congenially toward one who called himself the Mightiest Magician as well as the Gossiper of the Gods. But that Ningauble should let hang from his shoulders two bats whom he called Hugin and Munin, in open burlesque of Odin's ravens, was too much for him. It was more a patriotic than religious matter with Fafhrd. He believed in Odin only during moments of sentimental weakness.

"Slay the bats or send them slithering and I'll come, but not before," he dogmatized.

"Now I'll tell you nothing," said Ningauble pettishly, "for, as all know, my health will not permit bickering."

"But, Schoolmaster of Falsehood," purred the Mouser, darting a murderous glance at Fafhrd, "that is indeed to be regretted, especially since I was looking forward to regaling you with the intricate scandal that the Friday concubine of the satrap Philip withheld even from her body slave."

"Ah well," conceded the Many-Eyed One, "it is time for Hugin and Munin to feed."

The bats reluctantly unfurled their wings and flew lazily into the darkness.

Fafhrd stirred himself and moved forward, sustaining the scrutiny of the majority of the eyes, all six of which the Northman considered artfully manipulated puppet-orbs. The seventh no man had seen, or boasted of having seen, save the Mouser, who claimed it was Odin's other eye, stolen from sagacious Mimer—this not because he believed it, but to irk his northern comrade.

"Greetings, Snake Eyes," Fafhrd boomed.

"Oh, is it you, Hulk?" said Ningauble carelessly. "Sit down, both, and share my humble fire."

"Are we not to be invited beyond the Great Gate and share your fabulous comforts too?"

"Do not mock me, Gray One. As all know, I am poor, penurious Ningauble."

So with a sigh the Mouser settled himself on his heels, for he well knew that the Gossiper prized above all else a reputation for poverty, chastity, humility, and thrift, therefore playing his own doorkeeper, except on certain days when the Great Gate muted the tinkle of impious sistrum and the lascivious wail of flute and the giggles of those who postured in the shadow shows.

But now Ningauble coughed piteously and seemed to shiver and warmed his cloaked members at the fire. And the shadows flickered weakly against iron and stone, and the little creatures crept rustling in, making their eyes wide to see and their ears cupped to hear; and upon their rhythmically swinging, weaving stalks pulsated the six eyes. At intervals, too, Ningauble would pick up, seemingly at random, a potsherd from the great pile and rapidly scan the memorandum scribbled on it, without breaking the rhythm of the eye-stalks or, apparently, the thread of his attention.

As Fafhrd started to speak, Ningauble questioned rapidly, "And now, my children, you had something to tell me concerning the Friday concubine—"

"Ah yes, Artist of Untruth," the Mouser cut in hastily, "concerning not so much the concubine as three eunuch priests of Cybele and a slave-girl from Samos—a tasty affair of wondrous complexity, which you must give me leave to let simmer in my mind so that I may serve it up to you skimmed of the slightest fact of exaggeration and with all the spice of true detail."

"And while we wait for the Mouser's mind-pot to boil," said Fafhrd casually, at last catching the spirit of the thing, "you may the more merrily pass the time by advising us as to a trifling difficulty." And he gave a succinct account of their tantalizing bedevilment by sow- and snail-changed maidens.

"And you say that Chloe alone proved immune to the spell?" queried Ningauble thoughtfully, tossing a potsherd to the far side of the pile. "Now that brings to my mind—"

"The exceedingly peculiar remark at the end of Diotima's fourth epistle to Socrates?" interrupted the Mouser brightly. "Am I not right, Father?"

"You are not," replied Ningauble coldly. "As I was

about to observe, when this tick of the intellect sought to burrow the skin of my mind, there must be something that throws a protective influence around Chloe. Do you know of any god or demon in whose special favor she stands, or any incantation or rune she habitually mumbles, or any notable talisman, charm, or amulet she customarily wears or inscribes on her body?''

"She did mention one thing," the Mouser admitted diffidently after a moment. "An amulet given her years ago by some Persian, or Greco-Persian girl. Doubtless a trifle of no consequence."

"Doubtless. Now, when the first sow-change occurred, did Fafhrd laugh the laugh? He did? That was unwise, as I have many times warned you. Advertise often enough your connection with the Elder Gods and you may be sure that some greedy searcher from the pit . . ."

"But what *is* our connection with the Elder Gods?" asked the Mouser, eagerly, though not hopefully. Fafhrd grunted derisively.

"Those are matters best not spoken of," Ningauble ordained. "Was there anyone who showed a particular interest in Fafhrd's laughter?"

The Mouser hesitated. Fafhrd coughed. Thus prodded, the Mouser confessed, "Oh, there was a girl who was perhaps a trifle more attentive than the others to his bellowing. A Persian girl. In fact, as I recall, the same one who gave Chloe the amulet."

"Her name is Ahura," said Fafhrd. "The Mouser's in love with her."

"A fable!" the Mouser denied laughingly, double-daggering Fafhrd with a surreptitious glare. "I can assure you, Father, that she is a very shy, stupid girl, who cannot possibly be concerned in any way with our troubles."

"Of course, since you say so," Ningauble observed, his voice icily rebuking. "However, I can tell you this much:

the one who has placed the ignominious spell upon you is, insofar as he partakes of humanity, a man . . ."

(The Mouser was relieved. It was unpleasant to think of dark-haired, lithe Ahura being subjected to certain methods of questioning which Ningauble was reputed to employ. He was irked at his own clumsiness in trying to lead Ningauble's attention away from Ahura. Where she was concerned, his wit failed him.)

". . . and an adept," Ningauble concluded.

The Mouser started. Fafhrd groaned, "Again?"

"Again," Ningauble affirmed. "Though why, save for your connection with the Elder Gods, you should interest those most recondite of creatures, I cannot guess. They are not men who wittingly will stand in the glaringly illuminated foreground of history. They seek—"

"But who is it?" Fafhrd interjected.

"Be quiet, Mutilator of Rhetoric. They seek the shadows, and surely for good reason. They are the glorious amateurs of high magic, disdaining practical ends, caring only for the satisfaction of their insatiable curiosities, and therefore doubly dangerous. They are—"

"But what's his name?"

"Silence, Trampler of Beautiful Phrases. They are in their fashion fearless, irreligiously considering themselves the co-equals of destiny and having only contempt for the Demigoddess of Chance, the Imp of Luck, and the Demon of Improbability. In short, they are adversaries before whom you should certainly tremble and to whose will you should unquestionably bow."

"But his name, Father, his name!" Fafhrd burst out, and the Mouser, his impudence again in the ascendant, remarked, "It is he of the Sabihoon, is it not, Father?"

"It is not. The Sabihoon are an ignorant fisher folk who inhabit the hither shore of the far lake and worship the beast god Wheen, denying all others," a reply that tickled the Mouser, for to the best of his knowledge he had just invented the Sabihoon.

"No, his name is . . ." Ningauble paused and began to chuckle. "I was forgetting that I must under no circumstances tell you his name."

Fafhrd jumped up angrily. "What?"

"Yes, Children," said Ningauble, suddenly making his eye-stalks staringly rigid, stern, and uncompromising. "And I must furthermore tell you that I can in no way help you in this matter . . ." (Fafhrd clenched his fists) ". . . and I am very glad of it too . . ." (Fafhrd swore) ". . . for it seems to me that no more fitting punishment could have been devised for your abominable lecheries, which I have so often bemoaned . . ." (Fafhrd's hand went to his sword hilt) ". . . in fact, if it had been up to me to chastise you for your manifold vices, I would have chosen the very same enchantment . . ." (But now he had gone too far; Fafhrd growled, "Oh, so it is you who are behind it!" ripped out his sword, and began to advance slowly on the hooded figure) ". . . Yes, my children, you must accept your lot without rebellion or bitterness . . ." (Fafhrd continued to advance) ". . . Far better that you should retire from the world as I have and give yourselves to meditation and repentance. . . ." (The sword, flickering with firelight, was only a yard away) ". . . Far better that you should live out the rest of this incarnation in solitude, each surrounded by his faithful band of sows or snails . . ." (The sword touched the ragged robe) ". . . devoting your remaining years to the promotion of a better understanding between mankind and the lower animals. However—" (Ningauble sighed and the sword hesitated) ". . . if it is still your firm and foolhardy intention to challenge this adept, I suppose I must aid you with what little advice I can give, though warning you that it will plunge you into maelstroms of trouble and lay upon you geases you will grow grey in fulfilling, and incidentally be the means of your deaths.''

Fafhrd lowered his sword. The silence in the black cave grew heavy and ominous. Then, in a voice that was distant yet resonant, like the sound that came from the statue of Memnon at Thebes when the first rays of the morning sun fell upon it, Ningauble began to speak.

''It comes to me, confusedly, like a scene in a rusted mirror; nevertheless, it comes, and thus: You must first possess yourselves of certain trifles. The shroud of Ahriman, from the secret shrine near Persepolis—''

''But what about the accursed swordsmen of Ahriman, Father?'' put in the Mouser. ''There are twelve of them. Twelve, Father, and all very accursed and hard to persuade.''

''Do you think I am setting toss-and-fetch problems for puppy dogs?'' wheezed Ningauble angrily. ''To proceed: You must secondly obtain powdered mummy from the Demon Pharaoh, who reined for three horrid and unhistoried midnights after the death of Ikhnaton—''

''But, Father,'' Fafhrd protested, blushing a little, ''you know who owns that powdered mummy, and what she demands of any two men who visit her.''

''Shh! I'm your elder, Fafhrd, by eons. Thirdly, you must get the cup from which Socrates drank the hemlock, fourthly a sprig from the original Tree of Life, and lastly . . .'' He hesitated as if his memory had failed him, dipped up a potsherd from the pile, and read from it: ''And lastly, you must procure the woman who will come when she is ready.''

''What woman?''

''The woman who will come when she is ready.'' Ningauble tossed back the fragment, starting a small land-slide of shards.

''Corrode Loki's bones!'' cursed Fafhrd, and the Mouser

said, "But Father, no woman comes when she's ready. She always waits."

Ningauble sighed merrily and said, "Do not be downcast, Children. Is it ever the custom of your good friend the Gossiper to give simple advice?"

"It is not," said Fafhrd.

"Well, having all these things, you must go to the Lost City of Ahriman that lies east of Armenia—whisper not its name—"

"Is it Khatti?" whispered the Mouser.

"No, Blowfly. And furthermore, why are you interrupting me when you are supposed to be hard at work recalling all the details of the scandal of the Friday concubine, the three eunuch priests, and the slave girl from Samos?"

"Oh truly, Spy of the Unmentionable, I labor at that until my mind becomes a weariness and a wandering, and all for love of you." The Mouser was glad of Ningauble's question, for he had forgotten the three eunuch priests, which would have been most unwise, as no one in his senses sought to cheat the Gossiper of even a pinch of misinformation promised.

Ningauble continued, "Arriving at the Lost City, you must seek out the ruined black shrine, and place the woman before the great tomb, and wrap the shroud of Ahriman around her, and let her drink the powdered mummy from the hemlock cup, diluting it with a wine you will find where you find the mummy, and place in her hand the sprig from the Tree of Life, and wait for the dawn."

"And then?" rumbled Fafhrd.

"And then the mirror becomes all red with rust. I can see no farther, except that someone will return from a place which it is unlawful to leave, and that you must be wary of the woman."

"But Father, all this scavenging of magic trumpery is a

great bother," Fafhrd objected. "Why shouldn't we go at once to the Lost City?"

"Without the map on the shroud of Ahriman?" murmured Ningauble.

"And you still can't tell us the name of the adept we seek?" the Mouser ventured. "Or even the name of the woman? Puppy dog problems indeed! We give you a bitch, Father, and by the time you return her, she's dropped a litter."

Ningauble shook his head ever so slightly, the six eyes retreated under the hood to become an ominous multiple gleam, and the Mouser felt a shiver crawl on his spine.

"Why is it, Riddle-Vendor, that you always give us half knowledge?" Fafhrd pressed angrily. "Is it that at the last moment our blades may strike with half force?"

Ningauble chuckled.

"It is because I know you too well, Children. If I said one word more, Hulk, you could be cleaving with your great sword—at the wrong person. And your cat-comrade would be brewing his child's magic—the wrong child's magic. It is no simple creature you foolhardily seek, but a mystery, no single identity but a mirage, a stony thing that has stolen the blood and substance of life, a nightmare crept out of dream."

For a moment it was as if, in the far reaches of that nighted cavern, something that waited stirred. Then it was gone.

Ningauble purred complacently, "And now I have an idle moment, which, to please you, I will pass in giving ear to the story that the Mouser has been impatiently waiting to tell me."

So, there being no escape, the Mouser began, first explaining that only the surface of the story had to do with the concubine, the three priests, and the slave girl; the deeper portion touching mostly, though not entirely, on four infamous handmaidens of Ishtar and a dwarf who was richly compensated for his deformity. The fire grew low and a little, lemurlike creature came edging in to replenish it, and the hours stretched on, for the Mouser always warmed to his own tales. There came a place where Fafhrd's eyes bugged with astonishment, and another where Ningauble's paunch shook like a small mountain in earthquake, but eventually the tale came to an end, suddenly and seemingly in the middle, like a piece of foreign music.

Then farewells were said and final questions refused answer, and the two seekers started back the way they had come. And Ningauble began to sort in his mind the details of the Mouser's story, treasuring it the more because he knew it was an improvisation, his favorite proverb being, "He who lies artistically, treads closer to the truth than ever he knows."

Fafhrd and the Mouser had almost reached the bottom of the boulder stair when they heard a faint tapping and turned to see Ningauble peering down from the verge, supporting himself with what looked like a cane and rapping with another.

"Children," he called, and his voice was tiny as the note of the lone flute in the Temple of Baal, "it comes to me that something in the distant spaces lusts for something in you. You must guard closely what commonly needs no guarding."

"Yes, Godfather of Mystification."

"You will take care?" came the elfin note. "Your beings depend on it."

"Yes, Father."

And Ningauble waved once and hobbled out of sight. The little creatures of his great darkness followed him, but whether to report and receive orders or only to pleasure him with their gentle antics, no man could be sure. Some said that Ningauble had been created by the Elder Gods for men to guess about and so sharpen their imaginations for even tougher riddles. None knew whether he had the gift of foresight, or whether he merely set the stage for future events with such a bewildering cunning that only an efreet or an adept could evade acting the part given him.

3
The Woman Who Came

After Fafhrd and the Gray Mouser emerged from the Bottomless Caves into the blinding upper sunlight, their trail for a space becomes dim. Material relating to them has, on the whole, been scanted by annalists, since they were heroes too disreputable for classic myth, too cryptically independent ever to let themselves be tied to a folk, too shifty and improbable in their adventurings to please the historian, too often involved with a riff-raff of dubious demons, unfrocked sorcerors, and discredited deities—a veritable underworld of the supernatural. And it becomes doubly difficult to piece together their actions during a period when they were engaged in thefts requiring stealth, secrecy, and bold misdirection. Occasionally, however, one comes across the marks they left upon the year.

For instance, a century later the priests of Ahriman were chanting, although they were too intelligent to believe it themselves, the miracle of Ahriman's snatching of his own hallowed shroud. One night the twelve accursed swordsmen saw the blackly scribbled shroud rise like a pillar of cobwebs from the altar, rise higher than mortal man, although the form within seemed anthropoid. Then Ahriman spoke from the shroud, and they worshipped him, and he replied with obscure parables and finally strode giantlike from the secret shrine.

The shrewdest of the century-later priests remarked, "I'd say a man on stilts, or else—" (happy surmise!) "—one man on the shoulders of another."

Then there were the things that Nikri, body slave to the infamous False Laodice, told the cook while she anointed the bruises of her latest beating. Things concerning two strangers who visited her mistress, and the carousal her mistress proposed to them, and how they escaped the black eunuch scimitarmen she had set to slay them when the carousal was done.

"They were magicians, both of them," Nikri averred, "for at the peak of the doings they transformed my lady into a hideous, wiggly-horned sow, a horrid chimera of snail and swine. But that wasn't the worst, for they stole her chest of aphrodisiac wines. When she discovered that the demon mummia was gone with which she'd hoped to stir the lusts of Ptolemy, she screamed in rage and took her back-scratcher to me. Ow, but that hurts!"

The cook chuckled.

But as to who visited Hieronymus, the greedy tax farmer and connoisseur of Antioch, or in what guise, we cannot be sure. One morning he was found in his treasure room with his limbs stiff and chill, as if from hemlock, and there was a look of terror on his fat face, and the famous cup from which he had often caroused was missing, although there were circular stains on the table before him. He recovered, but would never tell what had happened.

The priests who tended the Tree of Life in Babylon were a little more communicative. One evening just after sunset they saw the topmost branches shake in the gloaming and heard the snick of a pruning knife. All around them, without other sound or movement, stretched the desolate city, from which the inhabitants had been herded to nearby

Seleucia three-quarters of a century before and to which the priests crept back only in great fear to fulfill their sacred duties. They instantly prepared, some of them to climb the Tree armed with tempered golden sickles, others to shoot down with gold-tipped arrows whatever blasphemer was driven forth, when suddenly a large gray batlike shape swooped from the Tree and vanished behind a jagged wall. Of course, it might conceivably have been a gray-cloaked man swinging on a thin, tough rope, but there were too many things whispered about the creatures that flapped by night through the ruins of Babylon for the priests to dare pursuit.

Finally Fafhrd and the Gray Mouser reappeared in Tyre, and a week later they were ready to depart on the ultimate stage of their quest. Indeed, they were already outside the gates, lingering at the landward end of Alexander's mole, spine of an ever-growing isthmus. Gazing at it, Fafhrd remembered how once an unintroduced stranger had told him a tale about two fabulous adventurers who had aided mightily in the foredoomed defense of Tyre against Alexander the Great more than a hundred years ago. The larger had heaved heavy stone blocks on the attacking ships, the smaller had dove to file through the chains with which they were anchored. Their names, the stranger had said, were Fafhrd and the Gray Mouser. Fafhrd had made no comment.

It was near evening, a good time to pause in adventurings, to recall past escapades, to hazard misty, wild, rosy speculations concerning what lay ahead.

"I think any woman would do," insisted the Mouser bickering. "Ningauble was just trying to be obscure. Let's take Chloe."

"If only she'll come when she's ready," said Fafhrd, half smiling.

The sun was dipping ruddy-golden into the rippling sea.

The merchants who had pitched shop on the landward side in order to get first crack at the farmers and inland traders on market day were packing up wares and taking down canopies.

"Any woman will eventually come when she's ready, even Chloe," retorted the Mouser. "We'd only have to take along a silk tent for her and a few pretty conveniences. No trouble at all."

"Yes," said Fafhrd, "we could probably manage it without more than one elephant."

Most of Tyre was darkly silhouetted against the sunset, although there were gleams from the roofs here and there, and the gilded peak of the Temple of Melkarth sent a little water-borne glitter track angling in toward the greater one of the sun. The fading Phoenician port seemed entranced, dreaming of past glories, only half listening to today's news of Rome's implacable eastward advance, and Philip of Macedon's loss of the first round at the Battle of the Dog's Heads, and now Antiochus preparing for the second, with Hannibal come to help him from Tyre's great fallen sister Carthage across the sea.

"I'm sure Chloe will come if we wait until tomorrow," the Mouser continued. "We'll have to wait in any case, because Ningauble said the woman wouldn't come until she was ready."

A cool little wind came out of the wasteland that was Old Tyre. The merchants hurried; a few of them were already going home along the mole, their slaves looking like hunchbacks and otherwise misshapen monsters because of the packs on their shoulders and heads.

"No," said Fafhrd, "we'll start. And if the woman doesn't come when she's ready, then she isn't the woman who will come when she's ready, or if she is, she'll have to hump herself to catch up."

The three horses of the adventurers moved restlessly and

the Mouser's whinnied. Only the great camel, on which were slung the wine-sacks, various small chests, and snugly-wrapped weapons, stood sullenly still. Fafhrd and the Mouser casually watched the one figure on the mole that moved against the homing stream; they were not exactly suspicious, but after the year's doings they could not overlook the possibility of death-dealing pursuers, taking the form either of accursed swordsmen, black eunuch scimitarmen, gold-weaponed Babylonian priests, or such agents as Hieronymus of Antioch might favor.

"Chloe would have come on time, if only you'd helped me persuade her," argued the Mouser. "She likes you, and I'm sure she must have been the one Ningauble meant, because she has that amulet which works against the adept."

The sun was a blinding sliver on the sea's rim, then went under. All the little glares and glitters on the roofs of Tyre winked out. The Temple of Melkarth loomed black against the fading sky. The last canopy was being taken down and most of the merchants were more than halfway across the mole. There was still only one figure moving shoreward.

"Weren't seven nights with Chloe enough for you?" asked Fafhrd. "Besides, it isn't she you'll be wanting when we kill the adept and get this spell off us."

"That's as it may be," retorted the Mouser. "But remember we have to catch your adept first. And it's not only I whom Chloe's company could benefit."

A faint shout drew their attention across the darkling water to where a lateen-rigged trader was edging into the Egyptian Harbor. For a moment they thought the landward end of the mole had been emptied. Then the figure moving away from the city came out sharp and black against the sea, a slight figure, not burdened like the slaves.

"Another fool leaves sweet Tyre at the wrong time," observed the Mouser. "Just think what a woman will

mean in those cold mountains we're going to, Fafhrd, a
woman to prepare dainties and stroke your forehead.''

Fafhrd said, ''It isn't your forehead, little man, you're
thinking of.''

The cool wind came again and the packed sand moaned
at its passing. Tyre seemed to crouch like a beast against
the threats of darkness. A last merchant searched the ground
hurriedly for some lost article.

Fafhrd put his hand on his horse's shoulder and said,
''Come on.''

The Mouser made a last point. ''I don't think Chloe
would insist on taking the slave girl to oil her feet, that is,
if we handled it properly.''

Then they saw that the other fool leaving sweet Tyre
was coming toward them, and that it was a woman, tall
and slender, dressed in stuffs that seemed to melt into the
waning light, so that Fafhrd found himself wondering
whether she truly came from Tyre or from some aerial
realm whose inhabitants may venture to earth only at
sunset. Then, as she continued to approach at an easy,
swinging stride, they saw that her face was fair and that
her hair was raven; and the Mouser's heart gave a great leap
and he felt that this was the perfect consummation of their
waiting, that he was witnessing the birth of an Aphrodite,
not from the foam but the dusk; for it was indeed his
dark-haired Ahura of the wine shops, no longer staring
with cold, shy curiosity, but eagerly smiling.

Fafhrd, not altogether untouched by similar feelings,
said slowly, ''So you are the woman who came when she
was ready?''

''Yes,'' added the Mouser gayly, ''and did you know
that in a minute more you'd have been too late?''

4
The Lost City

During the next week, one of steady northward journey-
ing along the fringe of the desert, they learned little more
of the motives or history of their mysterious companion
than the dubious scraps of information Chloe had provided. When asked why she had come, Ahura replied that
Ningauble had sent her, that Ningauble had nothing to do
with it and that it was all an accident, that certain dead
Elder Gods had dreamed her a vision, that she sought a
brother lost in a search for the Lost City of Ahriman; and
often her only answer was silence, a silence that seemed
sometimes sly and sometimes mystical. However, she stood
up well to hardship, proved a tireless rider, and did not
complain at sleeping on the ground with only a large cloak
snuggled around her. Like some especially sensitive mi-
gratory bird, she seemed possessed of an even greater urge
than their own to get on with the journey.

Whenever opportunity offered, the Mouser paid assidu-
ous court to her, limited only by the fear of working a
snail-change. But after a few days of this tantalizing pleasure, he noticed that Fafhrd was vying for it. Very swiftly
the two comrades became rivals, contesting as to who
should be the first to offer Ahura assistance on those rare
occasions when she needed it, striving to top each other's
brazenly boastful accounts of incredible adventures, con-
stantly on the alert lest the other steal a moment alone.
Such a spate of gallantry had never before been known on
their adventurings. They remained good friends—and they
were aware of that—but very surly friends—and they were
aware of that too. And Ahura's shy, or sly, silence encouraged them both.

They forded the Euphrates south of the ruins of Car-
chemish, and struck out for the headwaters of the Tigris,
intersecting but swinging east away from the route of
Xenophon and the Ten Thousand. It was then that their surli-
ness came to a head. Ahura had roamed off a little, letting
her horse crop the dry herbage, while the two sat on a
boulder, and expostulated in whispers, Fafhrd proposing
that they both agree to cease paying court to the girl until
their quest was over, the Mouser doggedly advancing his
prior claim. Their whispers became so heated that they did
not notice a white pigeon swooping toward them until it
landed with a downward beat of wings on an arm Fafhrd
had flung wide to emphasize his willingness to renounce
the girl temporarily—if only the Mouser would.

Fafhrd blinked, then detached a scrap of parchment
from the pigeon's leg, and read, "There is danger in the
girl. You must both forgo her."

The tiny seal was an impression of seven tangled eyes.

"Just *seven* eyes!" remarked the Mouser. "Pah, He is
modest!" And for a moment he was silent, trying to
picture the gigantic web of unknown strands by which the
Gossiper gathered his information and conducted his
business.

But this unexpected seconding of Fafhrd's argument
finally won from him a sulky consent, and they solemnly
pledged not to lay hand on the girl, or each in any way to
further his cause, until they had found and dealt with the
adept.

They were now in a townless land that caravans avoided,
a land like Xenophon's, full of chill misty mornings,
dazzling noons, and treacherous twilights, with hints of
shy, murderous, mountain-dwelling tribes recalling the omnipresent legends of "little people" as unlike men as cats
are unlike dogs. Ahura seemed unaware of the sudden

cessation of the attentions paid her, remaining as provoca-
tively shy and indefinite as ever.

The Mouser's attitude toward Ahura, however, began to
undergo a gradual but profound change. Whether it was
the souring of his inhibited passion, or the shrewder insight of a mind no longer abubble with the fashioning of
compliments and witticisms, he began to feel more and
more that the Ahura he loved was only a faint spark almost
lost in the darkness of a stranger who daily became more
riddlesome, dubious, and even, in the end, repellant. He
remembered the other name Chloe had given Ahura, and
found himself brooding oddly over the legend of Her-
maphroditus bathing in the Carian fountain and becoming
joined in one body with the nymph Salmacis. Now when
he looked at Ahura he could see only the avid eyes that
peered secretly at the world through a crevice. He began to
think of her chuckling soundlessly at night at the mortify-
ing spell that had been laid upon himself and Fafhrd. He
became obsessed with Ahura in a very different way, and
took to spying on her and studying her expression when
she was not looking, as if hoping in that way to penetrate
her mystery.

Fafhrd noticed it and instantly suspected that the Mouser
was contemplating going back on his pledge. He restrained
his indignation with difficulty and took to watching the
Mouser as closely as the Mouser watched Ahura. No
longer when it became necessary to procure provisions was
either willing to hunt alone. The easy amicability of their
friendship deteriorated. Then, late one afternoon while
they were traversing a shadowy ravine east of Armenia, a
hawk dove suddenly and sank its talons in Fafhrd's shoulder. The Northerner killed the creature in a flurry of
reddish feathers before he noticed that it too carried a
message.

"Watch out for the Mouser," was all it said, but cou-

pled with the smart of the talon-pricks, that was quite
enough for Fafhrd. Drawing up beside the Mouser while
Ahura's horse pranced skittishly away from the distur-
bance, he told the Mouser his full suspicions and warned
him that any violation of their agreement would at once
end their friendship and bring them into deadly collision.

The Mouser listened like a man in a dream, still moodily watching Ahura. He would have liked to have told
Fafhrd his real motives, but was doubtful whether he could
make them intelligible. Moreover, he was piqued at being
misjudged. So when Fafhrd's direful outburst was finished, he made no comment. Fafhrd interpreted this as an
admission of guilt and cantered on in a rage.

They were now nearing that rugged vantage-land from
which the Medes and the Persians had swooped down on
Assyria and Chaldea, and where, if they could believe
Ningauble's geography, they would find the forgotten lair
of the Lord of Eternal Evil. At first the archaic map on the
shroud of Ahriman proved more maddening than helpful,
but after a while, clarified in part by a curiously erudite
suggestion of Ahura, it began to make disturbing sense,
showing them a deep gorge where the foregoing terrain led
one to expect a saddle-backed crest, and a valley where
ought to have been a mountain. If the map held true, they
would reach the Lost City in a few days.

All the while, the Mouser's obsession deepened, and at
last took definite and startling form. He believed that
Ahura was a man.

It was very strange that the intimacy of camp life and
the Mouser's own zealous spying should not long ago have
turned up concrete proof or disproof of this clearcut suppo-
sition. Nevertheless, as the Mouser wonderingly realized on
reviewing events, they had not. Granted, Ahura's form
and movements, all her least little actions were those of a
woman, but he recalled painted and padded minions, sweet

not simpering, who had aped femininity almost as well.
Preposterous—but there it was. From that moment his
obsessive curiosity became a compulsive sweat and he
redoubled his moody peering, much to the anger of Fafhrd,
who took to slapping his sword hilt at unexpected intervals, though without ever startling the Mouser into looking
away. Each in his way stayed as surly-sullen as the camel
that displayed a more and more dour balkiness at this
preposterous excursion from the healthy desert.

Those were nightmare days for the Gray One, as they
advanced ever closer through gloomy gorges and over
craggy crests toward Ahriman's primeval shrine. Fafhrd
seemed an ominous, white-faced giant reminding him of
someone he had known in waking life, and their whole
quest a blind treading of the more subterranean routes of
dream. He still wanted to tell the giant his suspicions, but
could not bring himself to it, because of their monstrous-
ness and because the giant loved Ahura. And all the while
Ahura eluded him, a phantom fluttering just beyond reach;
though, when he forced his mind to make the comparison,
he realized that her behavior had in no way altered, except
for an intensification of the urge to press onward, like a
vessel nearing its home port.

Finally there came a night when he could bear his
torturing curiosity no longer. He writhed from under a
mountain of oppressive unremembered dreams and, propped
on an elbow, looked around him, quite as the creature for
which he was named.

It would have been cold if it had not been so still. The
fire had burned to embers. It was rather the moonlight that
showed him Fafhrd's tousled head and elbow outthrust
from shaggy bearskin cloak. And it was the moonlight that
struck full on Ahura stretched beyond the embers, her
lidded, tranquil face fixed on the zenith, seeming hardly to
breathe.

He waited a long time. Then, without making a sound,
he laid back his gray cloak, picked up his sword, went
around the fire, and kneeled beside her. Then, for another
space, he dispassionately scrutinized her face. But it remained the hermaphroditic mask that had tormented his
waking hours—if he were still sure of the distinction between waking and dream. Suddenly his hands grasped at
her—and as abruptly checked. Again he stayed motionless
for a long time. Then, with movements as deliberate and
rehearsed-seeming as a sleep-walker's, but more silent, he
drew back her woolen cloak, took a small knife from his
pouch, lifted her gown at the neck, careful not to touch her
skin, slit it to her knee, treating her chiton the same.

The breasts, white as ivory, that he had known would
not be there, were there. And yet, instead of his nightmare
lifting, it deepened.

It was something too profound for surprise, this wholly
unexpected further insight. For as he knelt there, somberly
studying, he knew for a certainty that this ivory flesh was a
mask, as cunningly fashioned as the face and for as
frighteningly incomprehensible a purpose.

The ivory eyelids did not flicker, but the edges of the
teeth showed in what he fancied was a deliberate, flickery
smile.

He was never more certain than at this moment that
Ahura was a man.

The embers crunched behind him.

Turning, the Mouser saw only the streak of gleaming
steel poised above Fafhrd's head, motionless for a moment, as if with superhuman forbearance a god should
give his creature a chance before loosing the thunderbolt.

The Mouser ripped out his own slim sword in time to
ward the titan blow. From hilt to point, the two blades
screamed.

And in answer to that scream, melting into, continuing,

and augmenting it, there came from the absolute calm of the west a gargantuan gust of wind that sent the Mouser staggering forward and Fafhrd reeling back, and rolled Ahura across the place where the embers had been.

Almost as suddenly the gale died. As it died, something whipped batlike toward the Mouser's face and he grabbed at it. But it was not a bat, or even a large leaf. It felt like papyrus.

The embers, blown into a clump of dry grass, had perversely started a blaze. To its flaring light he held the thin scrap that had fluttered out of the infinite west.

He motioned frantically to Fafhrd, who was clawing his way out of a scrub pine.

There was squid-black writing on the scrap, in large characters, above the tangled seal.

"By whatever gods you revere, give up this quarrel. Press onward at once. Follow the woman."

They became aware that Ahura was peering over their abutting shoulders. The moon came gleamingly from behind the small black tatter of cloud that had briefly obscured it. She looked at them, pulled together chiton and gown, belted them with her cloak. They collected their horses, extricated the fallen camel from the cluster of thorn bushes in which it was satisfiedly tormenting itself, and set out.

After that the Lost City was found almost too quickly; it seemed like a trap or the work of an illusionist. One moment Ahura was pointing out to them a boulder-studded crag; the next, they were looking down on a narrow valley choked with crazily-leaning, moonsilvered monoliths and their accomplice shadows.

From the first it was obvious that "city" was a misnomer. Surely men had never dwelt in those massive stone tents and huts, though they may have worshipped there. It was a habitation for Egyptian colossi, for stone automata.

But Fafhrd and the Mouser had little time to survey its entirety, for without warning Ahura sent her horse clattering and sliding down the slope.

Thereafter it was a hairbrained, drunken gallop, their horses plunging shadows, the camel a lurching ghost, through forests of crude-hewn pillars, past teetering single slabs big enough for palace walls, under lintels made for elephants, always following the elusive hoofbeat, never catching it, until they suddenly emerged into clear moonlight and drew up in an open space between a great sarcophagus-like block or box with steps leading up to it, and a huge, crudely man-shaped monolith.

But they had hardly begun to puzzle out the things around them before they became aware that Ahura was gesturing impatiently. They recalled Ningauble's instructions, and realized that it was almost dawn. So they unloaded various bundles and boxes from the shivering, snapping camel, and Fafhrd unfolded the dark, cobwebby shroud of Ahriman and wrapped it around Ahura as she stood wordlessly facing the tomb, her face a marble portrait of eagerness, as if she sprang from the stone around her.

While Fafhrd busied himself with other things, the Mouser opened the ebony chest they had stolen from the False Laodice. A fey mood came upon him and, dancing cumbrously in imitation of a eunuch serving man, he tastefully arrayed a flat stone with all the little jugs and jars and tiny amphorae that the chest contained. And in an appropriate falsetto he sang:

> "I laid a board for the Great Seleuce,
> I decked it pretty and abstruse;
> And he must have been pleased,
> For when stuffed, he wheezed,
> 'As punishment castrate the man.' "

Then Fafhrd handed him Socrates' cup and, still prancing and piping, the Mouser measured into it the mummy powder and added the wine and stirred them together and, dancing fantastically toward Ahura, offered it to her. When she made no movement, he held it to her lips and she greedily gulped it without taking her eyes from the tomb.

Then Fafhrd came with the sprig from the Babylonian Tree of Life, which still felt marvellously fresh and firm-leafed to his touch, as if the Mouser had only snipped it a moment ago. And he gently pried open her clenched fingers and placed the sprig inside them and folded them again.

Thus ready, they waited. The sky reddened at the edge and seemed for a moment to grow darker, the stars fading and the moon turning dull. The outspread aphrodisiacs chilled, refusing the night breeze their savor. And the woman continued to watch the tomb, and behind her, seeming to watch the tomb too, as if it were her fantastic shadow, loomed the man-shaped monolith, which the Mouser now and then scrutinized uneasily over his shoulder, being unable to tell whether it were of primevally crude workmanship or something that men had laboriously defaced because of its evil.

The sky paled until the Mouser could begin to make out some monstrous carvings on the side of the sarcophagus—of men like stone pillars and animals like mountains—and until Fafhrd could see the green of the leaves in Ahura's hand.

Then he saw something astounding. In an instant the leaves withered and the sprig became a curled and blackened stick. In the same instant Ahura trembled and grew paler still, snow pale, and to the Mouser it seemed that there was a tenuous black cloud forming around her head, that the riddlesome stranger he hated was pouring upward like a smoky jinni from her body, the bottle.

The thick stone cover of the sarcophagus groaned and began to rise.

Ahura began to move toward the sarcophagus. To the Mouser it seemed that the cloud was drawing her along like a black sail.

The cover was moving more swiftly, as if it were the upper jaw of a stone crocodile. The black cloud seemed to the Mouser to strain triumphantly toward the widening slit, dragging the white wisp behind it. The cover opened wide. Ahura reached the top and then either peered down inside or, as the Mouser saw it, was almost sucked in along with the black cloud. She shook violently. Then her body collapsed like an empty dress.

Fafhrd gritted his teeth, a joint cracked in the Mouser's wrist. The hilts of their swords, unconsciously drawn, bruised their palms.

Then, like an idler from a day of bowered rest, an Indian prince from the tedium of the court, a philosopher from quizzical discourse, a slim figure rose from the tomb. His limbs were clad in black, his body in silvery metal, his hair and beard raven and silky. But what first claimed the sight, like an ensign on a masked man's shield, was a chatoyant quality of his youthful olive skin, a silvery gleaming that turned one's thoughts to fishes' bellies and leprosy—that, and a certain familiarity.

For the face of this black and silver stranger bore an unmistakable resemblance to Ahura.

5
Anra Devadoris

Resting his long hands on the edge of the tomb, the newcomer surveyed them pleasantly and nodded as if they were intimates. Then he vaulted lightly over and came striding down the steps, treading on the shroud of Ahriman without so much as a glance at Ahura.

He eyed their swords. "You anticipate danger?" he asked, politely stroking the beard which, it seemed to the Mouser, could never have grown so bushily silky except in a tomb.

"You are an adept?" Fafhrd retorted, stumbling over the words a little.

The stranger disregarded the question and stopped to study amusedly the zany array of aphrodisiacs.

"Dear Ningauble," he murmured, "is surely the father of all seven-eyed Lechers. I suppose you know him well enough to guess that he had you fetch these toys because he wants them for himself. Even in his duel with me, he cannot resist the temptation of a profit on the side. But perhaps this time the old pander had curtsied to destiny unwittingly. At least, let us hope so."

And with that he unbuckled his sword belt and carelessly laid it by, along with the wondrously slim, silver-hilted sword. The Mouser shrugged and sheathed his own weapon, but Fafhrd only grunted.

"I do not like you," he said. "Are you the one who put the swine-curse on us?"

The stranger regarded him quizzically.

"You are looking for a cause," he said. "You wish to know the name of an agent you feel has injured you. You plan to unleash your rage as soon as you know. But behind

155

every cause is another cause, and behind the last agent is yet another agent. An immortal could not slay a fraction of them. Believe me, who have followed that trail farther than most and who have had some experience of the special obstacles that are placed in the way of one who seeks to live beyond the confines of his skull and the meager present—the traps that are set for him, the titanic enmities he awakens. I beseech you to wait a while before warring, as I shall wait before answering your second question. That I am an adept I freely admit."

At this last statement the Mouser felt another light-headed impulse to behave fantastically, this time in mimicry of a magician. Here was the rare creature on whom he could test the rune against adepts in his pouch! He wanted to hum a death spell between his teeth, to flap his arms in an incantational gesture, to spit at the adept and spin widdershins on his left heel thrice. But he too chose to wait.

"There is always a simple way of saying things," said Fafhrd ominously.

"But there is where I differ with you," returned the adept, almost animatedly. "There are no ways of saying certain things, and others are so difficult that a man pines and dies before the right words are found. One must borrow phrases from the sky, words from beyond the stars. Else were all an ignorant, imprisoning mockery."

The Mouser stared at the adept, suddenly conscious of a monstrous incongruity about him—as if one should glimpse a hint of double-dealing in the curl of Solon's lips, or cowardice in the eyes of Alexander, or imbecility in the face of Aristotle. For although the adept was obviously erudite, confident, and powerful, the Mouser could not help thinking of a child morbidly avid for experience, a timid, painfully curious small boy. And the Mouser had the further bewildering feeling that this was the secret for which he had spied so long on Ahura.

Fafhrd's sword-arm bulged and he seemed about to make an even pithier rejoinder. But instead he sheathed his sword, walked over to the woman, held his fingers to her wrists for a moment, then tucked his bearskin cloak around her.

"Her ghost has gone only a little way," he said. "It will soon return. What did you do to her, you black and silver popinjay?"

"What matters what I've done to her or you, or me?" retorted the adept, almost peevishly. "You are here, and I have business with you." He paused. "This, in brief, is my proposal: that I make you adepts like myself, sharing with you all knowledge of which your minds are capable, on condition only that you continue to submit to such spells as I have put upon you and may put upon you in future, to further our knowledge. What do you say to that?"

"Wait, Fafhrd!" implored the Mouser, grabbing his comrade's arm. "Don't strike yet. Let's first look at the statue from all sides. Why, magnanimous magician, have you chosen to make this offer to us, and why have you brought us out here to make it, instead of getting your yes or no in Tyre?"

"An adept," roared Fafhrd, dragging the Mouser along, "offers to make me an adept! And for that I should go on kissing swine! Go spit down Fenris' throat!"

"As to why I have brought you here," said the adept coolly, "there are certain limitations on my powers of movement, or at least on my powers of satisfactory communication. There is, moreover, a special reason, which I will reveal to you as soon as we have concluded our agreement—though I may tell you that, unknown to yourselves, you have already aided me."

"But why pick on *us?* Why?" persisted the Mouser, bracing himself against Fafhrd's tugging.

"Some whys, if you follow them far enough, lead over the rim of reality," replied the black and silver one. "I have sought knowledge beyond the dreams of ordinary men, I have ventured far into the darkness that encircles minds and stars. But now, midmost of the pitchy windings of that fearsome labyrinth, I find myself suddenly at my skein's end. The tyrant powers who ignorantly guard the secret of the universe without knowing what it is, have scented me. Those vile wardens of whom Ningauble is the merest agent and even Ormadz a cloudy symbol, have laid their traps and built their barricades. And my best torches have snuffed out, or proved too flickery-feeble. I need new avenues of knowledge."

He turned upon them eyes that seemed to be changing to twin holes in a curtain. "There is something in the inmost core of you, something that you, or others before you, have close-guarded down the ages. Something that lets you laugh in a way that only the Elder Gods ever laughed. Something that makes you see a kind of jest in horror and disillusionment and death. There is much wisdom to be gained by the unravelling of that something."

"Do you think us pretty woven scarves for your slick fingers to fray," snarled Fafhrd. "So you can piece out that rope you're at the end of, and climb all the way down to Niflheim?"

"Each adept must fray himself, before he may fray others," the stranger intoned unsmilingly. "You do not know the treasure you keep virgin and useless within you, or spill in senseless laughter. There is much richness in it, many complexities, destiny-threads that lead beyond the sky to realms undreamt." His voice became swift and invoking. "Have you no itch to understand, no urge for greater adventuring than schoolboy rambles? I'll give you gods for foes, stars for your treasure-trove, if only you will do as I command. All men will be your animals; the best, your hunting pack. Kiss snails and swine? That's but an overture. Greater than Pan, you'll frighten nations, rape the world. The universe will tremble at your lust, but you will master it and force it down. That ancient laughter will give you the might—"

"Filth-spewing pimp! Scabby-lipped pander! Cease!" bellowed Fafhrd.

"Only submit to me and to my will," the adept continued rapturously, his lips working so that his black beard twitched rhythmically. "All things we'll twist and torture, know their cause. The lechery of gods will pave the way we'll tramp through windy darkness 'til we find the one who lurks in senseless Odin's skull twitching the strings that move your lives and mine. All knowledge will be ours, all for us three. Only give up your wills, submit to me!"

For a moment the Mouser was hypnotized by the glint of ghastly wonders. Then he felt Fafhrd's biceps, which had slackened under his grasp—as if the Northerner were yielding too—suddenly tighten, and from his own lips he heard words projected coldly into the echoing silence.

"Do you think a rhyme is enough to win us over to your nauseous titillations? Do you think we care a jot for your high-flown muck-peering? Fafhrd, this slobberer offends me, past ills that he has done us aside. It only remains to determine which one of us disposes of him. I long to unravel him, beginning with the ribs."

"Do you not understand what I have offered you, the magnitude of the boon? Have we no common ground?"

"Only to fight on. Call up your demons, sorcerer, or else look to your weapon."

An unearthly lust receded, rippling from the adept's eyes, leaving behind only a deadliness. Fafhrd snatched up the cup of Socrates and dropped it for a lot, swore as it

rolled toward the Mouser, whose cat-quick hand went
softly to the hilt of the slim sword called Scalpel. Stoop-
ing, the adept groped blindly behind him and regained his
belt and scabbard, drawing from it a blade that looked as
delicate and responsive as a needle. He stood, a lank and
icy indolence, in the red of the risen sun, the black anthropomorphic monolith looming behind him for his second.

The Mouser drew Scalpel silently from its sheath, ran a
finger caressingly down the side of the blade, and in so
doing noticed an inscription in black crayon which read,
"I do not approve of this step you are taking. Ningauble."
With a hiss of annoyance the Mouser wiped it off on his
thigh and concentrated his gaze on the adept—so preoc-
cupiedly that he did not observe the eyes of the fallen
Ahura quiver open.

"And now, Dead Sorcerer," said the Gray One lightly,
"my name is the Gray Mouser."

"And mine is Anra Devadoris."

Instantly the Mouser put into action his carefully weighed
plan: to take two rapid skips forward and launch his blade-
tipped body at the adept's sword, which was to be deflected, and at the adept's throat, which was to be sliced.
He was already seeing the blood spurt when, in the middle
of the second skip, he saw, whirring like an arrow toward
his eyes, the adept's blade. With a belly-contorted effort
he twisted to one side and parried blindly. The adept's
blade whipped in greedily around Scalpel, but only far
enough to snag and tear the skin at the side of the Mouser's neck. The Mouser recovered balance crouching, his
guard wide open, and only a backward leap saved him
from Anra Devadoris' second serpentlike strike. As he
gathered himself to meet the next attack, he gaped amazedly,
for never before in his life had he been faced by superior
speed. Fafhrd's face was white. Ahura, however, her head
raised a little from the furry cloak, smiled with a weak and

incredulous, but evil joy—a frankly vicious joy wholly unlike her former sly, intangible intimations of cruelty.

But Anra Devadoris smiled wider and nodded with a patronizing gratefulness at the Mouser, before gliding in. And now it was the blade Needle that darted in unhurried lightning attack, and Scalpel that whirred in frenzied defense. The Mouser retreated in jerky, circling stages, his face sweaty, his throat hot, but his heart exulting, for never before had he fought this well—not even on that stifling morning when, his head in a sack, he had disposed of a whimsically cruel Egyptian kidnaper.

Inexplicably, he had had the feeling that his days spent in spying on Ahura were now paying off.

Needle came slipping in and for the moment the Mouser could not tell upon which side of Scalpel it skirred and so sprang backward, but not swiftly enough to escape a prick in the side. He cut viciously at the adept's withdrawing arm—and barely managed to jerk his own arm out of the way of a stop thrust.

In a nasty voice so low that Fafhrd hardly heard her, and the Mouser heard her not at all, Ahura called, "The spiders tickled your flesh ever so lightly as they ran, Anra."

Perhaps the adept hesitated almost imperceptibly, or perhaps it was only that his eyes grew a shade emptier. At all events, the Mouser was not given that opportunity, for which he was desperately searching, to initiate a counterattack and escape the deadly whirligig of his circling retreat. No matter how intently he peered, he could spy no gap in the sword-woven steel net his adversary was tirelessly casting towards him, nor could be discerned in the face behind the net any betraying grimace, any flicker of eye hinting at the next point of attack, any flaring of nostrils or distension of lips telling of gasping fatigue similar to his own. It was inhuman, unalive, the mask of a machine built by some Daedalus, or of a leprously silver automaton stepped out of myth. And like a machine, Devadoris seemed to be gaining strength and speed from the very rhythm that was sapping his own.

The Mouser realized that he must interrupt that rhythm by a counterattack, any counterattack, or fall victim to a swiftness become blinding.

And then he further realized that the proper opportunity for that counterattack would never come, that he would wait in vain for any faltering in his adversary's attack, that he must risk everything on a guess.

His throat burned, his heart pounded on his ribs for air, a stinging, numbing poison seeping through his limbs.

Devadoris started a feint, or a deadly thrust, at his face.

Simultaneously, the Mouser heard Ahura jeer, "They hung their webs on your beard and the worms knew your secret parts, Anra."

He guessed—and cut at the adept's knee.

Either he guessed right, or else something halted the adept's deadly thrust.

The adept easily parried the Mouser's cut, but the rhythm was broken and his speed slackened.

Again he developed speed, again at the last possible moment the Mouser guessed. Again Ahura eerily jeered, "The maggots made you a necklace, and each marching beetle paused to peer into your eye, Anra."

Over and over it happened, speed, guess, macabre jeer, but each time the Mouser gained only momentary respite, never the opportunity to start an extended counterattack. His circling retreat continued so uninterruptedly that he felt as if he had been caught in a whirlpool. With each revolution, certain fixed landmarks swept into view: Fafhrd's blanched agonized face; the hulking tomb; Ahura's hate-contorted, mocking visage; the red stab of the risen sun; the gouged, black, somber monolith, with its attendant stony soldiers and their gigantic stone tents; Fafhrd again. . . .

And now the Mouser knew his strength was failing for good and all. Each guessed counterattack brought him less respite, was less of a check to the adept's speed. The landmarks whirled dizzily, darkened. It was as if he had been sucked to the maelstrom's center, as if the black cloud which he had fancied pouring from Ahura were enveloping him vampirously, choking off his breath.

He knew that he would be able to make only one more counter-cut, and must therefore stake all on a thrust at the heart.

He readied himself.

But he had waited too long. He could not gather the necessary strength, summon the speed.

He saw the adept preparing the lightning death-stroke.

His own thrust was like the gesture of a paralyzed man seeking to rise from his bed.

Then Ahura began to laugh.

It was a horrible, hysterical laugh; a giggling, snickering laugh; a laugh that made him dully wonder why she should find such joy in his death; and yet, for all the difference, a laugh that sounded like a shrill, distorted echo of Fafhrd's or his own.

Puzzledly, he noted that Needle had not yet transfixed him, that Devadoris' lighting thrust was slowing, slowing, as if the hateful laughter were falling in cumbering swathes around the adept, as if each horrid peal dropped a chain around his limbs.

The Mouser leaned on his own sword and collapsed, rather than lunged, forward.

He heard Fafhrd's shuddering sigh.

Then he realized that he was trying to pull Scalpel from the adept's chest and that it was an almost insuperably difficult task, although the blade had gone in as easily as if

Anra Devadoris had been a hollow man. Again he tugged, and Scalpel came clear, fell from his nerveless fingers. His knees shook, his head sagged, and darkness flooded everything.

Fafhrd, sweat-drenched, watched the adept. Anra Devadoris' rigid body teetered like a stone pillar, slim cousin to the monolith behind him. His lips were fixed in a frozen, foreknowing smile. The teetering increased, yet for a while, as if he were an incarnation of death's ghastly pendulum, he did not fall. Then he swayed too far forward and fell like a pillar, without collapse. There was a horrid, hollow crash as his head struck the black pavement.

Ahura's hysterical laughter burst out afresh.

Fafhrd ran forward calling to the Mouser, anxiously shook the slumped form. Snores answered him. Like some spent Theban phalanx-man drowsing over his pike in the twilight of the battle, the Mouser was sleeping the sleep of complete exhaustion. Fafhrd found the Mouser's gray cloak, wrapped it around him, and gently laid him down.

Ahura was shaking convulsively.

Fafhrd looked at the fallen adept, lying there so formally outstretched, like a tomb-statue rolled over. Dead, Devadoris' lankness was skeletal. He had bled hardly at all from the wound given him by Scalpel, but his forehead was crushed like an eggshell. Fafhrd touched him. The skin was cold, the muscles hard as stone.

Fafhrd had seen men go rigid immediately upon death— Macedonians who had fought too desperately and too long. But they had become weak and staggering toward the end. Anra Devadoris had maintained the appearance of ease and perfect control up to the last moment, despite the poisons that must have been coursing through his veins almost to the exclusion of blood. All through the duel, his chest had hardly heaved.

"By Odin crucified!" Fafhrd muttered. "He was something of a man, even though he was an adept."

A hand was laid on his arm. He jerked around. It was Ahura come behind him. The whites showed around her eyes. She smiled at him crookedly, then lifted a knowing eyebrow, put her finger to her lips, and dropped suddenly to her knees beside the adept's corpse. Gingerly she touched the satin smooth surface of the tiny blood-clot on the adept's breast. Fafhrd, noting afresh the resemblance between the dead and the crazy face, sucked in his breath. Ahura scurried off like a startled cat.

Suddenly she froze like a dancer and looked back at him, and a gloating, transcendent vindictiveness came into her face. She beckoned to Fafhrd. Then she ran lightly up the steps to the tomb and pointed into it and beckoned again. Doubtfully the Northerner approached, his eyes on her strained and unearthly face, beautiful as an efreet's. Slowly he mounted the steps.

Then he looked down.

Looked down to feel that the wholesome world was only a film on primary abominations. He realized that what Ahura was showing him had somehow been her ultimate degradation and the ultimate degradation of the thing that had named itself Anra Devadoris. He remembered the bizarre taunts that Ahura had thrown at the adept during the duel. He remembered her laughter, and his mind eddied along the edge of suspicions of pit-spawned improprieties and obscene intimacies. He hardly noticed that Ahura had slumped over the wall of the tomb, her white arms hanging down as if pointing all ten slender fingers in limp horror. He did not know that the blackly puzzled eyes of the suddenly awakened Mouser were peering up at him.

Thinking back, he realized that Devadoris' fastidiousness and exquisitely groomed appearance had made him think of the tomb as an eccentric entrance to some luxurious underground palace.

But now he saw that there were no doors in that cramping cell into which he peered, nor cracks indicating where hidden doors might be. Whatever had come from there, had lived there, where the dry corners were thick with webs and the floor swarmed with maggots, dung beetles, and furry black spiders.

6
The Mountain

Perhaps some chuckling demon, or Ningauble himself, planned it that way. At all events, as Fafhrd stepped down from the tomb, he got his feet tangled in the shroud of Ahriman and bellowed wildly (the Mouser called it "bleating") before he noticed the cause, which was by that time ripped to tatters.

Next Ahura, aroused by the tumult, set them into a brief panic by screaming that the black monolith and its soldiery were marching toward them to grind them under stony feet.

Almost immediately afterwards the cup of Socrates momentarily froze their blood by rolling around in a semicircle, as if its learned owner were invisibly pawing for it, perhaps to wet his throat after a spell of dusty disputation in the underworld. Of the withered sprig from the Tree of Life there was no sign, although the Mouser jumped as far and as skittishly as one of his namesakes when he saw a large black walking-stick insect crawling away from where the sprig might have fallen.

But it was the camel that caused the biggest commotion,

by suddenly beginning to prance about clumsily in a most uncharacteristically ecstatic fashion, finally cavorting up eagerly on two legs to the mare, which fled in squealing dismay. Afterwards it became apparent that the camel must have gotten into the aphrodisiacs, for one of the bottles was pashed as if by a hoof, with only a scummy licked patch showing where its leaked contents had been, and two of the small clay jars were vanished entirely. Fafhrd set out after the two beasts on one of the remaining horses, hallooing crazily.

The Mouser, left alone with Ahura, found his glibness put to the test in saving her sanity by a barrage of small talk, mostly well-spiced Tyrian gossip, but including a wholly apocryphal tale of how he and Fafhrd and five small Ethiopian boys once played Maypole with the eye-stalks of a drunken Ningauble, leaving him peering about in the oddest directions. (The Mouser was wondering why they had not heard from their seven-eyed mentor. After victories Ningauble was always particularly prompt in getting in his demands for payment; and very exacting too—he would insist on a strict accounting for the three missing aphrodisiac containers.)

The Mouser might have been expected to take advantage of this opportunity to press his suit with Ahura, and if possible assure himself that he was now wholly free of the snail-curse. But, her hysterical condition aside, he felt strangely shy with her, as if, although this was the Ahura he loved, he were now meeting her for the first time. Certainly this was a wholly different Ahura from the one with whom they had journeyed to the Lost City, and the memory of how he had treated that other Ahura put a restraint on him. So he cajoled and comforted her as he might have some lonely Tyrian waif, finally bringing two funny little hand-puppets from his pouch and letting them amuse her for him.

And Ahura sobbed and stared and shivered, and hardly seemed to hear what nonsense the Mouser was saying, yet grew quiet and sane-eyed and appeared to be comforted.

When Fafhrd eventually returned with the still giddy camel and the outraged mare, he did not interrupt, but listened gravely, his gaze occasionally straying to the dead adept, the black monolith, the stone city, or the valley's downward slope to the north. High over their heads a flock of birds was flying in the same direction. Suddenly they scattered wildly, as if an eagle had dropped among them. Fafhrd frowned. A moment later he heard a whirring in the air. The Mouser and Ahura looked up too, momentarily glimpsed something slim hurtling downward. They cringed. There was a thud as a long whitish arrow buried itself in a crack in the pavement hardly a foot from Fafhrd and stuck there vibrating.

After a moment Fafhrd touched it with shaking hand. The shaft was crusted with ice, the feathers stiff, as if, incredibly, it had sped for a long time through frigid supramundane air. There was something tied snugly around the shaft. He detached and unrolled an ice-brittle sheet of papyrus, which softened under his touch, and read, "You must go farther. Your quest is not ended. Trust in omens. Ningauble."

Still trembling, Fafhrd began to curse thunderously. He crumpled the papyrus, jerked up the arrow, broke it in two, threw the parts blindly away. "Misbegotten spawn of a eunuch, an owl, and an octopus!" he finished. "First he tries to skewer us from the skies, then he tells us our quest is not ended—when we've just ended it!"

The Mouser, well knowing these rages into which Fafhrd was apt to fall after battle, especially a battle in which he had not been able to participate, started to comment coolly. Then he saw the anger abruptly drain from Fafhrd's eyes, leaving a wild twinkle which he did not like.

"Mouser!" said Fafhrd eagerly. "Which way did I throw the arrow?"

"Why, north," said the Mouser without thinking.

"Yes, and the birds were flying north, and the arrow was coated with ice!" The wild twinkle in Fafhrd's eyes became a berserk brilliance. "Omens, he said? We'll trust in omens all right! We'll go north, north, and still north!"

The Mouser's heart sank. Now would be a particularly difficult time to combat Fafhrd's long-standing desire to take him to "that wondrously cold land where only brawny, hot-blooded men may live and they but by the killing of fierce, furry animals"—a prospect poignantly disheartening to a lover of hot baths, the sun, and southern nights.

"This is the chance of all chances," Fafhrd continued, intoning like a skald. "Ah, to rub one's naked hide with snow, to plunge like walrus into ice-garnished water. Around the Caspian and over greater mountains than these goes a way that men of my race have taken. Thor's gut, but you will love it! No wine, only hot mead and savory smoking carcasses, skin-toughening furs to wear, cold air at night to keep dreams clear and sharp, and great strong-hipped women. Then to raise sail on a winter ship and laugh at the frozen spray. Why have we so long delayed? Come! By the icy member that begot Odin, we must start at once!"

The Mouser stifled a groan. "Ah, blood brother," he intoned, not a whit less brazen-voiced, "my heart leaps even more than yours at the thought of nerve-quickening snow and all the other niceties of the manly life I have long yearned to taste. But—" Here his voice broke sadly, "—we forget this good woman, whom in any case, even if we disregard Ningauble's injunction, we must take safely back to Tyre."

He smiled inwardly.

"But I don't want to go back to Tyre," interrupted Ahura, looking up from the puppets with an impishness so like a child's that the Mouser cursed himself for ever having treated her as one. "This lonely spot seems equally far from all builded places. North is as good a way as any."

"Flesh of Freya!" bellowed Fafhrd, throwing his arms wide. "Do you hear what she says, Mouser? By Idun, that was spoken like a true snow-land woman! Not one moment must be wasted now. We shall smell mead before a year is out. By Frigg, a woman! Mouser, you good for one so small, did you not notice the pretty way she put it?"

So it was bustle about and pack and (for the present, at least, the Mouser conceded) no way out of it. The chest of aphrodisiacs, the cup, and the tattered shroud were bundled back onto the camel, which was still busy ogling the mare and smacking its great leathery lips. And Fafhrd leaped and shouted and clapped the Mouser's back as if there were not an eon-old dead stone city around them and a lifeless adept warming in the sun.

In a matter of moments they were jogging off down the valley, with Fafhrd singing tales of snowstorms and hunting and monsters big as icebergs and giants as tall as frosty mountains, and the Mouser dourly amusing himself by picturing his own death at the hands of some overly affectionate "great strong-hipped" woman.

Soon the way became less barren. Scrub trees and the valley's downward trend hid the city behind them. A surge of relief which the Mouser hardly noticed went through him as the last stony sentinel dipped out of sight, particularly the black monolith left to brood over the adept. He turned his attention to what lay ahead—a conical mountain barring the valley's mouth and wearing a high cap of mist, a lonely thunderhead which his imagination shaped into incredible towers and spires.

Suddenly his sleepy thoughts snapped awake. Fafhrd and Ahura had stopped and were staring at something wholly unexpected—a low wooden windowless house pressed back among the scrubby trees, with a couple of tilled fields behind it. The rudely carved guardian spirits at the four corners of the roof and topping the kingposts seemed Persian, but Persian purged of all southern influence—ancient Persian.

And ancient Persian too appeared the thin features, straight nose, and black-streaked beard of the aged man watching them circumspectly from the low doorway. It seemed to be Ahura's face he scanned most intently—or tried to scan, since Fafhrd mostly hid her.

"Greetings, Father," called the Mouser. "Is this not a merry day for riding, and yours good lands to pass?"

"Yes," replied the aged man dubiously, using a rusty dialect. "Though there are none, or few, who pass."

"Just as well to be far from the evil stinking cities," Fafhrd interjected heartily. "Do you know the mountain ahead, Father? Is there an easy way past it that leads north?"

At the word "mountain" the aged man cringed. He did not answer.

"Is there something wrong about the path we are taking?" the Mouser asked quickly. "Or something evil about that misty mountain?"

The aged man started to shrug his shoulders, held them contracted, looked again at the travelers. Friendliness seemed to fight with fear in his face, and to win, for he leaned forward and said hurriedly, "I warn you, sons, not to venture farther. What is the steel of your swords, the speed of your steeds, against—but remember" (he raised his voice) "I accuse no one." He looked quickly from side to side. "I have nothing at all to complain of. To me the mountain is a great benefit. My fathers returned here because the land is shunned by thief and honest man alike.

There are no taxes on this land—no money taxes. I question nothing.''

"Oh well, Father, I don't think we'll go farther," sighed the Mouser wilily. "We're but idle fellows who follow our noses across the world. And sometimes we smell a strange tale. And that reminds me of a matter in which you may be able to give us generous lads some help." He chinked the coins in his pouch. "We have heard a tale of a demon that inhabits here—a young demon dressed in black and silver, pale, with a black beard."

As the Mouser was saying these things the aged man was edging backward and at the finish he dodged inside and slammed the door, though not before they saw someone pluck at his sleeve. Instantly there came muffled angry expostulation in a girl's voice.

The door burst open. They heard the aged man say ". . . bring it down upon us all." Then a girl of about fifteen came running toward them. Her face was flushed, her eyes anxious and scared.

"You must turn back!" she called to them as she ran. "None but wicked things go to the mountain—or the doomed. And the mist hides a great horrible castle. And powerful, lonely demons live there. And one of them—"

She clutched at Fafhrd's stirrup. But just as her fingers were about to close on it, she looked beyond him straight at Ahura. An expression of abysmal terror came into her face. She screamed, "He! The Black Beard!" and crumpled to the ground.

The door slammed and they heard a bar drop into place.

They dismounted. Ahura quickly knelt by the girl, signed to them after a moment that she had only fainted. Fafhrd approached the barred door, but it would not open to any knocking, pleas, or threats. He finally solved the riddle by kicking it down. Inside he saw: the aged man cowering in a dark corner; a woman attempting to conceal a young child in a pile of straw; a very old woman sitting on a stool, obviously blind, but frightenedly peering about just the same; and a young man holding an axe in trembling hands. The family resemblance was very marked.

Fafhrd stepped out of the way of the young man's feeble axe-blow and gently took the weapon from him.

The Mouser and Ahura brought the girl inside. At sight of Ahura there were further horrified shrinkings.

They laid the girl on the straw, and Ahura fetched water and began to bathe her head.

Meanwhile, the Mouser, by playing on her family's terror and practically identifying himself as a mountain demon, got them to answer his questions. First he asked about the stone city. It was a place of ancient devil-worship, they said, a place to be shunned. Yes, they had seen the black monolith of Ahriman, but only from a distance. No, they did not worship Ahriman—see the fire-shrine they kept for his adversary Ormadz? But they dreaded Ahriman, and the stones of the devil-city had a life of their own.

Then he asked about the misty mountain, and found it harder to get satisfactory answers. The cloud always shrouded its peak, they insisted. Though once toward sun-set, the young man admitted, he thought he had glimpsed crazily leaning green towers and twisted minarets. But there was danger up there, horrible danger. What danger? He could not say.

The Mouser turned to the aged man. "You told me," he said harshly, "that my brother demons exact no money tax from you for this land. What kind of tax, then, do they exact?"

"Lives," whispered the aged man, his eyes showing more white.

"Lives, eh? How many? And when do they come for them?"

"They never come. We go. Maybe every ten years, maybe every five, there comes a yellow-green light on the mountaintop at night, and a powerful calling in the air. Sometimes after such a night one of us is gone—one who was too far from the house when the green light came. To be in the house with others helps resist the calling. I never saw the light except from our door, with a fire burning bright at my back and someone holding me. My brother went when I was a boy. Then for many years afterwards the light never came, so that even I began to wonder whether it was not a boyhood legend or illusion.

"But seven years ago," he continued quaveringly, staring at the Mouser, "there came riding late one afternoon, on two gaunt and death-wearied horses, a young man and an old—or rather the semblances of a young man and an old, for I knew without being told, knew as I crouched trembling inside the door, peering through the crack, that the masters were returning to the Castle Called Mist. The old man was bald as a vulture and had no beard. The young man had the beginnings of a silky black one. He was dressed in black and silver, and his face was very pale. His features were like—" Here his gaze flickered fearfully toward Ahura. "He rode stiffly, his lanky body rocking from side to side. He looked as if he were dead.

"They rode on toward the mountain without a sideward glance. But ever since that time the greenish-yellow light has glowed almost nightly from the mountaintop, and many of our animals have answered the call—and the wild ones too, to judge from their diminishing numbers. We have been careful, always staying near the house. It was not until three years ago that my eldest son went. He strayed too far in hunting and let darkness overtake him.

"And we have seen the black-bearded young man many times, usually at a distance, treading along the skyline or standing with head bowed upon some crag. Though once when my daughter was washing at the stream she looked up from her clothes-pounding and saw his dead eyes peering through the reeds. And once my eldest son, chasing a wounded snow-leopard into a thicket, found him talking with the beast. And once, rising early on a harvest morning, I saw him sitting by the well, staring at our doorway, although he did not seem to see me emerge. The old man we have seen too, though not so often. And for the last two years we have seen little or nothing of either, until—'' And once again his gaze flickered helplessly toward Ahura.

Meanwhile the girl had come to her senses. This time her terror of Ahura was not so extreme. She could add nothing to the aged man's tale.

They prepared to depart. The Mouser noted a certain veiled vindictiveness toward the girl, especially in the eyes of the woman with the child, for having tried to warn them. So turning in the doorway he said, "If you harm one hair of the girl's head, we will return, and the black-bearded one with us, and the green light to guide us by and wreak terrible vengeance."

He tossed a few coins on the floor and departed.

(And so, although or rather because her family looked upon her as an ally of demons, the girl from then on led a pampered life, and came to consider her blood as superior to theirs, and played shamelessly on their fear of the Mouser and Fafhrd and Black-beard, and finally made them give her all the golden coins, and with them purchased seductive garments after fortunate passage to a faraway city, where by clever stratagem she became the wife of a satrap and lived sumptuously ever afterwards— something that is often the fate of romantic people, if only they are romantic enough.)

Emerging from the house, the Mouser found Fafhrd making a brave attempt to recapture his former berserk mood. "Hurry up, you little apprentice-demon!" he welcomed. "We've a tryst with the good land of snow and cannot lag on the way!"

As they rode off, the Mouser rejoined good-naturedly, "But what about the camel, Fafhrd? You can't very well take it to the ice country. It'll die of the phlegm."

"There's no reason why snow shouldn't be as good for camels as it is for men," Fafhrd retorted. Then, rising in his saddle and turning back, he waved toward the house and shouted, "Lad! You that held the axe! When in years to come your bones feel a strange yearning, turn your face to the north. There you will find a land where you can become a man indeed."

But in their hearts both knew that this talk was a pretense, that other planets now loomed in their horoscopes—in particular one that shone with a greenish-yellow light. As they pressed on up the valley, its silence and the absence of animal and insect life now made sinister, they felt mysteries hovering all around. Some, they knew, were locked in Ahura, but both refrained from questioning her, moved by vague apprehensions of terrifying upheavals her mind had undergone.

Finally the Mouser voiced what was in the thoughts of both of them. "Yes, I am much afraid that Anra Devadoris, who sought to make us his apprentices, was only an apprentice himself and apt, apprentice-wise, to take credit for his master's work. Black-beard is gone, but the beardless one remains. What was it Ningauble said? . . . no simple creature, but a mystery? . . . no single identity, but a mirage?"

"Well, by all the fleas that bite the Great Antiochus, and all the lice that tickle his wife!" remarked a shrill, insolent voice behind them. "You doomed gentlemen already know what's in this letter I have for you."

They whirled around. Standing beside the camel—he might conceivably have been hidden, it is true, behind a nearby boulder—was a pertly grinning brown urchin, so typically Alexandrian that he might have stepped this minute out of Rakotis with a skinny mongrel sniffing at his heels. (The Mouser half expected such a dog to appear at the next moment.)

"Who sent you, boy?" Fafhrd demanded. "How did you get here?"

"Now who and how would you expect?" replied the urchin. "Catch." He tossed the Mouser a wax tablet. "Say, you two, take my advice and get out while the getting's good. I think so far as your expedition's concerned, Ningauble's pulling up his tent pegs and scuttling home. Always a friend in need, my dear employer."

The Mouser ripped the cords, unfolded the tablet, and read:

"Greetings, my brave adventurers. You have done well, but the best remains to be done. Hark to the calling. Follow the green light. But be very cautious afterwards. I wish I could be of more assistance. Send the shroud, the cup, and the chest back with the boy as first payment."

"Loki-brat! Regin-spawn!" burst out Fafhrd. The Mouser looked up to see the urchin lurching and bobbing back toward the Lost City on the back of the eagerly fugitive camel. His impudent laughter returned shrill and faint.

"There," said the Mouser, "rides off the generosity of poor, penurious Ningauble. Now we know what to do with the camel."

"Zutt!" said Fafhrd. "Let him have the brute and the toys. Good riddance to his gossiping!"

"Not a very high mountain," said the Mouser an hour later, "but high enough. I wonder who carved this neat little path and who keeps it clear?"

As he spoke, he was winding loosely over his shoulder a long thin rope of the sort used by mountain climbers, ending in a hook.

It was sunset, with twilight creeping at their heels. The little path, which had grown out of nothing, only gradually revealing itself, now led them sinuously around great boulders and along the crests of ever steeper rock-strewn slopes. Conversation, which was only a film on wariness, had played with the methods of Ningauble and his agents—whether they communicated with one another directly, from mind to mind, or by tiny whistles that emitted a note too high for human ears to hear, but capable of producing a tremor in any brother whistle or in the ear of the bat.

It was a moment when the whole universe seemed to pause. A spectral greenish light gleamed from the cloudy top ahead—but that was surely only the sun's sky-reflected afterglow. There was a hint of all-pervading sound in the air, a mighty susurrus just below the threshold of hearing, as if an army of unseen insects were tuning up their instruments. These sensations were as intangible as the force that drew them onward, a force so feeble that they knew they could break it like a single spider-strand, yet did not choose to try.

As if in response to some unspoken word, both Fafhrd and the Mouser turned toward Ahura. Under their gaze she seemed to be changing momently, opening like a night flower, becoming ever more childlike, as if some master hypnotist were stripping away the outer, later petals of her mind, leaving only a small limpid pool, from whose unknown depths, however, dark bubbles were dimly rising.

They felt their infatuation pulse anew, but with a shy restraint on it. And their hearts fell silent as the hooded heights above, as she said, "Anra Devadoris was my twin brother."

7
Ahura Devadoris

"I never knew my father. He died before we were born. In one of her rare fits of communicativeness my mother told me, 'Your father was a Greek, Ahura. A very kind and learned man. He laughed a great deal.' I remember how stern she looked as she said that, rather than how beautiful, the sunlight glinting from her ringletted, black-dyed hair.

"But it seemed to me that she had slightly emphasized the word 'Your.' You see, even then I wondered about Anra. So I asked Old Berenice the housekeeper about it. She told me she had seen Mother bear us, both on the same night.

"Old Berenice went on to tell me how my father had died. Almost nine months before we were born, he was found one morning beaten to death in the street just outside the door. A gang of Egyptian longshoremen who were raping and robbing by night were supposed to have done it, although they were never brought to justice—that was back when the Ptolemies had Tyre. It was a horrible death. He was almost pashed to a pulp against the cobbles.

"At another time Old Berenice told me something about my mother, after making me swear by Athena and by Set and by Moloch, who would eat me if I did, never to tell. She said that Mother came from a Persian family whose first daughters in the old times were all priestesses, dedicated from birth to be the wives of an evil Persian god, forbidden the embraces of mortals, doomed to spend their nights alone with the stone image of the god in a lonely temple 'half-way across the world,' she said. Mother was away that day and Old Berenice dragged me down into a

little basement under Mother's bedroom and pointed out
three ragged gray stones set among the bricks and told me
they came from the temple. Old Berenice liked to frighten
me, although she was deathly afraid of Mother.

"Of course I instantly went and told Anra, as I always
did."

The little path was leading sharply upward now, along
the spine of a crest. Their horses went at a walk, first
Fafhrd's, then Ahura's, last the Mouser's. The lines were
smoothed in Fafhrd's face, although he was still very
watchful, and the Mouser looked almost like a quaint
child.

Ahura continued, "It is hard to make you understand
my relationship with Anra, because it was so close that
even the word 'relationship' spoils it. There was a game
we would play in the garden. He would close his eyes and
guess what I was looking at. In other games we would
change sides, but never in this one.

"He invented all sorts of versions of the game and
didn't want to play any others. Sometimes I would climb
up by the olive tree onto the tiled roof—Anra couldn't
make it—and watch for an hour. Then I'd come down and
tell him what I'd seen—some dyers spreading out wet
green cloth for the sun to turn it purple, a procession of
priests around the Temple of Melkarth, a galley from
Pergamum setting sail, a Greek official impatiently explaining something to his Egyptian scribe, two henna-
handed ladies giggling at some kilted sailors, a mysterious
and lonely Jew—and he would tell me what kind of people
they were and what they had been thinking and what they
were planning to do. It was a very special kind of imagination, for afterwards when I began to go outside I found out
that he was usually right. At the time I remember thinking
that it was as if he were looking at the pictures in my mind

and seeing more than I could. I liked it. It was such a gentle feeling.

"Of course our closeness was partly because Mother, especially after she changed her way of life, wouldn't let us go out at all or mix with other children. There was more reason for that than just her strictness. Anra was very delicate. He once broke his wrist and it was a long time healing. Mother had a slave come in who was skilled in such things, and he told Mother he was afraid that Anra's bones were becoming too brittle. He told about children whose muscles and sinews gradually turned to stone, so that they became living statues. Mother struck him in the face and drove him from the house—an action that cost her a dear friend, because he was an important slave.

"And even if Anra had been allowed to go out, he couldn't have. Once after I had begun to go outside I persuaded him to come with me. He didn't want to, but I laughed at him, and he could never stand laughter. As soon as we climbed over the garden wall he fell down in a faint and I couldn't rouse him from it though I tried and tried. Finally I climbed back so I could open the door and drag him in, and Old Berenice spotted me and I had to tell her what had happened. She helped me carry him in, but afterwards she whipped me because she knew I'd never dare tell Mother I'd taken him outside. Anra came to his senses while she was whipping me, but he was sick for a week afterwards. I don't think I ever laughed at him after that, until today.

"Cooped up in the house, Anra spent most of the time studying. While I watched from the roof or wheedled stories from Old Berenice and the other slaves, or later on went out to gather information for him, he would stay in Father's library, reading, or learning some new language from Father's grammars and translations. Mother taught both of us to read Greek, and I picked up a speaking

knowledge of Aramaic and scraps of other tongues from
the slaves and passed them on to him. But Anra was far
cleverer than I at reading. He loved letters as passionately
as I did the outside. For him, they were alive. I remember
him showing me some Egyptian hieroglyphs and telling
me that they were all animals and insects. And then he
showed me some Egyptian hieratics and demotics and told
me those were the same animals in disguise. But Hebrew,
he said, was best of all, for each letter was a magic charm.
That was before he learned Old Persian. Sometimes it was
years before we found out how to pronounce the languages
he learned. That was one of my most important jobs when
I started to go outside for him.

    "Father's library had been kept just as it was when he
died. Neatly stacked in cannisters were all the renowned
philosophers, historians, poets, rhetoricians, and grammar-
ians. But tossed in a corner along with potsherds and
papyrus scraps like so much trash, were rolls of a very
different sort. Across the back of one of them my father
had scribbled, derisively I'm sure, in his big impulsive
hand, 'Secret Wisdom!' It was those that from the first
captured Anra's curiosity. He would read the respectable
books in the cannisters, but chiefly so he could go back
and take a brittle roll from the corner, blow off the dust,
and puzzle out a little more.

    "They were very strange books that frightened and
disgusted me and made me want to giggle all at once.
Many of them were written in a cheap and ignorant style.
Some of them told what dreams meant and gave directions
for working magic—all sorts of nasty things to be cooked
together. Others—Jewish rolls in Aramaic—were about
the end of the world and wild adventures of evil spirits and
mixed-up, messy monsters—things with ten heads and
jeweled cartwheels for feet, things like that. Then there
were Chaldean star-books that told how all the lights in the

sky were alive and their names and what they did to you. And one jerky, half illiterate roll in Greek told about something horrible, which for a long while I couldn't understand, connected with an ear of corn and six pomegranate seeds. It was in another of those sensational Greek rolls that Anra first found out about Ahriman and his eternal empire of evil, and after that he couldn't wait until he'd mastered Old Persian. But none of the few Old Persian rolls in Father's library were about Ahriman, so he had to wait until I could steal such things for him outside.

"My going outside was after Mother changed her way of life. That happened when I was seven. She was always a very moody and frightening woman, though sometimes she'd be very affectionate toward me for a little while, and she always spoiled and pampered Anra, though from a distance, through the slaves, almost as if she were afraid of him.

"Now her moods became blacker and blacker. Sometimes I'd surprise her looking in horror at nothing, or beating her forehead while her eyes were closed and her beautiful face was all taut, as if she were going mad. I had the feeling she'd been backed up to the end of some underground tunnel and must find a door leading out, or lose her mind.

"Then one afternoon I peeked into her bedroom and saw her looking into her silver mirror. For a long, long while she studied her face in it and I watched her without making a sound. I knew that something important was happening. Finally she seemed to make some sort of difficult inward effort and the lines of anxiety and sternness and fear disappeared from her face, leaving it smooth and beautiful as a mask. Then she unlocked a drawer I'd never seen into before and took out all sorts of little pots and vials and brushes. With these she colored and whitened her face and carefully smeared a dark, shining powder around her eyes and painted her lips reddish-orange. All this time my heart was pounding and my throat was choking up, I didn't know why. Then she laid down her brushes and dropped her chiton and felt of her throat and breasts in a thoughtful way and took up the mirror and looked at herself with a cold satisfaction. She was very beautiful, but it was a beauty that terrified me. Until now I'd always thought of her as hard and stern outside, but soft and loving within, if only you could manage to creep into that core. But now she was all turned inside out. Strangling my sobs, I ran to tell Anra and find out what it meant. But this time his cleverness failed him. He was as puzzled and disturbed as I.

"It was right afterwards that she became even stricter with me, and although she continued to spoil Anra from a distance, kept us shut up from the world more than ever. I wasn't even allowed to speak to the new slave she'd bought, an ugly, smirking, skinny-legged girl named Phryne who used to massage her and sometimes play the flute. There were all sorts of visitors coming to the house now at night, but Anra and I were always locked in our little bedroom high up by the garden. We'd hear them yelling through the wall and sometimes screaming and bumping around the inner court to the sound of Phryne's flute. Sometimes I'd lie staring at the darkness in an inexplicable sick terror all night long. I tried every way to get Old Berenice to tell me what was happening, but for once her fear of Mother's anger was too great. She'd only leer at me.

"Finally Anra worked out a plan for finding out. When he first told me about it, I refused. It terrified me. That was when I discovered the power he had over me. Up until that time the things I had done for him had been part of a game I enjoyed as much as he. I had never thought of myself as a slave obeying commands. But now when I rebelled, I found out not only that my twin had an obscure power over my limbs, so that I could hardly move them at all, or imagined I couldn't, if he were unwilling, but also that I couldn't bear the thought of him being unhappy or frustrated.

"I realize now that he had reached the first of those crises in his life when his way was blocked and he pitilessly sacrificed his dearest helper to the urgings of his insatiable curiosity.

"Night came. As soon as we were locked in I let a knotted cord out the little high window and wriggled out and climbed down. Then I climbed the olive tree to the roof. I crept over the tiles down to the square skylight of the inner court and managed to squirm over the edge—I almost fell—into a narrow, cobwebby space between the ceiling and the tiles. There was a faint murmur of talk from the dining room, but the court was empty. I lay still as a mouse and waited."

Fafhrd uttered a smothered exclamation and stopped his horse. The others did the same. A pebble rattled down the slope, but they hardly heard it. Seeming to come from the heights above them and yet to fill the whole darkening sky was something that was not entirely a sound, something that tugged at them like the Sirens' voices at fettered Odysseus. For a while they listened incredulously, then Fafhrd shrugged and started forward again, the others following.

Ahura continued, "For a long time nothing happened, except occasionally slaves hurried in and out with full and empty dishes, and there was some laughter, and I heard Phryne's flute. Then suddenly the laughter grew louder and changed to singing, and there was the sound of couches pushed back and the patter of footsteps, and there swept into the court a Dionysiac rout.

"Phryne, naked, piped the way. My mother followed,

laughing, her arms linked with those of two dancing young men, but clutching to her bosom a large silver wine-bowl. The wine sloshed over and stained purple her white silk chiton around her breasts, but she only laughed and reeled more wildly. After those came many others, men and women, young and old, all singing and dancing. One limber young man skipped high, clapping his heels, and one fat old grinning fellow panted and had to be pulled by girls, but they kept it up three times around the court before they threw themselves down on the couches and cushions. Then while they chattered and laughed and kissed and embraced and played pranks and watched a naked girl prettier than Phryne dance, my mother offered the bowl around for them to dip their wine cups.

"I was astounded—and entranced. I had been almost dead with fear, expecting I don't know what cruelties and horrors. Instead, what I saw was wholly lovely and natural. The revelation burst on me, 'So this is the wonderful and important thing that people do.' My mother no longer frightened me. Though she still wore her new face, there was no longer any hardness about her, inside or out, only joy and beauty. The young men were so witty and gay I had to put my fist in my mouth to keep from screaming with laughter. Even Phryne, squatting on her heels like a skinny boy as she piped, seemed for once unmalicious and likable. I couldn't wait to tell Anra.

"There was only one disturbing note, and that was so slight I hardly noticed it. Two of the men who took the lead in the joking, a young red-haired fellow and an older chap with a face like a lean satyr, seemed to have something up their sleeves. I saw them whisper to some of the others. And once the younger grinned at Mother and shouted, 'I know something about you from way back!' And once the older called at her mockingly, 'I know something about your great-grandmother, you old Persian, you!' Each time Mother laughed and waved her hand derisively, but I could see that she was bothered underneath. And each time some of the others paused momentarily, as if they had an inkling of something, but didn't want to let on. Eventually the two men drifted out, and from then on there was nothing to mar the fun.

"The dancing became wilder and staggering, the laughter louder, more wine was spilt than drank. Then Phryne threw away her flute and ran and landed in the fat man's lap with a jounce that almost knocked the wind out of him. Four or five of the others tumbled down.

"Just at that moment there came a crashing and a loud rending of wood, as if a door were being broken in. Instantly everyone was as still as death. Someone jerked around and a lamp snuffed out, throwing half the court into shadow.

"Then loud, shaking footsteps, like two paving blocks walking, sounded through the house, coming nearer and nearer.

"Everyone was frozen, staring at the doorway. Phryne still had her arm around the fat man's neck. But it was in Mother's face that the truly unbearable terror showed. She had retreated to the remaining lamp and dropped to her knees there. The whites showed around her eyes. She began to utter short, rapid screams, like a trapped dog.

"Then through the doorway clomped a great ragged-edged, square-limbed, naked stone man fully seven feet high. His face was just expressionless black gashes in a flat surface, and before him was thrust a mortary stone member. I couldn't bear to look at him, but I had to. He tramped echoingly across the room to Mother, jerked her up, still screaming, by the hair, and with the other hand ripped down her wine-stained chiton. I fainted.

"But it must have ended about there, for when I came to, sick with terror, it was to hear everyone laughing uproariously. Several of them were bending over Mother, at once reassuring and mocking her, the two men who had gone out among them, and to one side was a jumbled heap of cloth and thin boards, both crusted with mortar. From what they said I understood that the red-haired one had worn the horrible disguise, while satyr-face had made the footsteps by rhythmically clomping on the floor with a brick, and had simulated the breaking door by jumping on a propped-up board.

" 'Now tell us your great-grandmother wasn't married to a stupid old stone demon back in Persia!' he jeered pleasantly, wagging his finger.

"Then came something that tortured me like a rusty dagger and terrified me, in a very quiet way, as much as the image. Although she was white as milk and barely able to totter, Mother did her best to pretend that the loathsome trick they'd played on her was just a clever joke. I knew why. She was horribly afraid of losing their friendship and would have done anything rather than be left alone.

"Her pretense worked. Although some of them left, the rest yielded to her laughing entreaties. They drank until they sprawled out snoring. I waited until almost dawn, then summoned all my courage, made my stiff muscles pull me up onto the tiles, cold and slippery with dew, and with what seemed the last of my strength, dragged myself back to our room.

"But not to sleep. Anra was awake and avid to hear what had happened. I begged him not to make me, but he insisted. I had to tell him everything. The pictures of what I'd seen kept bobbing up in my wretchedly tired mind so vividly that it seemed to be happening all over again. He asked all sorts of questions, wouldn't let me miss a single detail. I had to relive the first thrilling revelation of joy, tainted now by the knowledge that the people were mostly sly and cruel.

"When I got to the part about the stone image, Anra became terribly excited. But when I told him about it all being a nasty joke, he seemed disappointed. He became angry, as if he suspected me of lying.

"Finally he let me sleep.

"The next night I went back to my cubbyhole under the tiles."

Again Fafhrd stopped his horse. The mist masking the mountaintop had suddenly begun to glow, as if a green moon were rising, or as if it were a volcano spouting green flames. The hue tinged their upturned faces. It lured like some vast cloudy jewel. Fafhrd and the Mouser exchanged a glance of fatalistic wonder. Then all three proceeded up the narrowing ridge.

Ahura continued, "I'd sworn by all the gods I'd never do it. I'd told myself I'd rather die. But . . . Anra made me.

"Daytimes I wandered around like a stupefied little ghost-slave. Old Berenice was puzzled and suspicious and once or twice I thought Phryne grimaced knowingly. Finally even Mother noticed and questioned me and had a physician in.

"I think I would have gotten really sick and died, or gone mad, except that then, in desperation at first, I started to go outside, and a whole new world opened to me."

As she spoke on, her voice rising in hushed excitement at the memory of it, there was painted in the minds of Fafhrd and the Mouser a picture of the magic city that Tyre must have seemed to the child—the waterfront, the riches, the bustle of trade, the hum of gossip and laughter, the ships and strangers from foreign lands.

"Those people I had watched from the roof—I could touch them now, follow them around corners, make friends with them—and I soon found that I could make friends almost anywhere. Every person I met seemed a wonderful mystery, something to be smiled and chattered at. I dressed as a slave-child, and all sorts of folk got to know me and expect my coming—other slaves, tavern wenches and sellers of sweetmeats, street merchants and scribes, errand boys and boatmen, seamstresses and cooks. I made myself useful, ran errands myself, listened delightedly to their endless talk, passed on gossip I'd heard, gave away bits of food I'd stolen at home, became a favorite. It seemed to me I could never get enough of Tyre. I scampered from morning to night. It was generally twilight before I climbed back over the garden wall.

"I couldn't fool Old Berenice, but after a while I found a way to escape her whippings. I threatened to tell Mother it was she who had told red-hair and satyr-face about the stone image. I don't know if I guessed right or not, but the threat worked. After that, she would only mumble venomously whenever I sneaked in after sunset. As for Mother, she was getting farther away from us all the time, alive only by night, lost by day in frightened brooding.

"Then, each evening, came another delight. I would tell Anra everything I had heard and seen, each new adventure, each little triumph. Like a magpie I brought home for him all the bright colors, sounds, and odors. Like a magpie I repeated for him the babble of strange languages I'd heard, the scraps of learned talk I'd caught from priests and scholars. I forgot what he'd done to me. We were playing the game again, the most wonderful version of all. Often he helped me, suggesting new places to go, new things to watch for, and once he even saved me from being kidnapped by a couple of ingratiating Alexandrian slave-dealers whom anyone but I would have suspected.

"It was odd how that happened. The two had made much of me, were promising me sweetmeats if I would go somewhere nearby with them, when I thought I heard

Anra's voice whisper 'Don't.' I became cold with terror and darted down an alley.

"It seemed as though Anra were now able sometimes to see the pictures in my mind even when I was away from him. I felt ever so close to him.

"I was wild for him to come out with me, but I've told you what happened the one time he tried. And as the years passed, he seemed to become tied even tighter to the house. Once when Mother vaguely talked of moving to Antioch, he fell ill and did not recover until she had promised we would never, never go.

"Meanwhile he was growing up into a slim and darkly handsome youth. Phryne began to make eyes at him and sought excuses to go to his room. But he was frightened and rebuffed her. However, he coaxed me to make friends with her, although Mother had forbidden it, to go to her room, talk to her, be near her, even share her bed those nights when Mother did not want her. He seemed to like that.

"You know the restlessness that comes to a maturing child, when he seeks love, or adventure, or the gods, or all three. That restlessness had come to Anra, but his only gods were in those dusty, dubious rolls my father had labeled 'Secret Wisdom!' I hardly knew what he did by day any more except that there were odd ceremonies and experiments mixed with his studies. Some of them he conducted in the little basement where the three gray stones were. At such times he had me keep watch. He no longer told me what he was reading or thinking, and I was so busy in my new world that I hardly noticed the difference.

"And yet I could see the restlessness growing. He sent me on longer and more difficult missions, had me inquire after books the scribes had never heard of, seek out all manner of astrologers and wise-women, required me to steal or buy stranger and stranger ingredients from the herb doctors. And when I did win such treasures for him, he would only snatch them from me unjoyfully and be twice as gloomy the evening after. Gone were such days of rejoicing as when I had brought him the first Persian rolls about Ahriman, the first lodestone, or repeated every syllable I had overheard of the words of a famous philosopher from Athens. He was beyond all that now. He sometimes hardly listened to my detailed reports, as if he had already glanced through them and knew they contained nothing to interest him.

"He grew haggard and sick. His restlessness took the form of a frantic pacing. I was reminded of my mother trapped in that blocked-off, underground corridor. It made my heart hurt to watch him. I longed to help him, to share with him my new exciting life, to give him the thing he so desperately wanted.

"But it was not my help he needed. He had embarked on a dark, mysterious quest I did not understand, and he had reached a bitter, corroding impasse where of his own experience he could go no farther.

"He needed a teacher."

8
The Old Man Without a Beard

"I was fifteen when I met the Old Man Without a Beard. I called him that then and I still call him that, for there is no other distinguishing characteristic my mind can seize and hold. Whenever I think of him, even whenever I look at him, his face melts into the mob. It is as if a master actor, after portraying every sort of character in the world, should have hit on the simplest and most perfect of disguises.

"As to what lies behind that too-ordinary face—the something you can sometimes sense but hardly grasp—all I can say is a satiety and an emptiness that are not of this world."

Fafhrd caught his breath. They had reached the end of the ridge. The leftward slope had suddenly tilted uward, become the core of the mountain. While the rightward slope had swung downward and out of sight, leaving an unfathomable black abyss. Between, the path continued upward, a stony strip only a few feet wide. The Mouser touched reassuringly the coil of rope over his shoulder. For a moment their horses hung back. Then, as if the faint green glow and the ceaseless murmuring that bathed them were an intangible net, they were drawn on.

"I was in a wine shop. I had just carried a message to one of the men-friends of the Greek girl Chloe, hardly older than myself, when I noticed him sitting in a corner. I asked Chloe about him. She said he was a Greek chorister and commercial poet down on his luck, or, no, that he was an Egyptian fortuneteller, changed her mind again, tried to remember what a Samian pander had told her about him, gave him a quick puzzled look, decided that she didn't really know him at all and that it didn't matter.

"But his very emptiness intrigued me. Here was a new kind of mystery. After I had been watching him for some time, he turned around and looked at me. I had the impression that he had been aware of my inquiring gaze from the beginning, but had ignored it as a sleepy man a buzzing fly.

"After that one glance he slumped back into his former position, but when I left the shop he walked at my side.

" 'You're not the only one who looks through your eyes, are you?' he said quietly.

"I was so startled by his question that I didn't know how to reply, but he didn't require me to. His face brightened without becoming any more individualized and he immediately began to talk to me in the most charming and humorous way, though his words gave no clue as to who he was or what he did.

"However, I gathered from hints he let fall that he possessed some knowledge of those odd sorts of things that always interested Anra and so I followed him willingly, my hand in his.

"But not for long. Our way led up a narrow twisting alley, and I saw a sideways glint in his eye, and felt his hand tighten on mine in a way I did not like. I became somewhat frightened and expected at any minute the danger warning from Anra.

"We passed a lowering tenement and stopped at a rickety three-story shack leaning against it. He said his dwelling was at the top. He was drawing me toward the ladder that served for stairs, and still the danger warning did not come.

"This his hand crept toward my wrist and I did not wait any longer, but jerked away and ran, my fear growing greater with every step.

"When I reached home, Anra was pacing like a leopard. I was eager to tell him all about my narrow escape, but he kept interrupting me to demand details of the Old Man and angrily flirting his head because I could tell him so little. Then, when I came to the part about my running away, an astounding look of tortured betrayal contorted his features, he raised his hands as if to strike me, then threw himself down on the couch, sobbing.

"But as I leaned over him anxiously, his sobs stopped. He looked around at me, over his shoulder, his face white but composed, and said, 'Ahura, I must know everything about him.'

"In that one moment I realized all that I had overlooked for years—that my delightful airy freedom was a sham—

that it was not Anra, but I, that was tethered—that the
game was not a game, but a bondage—that while I had
gone about so open and eager, intent only on sound and
color, form and movement, he had been developing the
side I had no time for, the intellect, the purpose, the
will—that I was only a tool to him, a slave to be sent on
errands, an unfeeling extension of his own body, a tentacle
he could lose and grow again, like an octopus—that even
my misery at his frantic disappointment, my willingness to
do anything to please him, was only another level to be
coldly used against me—that our very closeness, so that
we were only two halves of one mind, was to him only
another tactical advantage.

"He had reached the second great crisis of his life, and
again he unhesitatingly sacrificed his nearest.

"There was something uglier to it even than that, as I
could see in his eyes as soon as he was sure he had me.
We were like brother and sister kings in Alexandria or
Antioch, playmates from infancy, destined for each other,
but unknowingly, and the boy crippled and impotent—and
now, too soon and horridly had come the bridal night.

"The end was that I went back to the narrow alley, the
lowering tenement, the rickety shack, the ladder, the third
story, and the Old Man Without a Beard.

"I didn't give in without a struggle. Once I was out of
the house I fought every inch of the way. Up until now,
even in the cubbyhole under the tiles, I had only to spy
and observe for Anra. I had not to do things.

"But in the end it was the same. I dragged myself up
the last rung and knocked on the warped door. It swung
open at my touch. Inside, across a fumy room, behind a
large empty table, by the light of a single ill-burning lamp,
his eyes as unwinking as a fish's, and upon me, sat the
Old Man Without a Beard."

Ahura paused, and Fafhrd and the Mouser felt a clamminess descend upon their skins. Looking up, they saw uncoiling downward from dizzy heights, like the ghosts of constrictive snakes or jungle vines, thin tendrils of green mist.

"Yes," said Ahura, "there is always mist or smokiness of some sort where he is.

"Three days later I returned to Anra and told him everything—a corpse giving testimony as to its murderer. But in this instance the judge relished the testimony, and when I told him of a certain plan the Old Man had in mind, an unearthly joy shimmered on his face.

"The Old Man was to be hired as a tutor and physician for Anra. This was easily arranged, as Mother always acceded to Anra's wishes and perhaps still had some hope of seeing him stirred from his seclusion. Moreover, the Old Man had a mixture of unobtrusiveness and power that I am sure would have won him entry everywhere. Within a matter of weeks he had quietly established a mastery over everyone in the house—some, like Mother, merely to be ignored; others, like Phryne, ultimately to be used.

"I will always remember Anra on the day the Old Man came. This was to be his first contact with the reality beyond the garden wall, and I could see that he was terribly frightened. As the hours of waiting passed, he retreated to his room, and I think it was mainly pride that kept him from calling the whole thing off. We did not hear the Old Man coming—only Old Berenice, who was counting the silver outside, stopped her muttering. Anra threw himself back on the couch in the farthest corner of the room, his hands gripping its edge, his eyes fixed on the doorway. A shadow lurched into sight there, grew darker and more definite. Then the Old Man put down on the threshold the two bags he was carrying and looked beyond me at Anra. A moment later my twin's painful gasps died in a faint hiss of expired breath. He had fainted.

"That evening his new education began. Everything that had happened was, as it were, repeated on a deeper, stranger level. There were languages to be learned, but not any languages to be found in human books; rituals to be intoned, but not to any gods that ordinary men have worshipped; magic to be brewed, but not with herbs that I could buy or steal. Daily Anra was instructed in the ways of inner darkness, the sicknesses and unknown powers of the mind, the eon-buried emotions that must be due to insidious impurities the god overlooked in the earth from which they made man. By silent stages our home became a temple of the abominable, a monastery of the unclean.

"Yet there was nothing of tainted orgy, of vicious excess, about their actions. Whatever they did, was done with strict self-discipline and mystic concentration. There was no looseness anywhere about them. They aimed at a knowledge and a power, born of darkness, true, but one which they were willing to make any self-sacrifice to obtain. They were religious, with this difference: their ritual was degradation, their aim a world chaos played upon like a broken lyre by their master minds, their god the quintessence of evil, Ahriman, the ultimate pit.

"As if performed by sleepwalkers, the ordinary routine of our home went on. Indeed, I sometimes felt that we were all of us, except Anra, merely dreams behind the Old Man's empty eyes—actors in a deliberate nightmare where men portrayed beasts; beasts, worms; worms, slime.

"Each morning I went out and made my customary way through Tyre, chattering and laughing as before, but emptily, knowing that I was no more free than if visible chains leashed me to the house, a puppet dangled over the garden wall. Only at the periphery of my masters' intentions did I dare oppose them even passively—once I smuggled the girl Chloe a protective amulet because I fancied they were considering her as a subject for such experiments as they had tried on Phryne. And daily the periphery of their intentions widened—indeed, they would long since have left the house themselves, except for Anra's bondage to it.

"It was to the problem of breaking that bondage that they now devoted themselves. I was not told how they hoped to manage it, but I soon realized that I was to play a part.

"They would shine glittering lights into my eyes and Anra would chant until I slept. Hours or even days later I would awake to find that I had gone unconsciously about my daily business, my body a slave to Anra's commands. At other times Anra would wear a thin leather mask which covered all his features, so that he could only see, if at all, through my eyes. My sense of oneness with my twin grew steadily with my fear of him.

"Then came a period in which I was kept closely pent up, as if in some savage prelude to maturity or death or birth, or all three. The Old Man said something about 'not to see the sun or touch the earth.' Again I crouched for hours in the cubbyhole under the tiles or on reed mats in the little basement. And now it was my eyes and ears that were covered rather than Anra's. For hours I, whom sights and sounds had nourished more than food, could see nothing but fragmentary memories of the child-Anra sick, or the Old Man across the fumy room, or Phryne writhing on her belly and hissing like a snake. But worst of all was my separation from Anra. For the first time since our birth I could not see his face, hear his voice, feel his mind. I withered like a tree from which the sap is withdrawn, an animal in which the nerves have been killed.

"Finally came a day or night, I know not which, when the Old Man loosened the mask from my face. There could hardly have been more than a glimmer of light, but my long-blindfolded eyes made out every detail of the little basement with a painful clarity. The three gray stones had been dug out of the pavement. Supine beside them lay

Anra, emaciated, pale, hardly breathing, looking as though he were about to die.''

The three climbers stopped, confronted by a ghostly green wall. The narrow path had emerged onto what must be the mountain's tablelike top. Ahead stretched a level expanse of dark rock, mist-masked after the first few yards. Without a word they dismounted and led their trembling horses forward into a moist realm which, save that the water was weightless, most resembled a faintly phosphorescent sea-bottom.

"My heart leaped out toward my twin in pity and horror. I realized that despite all tyranny and torment I still loved him more than anything in the world, loved him as a slave loves the weak, cruel master who depends for everything on that slave, loved him as the ill-used body loves the despot mind. And I felt more closely linked to him, our lives and deaths interdependent, than if we had been linked by bonds of flesh and blood, as some rare twins are.

"The Old Man told me I could save him from death if I chose. For the present I must merely talk to him in my usual fashion. This I did, with an eagerness born of days without him. Save for an occasional faint fluttering of his sallow eyelids, Anra did not move, yet I felt that never before had he listened as intently, never before had he understood me as well. It seemed to me that all my previous speech with him had been crude by contrast. Now I remembered and told him all sorts of things that had escaped my memory or seemed too subtle for language. I talked on and on, haphazardly, chaotically, ranging swiftly from local gossip to world history, delving into myriad experiences and feelings, not all of them my own.

"Hours, perhaps days, passed—the Old Man may have put some spell of slumber or deafness on the other inmates of the house to guard against interruption. At times my throat grew dry and he gave me drink, but I hardly dared

pause for that, since I was appalled at the slight but
unremitting change for the worse that was taking place in
my twin and I had become possessed with the idea that my
talking was the cord between life and Anra, that it created
a channel between our bodies, across which my strength
could flow to revive him.

"My eyes swam and blurred, my body shook, my voice
ran the gamut of hoarseness down to an almost inaudible
whisper. Despite my resolve I would have fainted, save
that the Old Man held to my face burning aromatic herbs
which caused me to come shudderingly awake.

"Finally I could no longer speak, but that was no
release, as I continued to twitch my cracked lips and think
on and on in a rushing feverish stream. It was as if I jerked
and flung from the depths of my mind scraps of ideas from
which Anra sucked the tiny life that remained to him.

"There was one persistent image—of a dying Hermaphro-
ditus approaching Salmacis' pool, in which he would become one with the nymph.

"Farther and farther I ventured out along the talk-created
channel between us, nearer and nearer I came to Anra's
pale, delicate, cadaverous face, until, as with a despairing
burst of effort I hurled my last strength to him, it loomed
large as a green-shadowed ivory cliff falling to engulf
me—"

Ahura's words broke off in a gasp of horror. All three
stood still and stared ahead. For rearing up before them in
the thickening mist, so near that they felt they had been
ambushed, was a great chaotic structure of whitish, faintly
yellowed stone, through whose narrow windows and wide-
open door streamed a baleful greenish light, source of the
mist's phosphorescent glow. Fafhrd and the Mouser thought
of Karnak and its obelisks, of the Pharos lighthouse, of the
Acropolis, of the Ishtar Gate in Babylon, of the ruins of
Khatti, of the Lost City of Ahriman, of those doomful

mirage-towers that seamen see where are Scylla and
Charybdis. Of a truth, the architecture of the strange structure varied so swiftly and to such unearthly extremes that it
was lifted into an insane stylistic realm all its own. Mist-
magnified, its twisted ramps and pinnacles, like a fluid
face in a nightmare, pushed upward toward where the stars
should have been.

9
The Castle Called Mist

"What happened next was so strange that I felt sure I
had plunged from feverish consciousness into the cool
retreat of a fanciful dream," Ahura continued as, having
tethered their horses, they mounted a wide stairway toward
that open door which mocked alike sudden rush and cautious reconnoitering. Her story went on with as calm and
drugged a fatalism as their step-by-step advance. "I was
lying on my back beside the three stones and watching my
body move around the little basement. I was terribly weak,
I could not stir a muscle, and yet I felt delightfully
refreshed—all the dry burning and aching in my throat
was gone. Idly, as one will in a dream, I studied my face.
It seemed to be smiling in triumph, very foolishly I thought.
But as I continued to study it, fear began to intrude into
my pleasant dream. The face was mine, but there were
unfamiliar quirks of expression. Then, becoming aware of
my gaze, it grimaced contemptuously and turned and said
something to the Old Man, who nodded matter-of-factly.
The intruding fear engulfed me. With a tremendous effort I
managed to roll my eyes downward and look at my real
body, the one lying on the floor.

"It was Anra's."

They entered the doorway and found themselves in a huge, many-nooked and -niched stone room—though seemingly no nearer the ultimate source of the green glow, except that here the misty air was bright with it. There were stone tables and benches and chairs scattered about, but the chief feature of the place was the mighty archway ahead, from which stone groinings curved upward in baffling profusion. Fafhrd's and the Mouser's eyes momentarily sought the keystone of the arch, both because of its great size and because there was an odd dark recess toward its top.

The silence was portentous, making them feel uneasily for their swords. It was not merely that the luring music had ceased—here in the Castle Called Mist there was literally no sound, save what rippled out futilely from their own beating hearts. There was instead a fogbound concentration that froze into the senses, as though they were inside the mind of a titanic thinker, or as if the stones themselves were entranced.

Then, since it seemed as unthinkable to wait in that silence as for lost hunters to stand motionless in deep winter cold, they passed under the archway and took at random an upward-leading ramp.

Ahura continued, "Helplessly I watched them make certain preparations. While Anra gathered some small bundles of manuscripts and clothing, the Old Man lashed together the three mortar-crusted stones.

"It may have been that in the moment of victory he relaxed habitual precautions. At all events, while he was still bending over the stones, my mother entered the room. Crying out, 'What have you done to him?' she threw herself down beside me and felt at me anxiously. But that was not to the Old Man's liking. He grabbed her by the shoulders and roughly jerked her back. She lay huddled

against the wall, her eyes wide, her teeth chattering—
especially when she saw Anra, in my body, grotesquely
lift the lashed stones. Meanwhile the Old Man hoisted me,
in my new, wasted form, to his shoulder, picked up the
bundles, and ascended the short stair.

"We walked through the inner court, rose-strewn and
filled with Mother's perfumed, wine-splashed friends, who
stared at us in befuddled astonishment, and so out of the
house. It was night. Five slaves waited with a curtained
litter in which the Old Man placed me. My last glimpse
was of Mother's face, its paint tracked by tears, peering
horrifiedly through the half open door."

The ramp issued onto an upper level and they found
themselves wandering aimlessly through a mazy series of
rooms. Of little use to record here the things they thought
they saw through shadowy doorways, or thought they
heard through metal doors with massy complex bolts whose
drawing they dared not fathom. There was a disordered,
high-shelved library, certain of the rolls seeming to smoke
and fume as though they held in their papyrus and ink the
seeds of a holocaust; the corners were piled with sealed
cannisters of greenish stone and age-verdigrised brass tab-
lets. There were instruments that Fafhrd did not even
bother to warn the Mouser against touching. Another room
exuded a fearful animal stench; upon its slippery floor they
noted a sprinkling of short, incredibly thick black bristles.
But the only living creature they saw at any time was a
little hairless thing that looked as if it had once sought to
become a bear cub; when Fafhrd stooped to pet it, it
flopped away whimpering. There was a door that was
thrice as broad as it was high, and its height hardly that of
a man's knee. There was a window that let upon a blackness that was neither of mist nor of night, and yet seemed
infinite; peering in, Fafhrd could faintly see rusted iron
handholds leading upward. The Mouser uncoiled his climb-

ing rope to its full length and swung it around inside the window, without the hook striking anything.

Yet the strangest impression this ominously empty stronghold begot in them was also the subtlest, and one which each new room or twisting corridor heightened—a feeling of architectural inadequacy. It seemed impossible that the supports were equal to the vast weights of the great stone floors and ceilings, so impossible that they almost became convinced that there were buttresses and retaining walls they could not see, either invisible or existing in some other world altogether, as if the Castle Called Mist had only partially emerged from some unthinkable outside. That certain bolted doors seemed to lead where no space could be, added to this hinting.

They wandered through passages so distorted that, though they retained a precise memory of landmarks, they lost all sense of direction.

Finally Fafhrd said, "This gets us nowhere. Whatever we seek, whomever we wait for—Old Man or demon—it might as well be in that first room of the great archway."

The Mouser nodded as they turned back, and Ahura said, "At least we'll be at no greater disadvantage there. Ishtar, but the Old Man's rhyme is true! 'Each chamber is a slavering maw, each arch a toothy jaw.' I always greatly feared this place, but never thought to find a mazy den that sure as death has stony mind and stony claws.

"They never chose to bring me here, you see, and from the night I left our home in Anra's body, I was a living corpse, to be left or taken where they wished. They would have killed me, I think, at least there came a time when Anra would, except it was necessary that Anra's body have an occupant—or my rightful body when he was out of it, for Anra was able to re-enter his own body and walk about in it in this region of Ahriman. At such times I was kept drugged and helpless at the Lost City. I believe that something was done to his body at that time—the Old Man talked of making it invulnerable—for after I returned to it, I found it seeming both emptier and stonier than before."

Starting back down the ramp, the Mouser thought he heard from somewhere ahead, against the terrible silence, the faintest of windy groans.

"I grew to know my twin's body very well, for I was in it most of seven years in the tomb. Somewhere during that black period all fear and horror vanished—I had become habituated to death. For the first time in my life my will, my cold intelligence, had time to grow. Physically fettered, existing almost without sensation, I gained inward power. I began to see what I could never see before—Anra's weaknesses.

"For he could never cut me wholly off from him. The chain he had forged between our minds was too strong for that. No matter how far away he went, no matter what screens he raised up, I could always see into some sector of his mind, dimly, like a scene at the end of a long, narrow, shadowy corridor.

"I saw his pride—a silver-armored wound. I watched his ambition stalk among the stars as if they were jewels set on black velvet in his treasure house to be. I felt, almost as if it were my own, his choking hatred of the bland, miserly gods—almighty fathers who lock up the secrets of the universe, smile at our pleas, frown, shake their heads, forbid, chastise; and his groaning rage at the bonds of space and time, as if each cubit he could not see and tread upon were a sliver manacle on his wrist, as if each moment before or after his own life were a silver crucifying nail. I walked through the gale-blown halls of his loneliness and glimpsed the beauty that he cherished—shadowy, glittering forms that cut the soul like knives—and once I came upon the dungeon of his love, where no light came to show it was corpses that were fondled and bones kissed. I grew familiar with his desires, which demanded a universe of miracles peopled by unveiled gods. And his lust, which quivered at the world as at a woman, frantic to know each hidden part.

"Happily, for I was learning at long last to hate him, I noted how, though he possessed my body, he could not use it easily and bravely as I had. He could not laugh, or love, or dare. He must instead hang back, peer, purse his lips, withdraw."

More than halfway down the ramp, it seemed to the Mouser that the groan was repeated, louder, more whistlingly.

"He and the Old Man started on a new cycle of study and experience that took them, I think, to all corners of the world and that they were confident, I'm sure, would open to them those black realms wherein their powers would become infinite. Anxiously from my cramped vantagepoint I watched their quest ripen and then, to my delight, rot. Their outstretched fingers just missed the next handhold in the dark. There was something that both of them lacked. Anra became bitter, blamed the Old Man for their lack of success. They quarreled.

"When I saw Anra's failure become final, I mocked him with my laughter, not of lips but of mind. From here to the stars he could not have escaped it—it was then he would have killed me. But he dared not while I was in his own body, and I now had the power to bar him from that.

"Perhaps it was my faint thought-laughter that turned his desperate mind to you and to the secret of the laughter of the Elder Gods—that, and his need of magical aid in regaining his body. For a while then I almost feared he had found a new avenue of escape—or advance—until this morning before the tomb, with sheer cruel joy, I saw you spit on his offers, challenge, and, helped by my laughter, kill him. Now there is only the Old Man to fear."

Passing again under the massive multiple archway with its oddly recessed keystone, they heard the whistling groan once more repeated, and this time there was no mistaking its reality, its nearness, its direction. Hastening to a shadowy and particularly misty corner of the chamber, they made out an inner window set level with the floor, and in that window they saw a face that seemed to float bodyless on the thick fog. Its features defied recognition—it might have been a distillation of all the ancient, disillusioned faces in the world. There was no beard below the sunken cheeks.

Coming close as they dared, they saw that it was perhaps not entirely bodyless or without support. There was the ghostly suggestion of tatters of clothing or flesh trailing off, a pulsating sack that might have been a lung, and silver chains with hooks or claws.

Then the one eye remaining to that shameful fragment opened and fixed upon Ahura, and the shrunken lips twisted themselves into the caricature of a smile.

"Like you, Ahura," the fragment murmured in the highest of falsettos, "he sent me on an errand I did not want to run."

As one, moved by a fear they dared not formulate, Fafhrd and the Mouser and Ahura half turned round and peered over their shoulders at the mist-clogged doorway leading outside. For three, four heartbeats they peered. Then, faintly, they heard one of the horses whinny. Whereupon they turned fully round, but not before a dagger, sped by the yet unshaking hand of Fafhrd, had buried itself in the open eye of the tortured thing in the inner window.

Side by side they stood, Fafhrd wild-eyed, the Mouser taut, Ahura with the look of someone who, having successfully climbed a precipice, slips at the very summit.

A slim shadowy bulk mounted into the glow outside the doorway.

"Laugh!" Fafhrd hoarsely commanded Ahura. "Laugh!" He shook her, repeating the command.

Her head flopped from side to side, the cords in her neck jerked, her lips twitched, but from them came only a dry croaking. She grimaced despairingly.

"Yes," remarked a voice they all recognized, "there are times and places where laughter is an easily-biunted weapon—as harmless as the sword which this morning pierced me through."

Death-pale as always, the tiny blood-clot over his heart, his forehead crumpled in, his black garb travel-dusted, Anra Devadoris faced them.

"And so we come back to the beginning," he said slowly. "But now a wider circle looms ahead."

Fafhrd tried to speak, to laugh, but the words and laughter choked in his throat.

"Now you have learned something of my history and my power, as I intended you should," the adept continued. "You have had time to weigh and reconsider. I still await your answer."

This time it was the Mouser who sought to speak or laugh and failed.

For a moment the adept continued to regard them, smiling confidently. Then his gaze wandered beyond them. He frowned suddenly and strode forward, pushed past them, knelt by the inner window.

As soon as his back was turned Ahura tugged at the Mouser's sleeve, tried to whisper something—with no more success than one deaf and dumb.

They heard the adept sob, "He was my nicest."

The Mouser drew a dagger, prepared to steal on him from behind, but Ahura dragged him back, pointing in a very different direction.

The adept whirled on them. "Fools!" he cried, "have you no inner eye for the wonders of darkness, no sense of the grandeur of horror, no feeling for a quest beside which all other adventurings fade in nothingness, that you should destroy my greatest miracle—slay my dearest oracle? I let you come here to Mist, confident its mighty music and glorious vistas would win you to my view—and thus I am repaid. The jealous, ignorant powers ring me round—you are my great hope fallen. There were unfavorable portents as I walked from the Lost City. The white, idiot glow of Ormadz faintly dirtied the black sky. I heard in the wind the senile clucking of the Elder Gods. There was a fumbling abroad, as if even incompetent Ningauble, last and stupidest of the hunting pack, were catching up. I had a charm in reserve to thwart them, but it needed the Old Man to carry it. Now they close in for the kill. But there are still some moments of power left me and I am not wholly yet without allies. Though I am doomed, there are still those bound to me by such ties that they must answer me if I call upon them. You shall not see the end, if end there be.'' With that he lifted his voice in a great eerie shout, ''Father! Father!''

The echoes had not died before Fafhrd rushed at him, his great sword singing.

The Mouser would have followed suit except that, just as he shook Ahura off, he realized at what she was so insistently pointing.

The recess in the keystone above the mighty archway.

Without hesitation he unslipped his climbing rope, and running lightly across the chamber, made a whistling cast.

The hook caught in the recess.

Hand over hand he climbed up.

Behind him he heard the desperate skirl of swords, heard also another sound, far more distant and profound.

His hand gripped the lip of the recess, he pulled himself up and thrust in head and shoulders, steadying himself on hip and elbow. After a moment, with his free hand, he whipped out his dagger.

Inside, the recess was hollowed like a bowl. It was filled with a foul greenish liquid and incrusted with glowing minerals. At the bottom, covered by the liquid, were several objects—three of them rectangular, the others irregularly round and rhythmically pulsating.

He raised his dagger, but for the moment did not, could not, strike. There was too crushing a weight of things to be realized and remembered—what Ahura had told about the ritual marriage in her mother's family—her suspicion that, although she and Anra were born together, they were not children of the same father—how her Greek father had died (and now the Mouser guessed at the hands of what) —the strange affinity for stone the slave-physician had noted in Anra's body—what she had said about an operation performed on him—why a heart-thrust had not killed him—why his skull had cracked so hollowly and egg-shell easy—how he had never seemed to breathe—old legends of other sorcerors who had made themselves invulnerable by hiding their hearts—above all, the deep kinship all of them had sensed between Anra and this half-living castle— the black, man-shaped monolith in the Lost City—

As if pinioned by a nightmare, he helplessly heard the clash of swords rise toward a climax, heard it blotted out by the other sound—a gargantuan stony clomping that seemed to be following their course up the mountain, like a pursuing earthquake—

The Castle Called Mist began to tremble, and still he could not strike—

Then, as if surging across infinity from that utmost rim beyond which the Elder Gods had retreated, relinquishing the world to younger deities, he heard a mighty, star-shaking laughter that laughed at all things, even at this;

and there was power in the laughter, and he knew the power was his to use.

With a downward sweep of his arm he sent his dagger plunging into the green liquid and tearing through the stone-crusted heart and brain and lungs and guts of Anra Devadoris.

The liquid foamed and boiled, the castle rocked until he was almost shaken from the niche, the laughter and stony clomping rose to a pandemonium.

Then, in an instant it seemed, all sound and movement ceased. The Mouser's muscles went weak. He half fell, half slid, to the floor. Looking about dazedly, making no attempt to rise, he saw Fafhrd wrench his sword from the fallen adept and totter back until his groping hand found the support of a table-edge, saw Ahura, still gasping from the laughter that had possessed her, go up and kneel beside her brother and cradle his crushed head on her knees.

No word was spoken. Time passed. The green mist seemed to be slowly thinning.

Then a small black shape swooped into the room through a high window and the Mouser grinned.

"Hugin," he called luringly.

The shape swooped obediently to his sleeve and clung there, head down. He detached from the bat's leg a tiny parchment.

"Fancy, Fafhrd, it's from the commander of our rear guard," he announced gayly. "Listen:

" 'To my agents Fafhrd and the Gray Mouser, funeral greetings! I have regretfully given up all hope for you, and yet—token of my great affection—I risk my own dear Hugin in order to get his last message through. Incidentally, Hugin, if given opportunity, will return to me from Mist—something I am afraid you will not be able to do. So if, before you die, you see anything interesting—and I am sure you will—kindly scribble me a memorandum.

Remember the proverb: Knowledge takes precedence over death. Farewell for two thousand years, dearest friends. Ningauble.' ''

"That demands drink," said Fafhrd, and walked out into the darkness. The Mouser yawned and stretched himself, Ahura stirred, printed a kiss on the waxen face of her brother, lifted the trifling weight of his head from her lap, and laid it gently on the stone floor. From somewhere in the upper reaches of the castle they heard a faint crackling.

Presently Fafhrd returned, striding more briskly, with two jars of wine under his arm.

"Friends," he announced, "the moon's come out, and by its light this castle begins to look remarkably small. I think the mist must have been dusted with some green drug that made us see sizes wrong. We must have been drugged, I'll swear, for we never saw something that's standing plain as day at the bottom of the stairs with its foot on the first step—a black statue that's twin brother to the one in the Lost City."

The Mouser lifted his eyebrows. "And if we went back to the Lost City . . . ?" he asked.

"Why," said Fafhrd, "we might find that those fool Persian farmers, who admitted hating the thing, had knocked down the statue there, and broken it up, and hidden the pieces." He was silent for a moment. Then, "Here's wine," he rumbled, "to sluice the green drug from our throats."

The Mouser smiled. He knew that hereafter Fafhrd would refer to their present adventure as "the time we were drugged on a mountaintop."

They all three sat on a table-edge and passed the two jars endlessly round. The green mist faded to such a degree that Fafhrd, ignoring his claims about the drug, began to argue that even it was an illusion. The crackling from above increased in volume; the Mouser guessed that

the impious rolls in the library, no longer shielded by the
damp, were bursting into flame. Some proof of this was
given when the abortive bear cub, which they had completely forgotten, came waddling frightenedly down the
ramp. A trace of decorous down was already sprouting
from its naked hide. Fafhrd dribbled some wine on its
snout and held it up to the Mouser.

"It wants to be kissed," he rumbled.

"Kiss it yourself, in memory of pig-trickery," replied
the Mouser.

This talk of kissing turned their thoughts to Ahura.
Their rivalry forgotten, at least for the present, they persuaded her to help them determine whether her brother's
spells were altogether broken. A moderate number of hugs
demonstrated this clearly.

"Which reminds me," said the Mouser brightly, "now
that our business here is over, isn't it time we started,
Fafhrd, for your lusty Northland and all that bracing snow?"

Fafhrd drained one jar dry and picked up the other.

"The Northland?" he ruminated. "What is it but a
stamping ground of petty, frost-whiskered kinglets who
know not the amenities of life. That's why I left the place.
Go back? By Thor's smelly jerkin, not now!"

The Mouser smiled knowingly and sipped from the
remaining jar. Then, noticing the bat still clinging to his
sleeve, he took stylus, ink, and a scrap of parchment from
his pouch, and, with Ahura giggling over his shoulder,
wrote:

"To my aged brother in petty abominations, greetings!
It is with the deepest regret that I must report the outra-
geously lucky and completely unforeseen escape of two rude
and unsympathetic fellows from the Castle Called Mist.
Before leaving, they expressed to me the intention of
returning to someone called Ningauble—you are Ningauble,
master, are you not?—and lopping off six of his seven

eyes for souvenirs. So I think it only fair to warn you. Believe me, I am your friend. One of the fellows was very tall and at times his bellowings seemed to resemble speech. Do you know him? The other fancied a gray garb and was of extreme wit and personal beauty, given to . . ."

Had any of them been watching the corpse of Anra Devadoris at this moment, they would have seen a slight twitching of the lower jaw. At last the mouth came open, and out leapt a tiny black mouse. The cub-like creature, to whom Fafhrd's fondling and the wine had imparted the seeds of self-confidence, lurched drunkenly at it, and the mouse began a squeaking scurry toward the wall. A wine jar, hurled by Fafhrd, shattered on the crack into which it shot; Fafhrd had seen, or thought he had seen, the untoward place from which the mouse had come.

"Mice in his mouth," he hiccuped. "What dirty habits for a pleasant young man! A nasty, degrading business, this thinking oneself an adept."

"I am reminded," said the Mouser, "of what a witch told me about adepts. She said that, if an adept chances to die, his soul is reincarnated in a mouse. If, as a mouse, he managed to kill a rat, his soul passes over into a rat. As a rat, he must kill a cat; as a cat, a wolf; as a wolf, a panther; and as a panther, a man. Then he can recommence his adeptry. Of course, it seldom happens that anyone gets all the way through the sequence and in any case it takes a very long time. Trying to kill a rat is enough to satisfy a mouse with mousedom."

Fafhrd solemnly denied the possibility of any such foolery, and Ahura cried until she decided that being a mouse would interest rather than dishearten her peculiar brother. More wine was drunk from the remaining jar. The crackling from the rooms above had become a roar, and a bright red glow consumed the dark shadows. The three adventurers prepared to leave the place.

Meantime the mouse, or another very much like it, thrust its head from the crack and began to lick the wine-damp shards, keeping a fearful eye upon those in the great room, but especially upon the strutting little would-be bear.

A great blast of wind, cold and pure, blew away the last lingering of Mist. As they went through the doorway they saw, outspread above them, the self-consistent stars.

Editor's Introduction to

"Wet Magic"

*R*ay Bradbury has called Henry Kuttner "a neglected master." While Bradbury's high praise for Kuttner is understandable—it was under Kuttner's tutelage and encouragement that Bradbury broke into print—and while such terms as "undeservedly neglected" and "unjustly forgotten" are sometimes too generously applied, in the case of Henry Kuttner these judgments are sad statement of fact.

Born in Los Angeles on April 7, 1915, Henry Kuttner attracted notice with his first sale to Weird Tales—the oft-reprinted minor classic, "The Graveyard Rats" (March 1936). As was the case with many youthful writers of the period, Kuttner's earliest work was heavily influenced by the writings of H. P. Lovecraft. His own writing career would span the next twenty-two years, his typewriter generating hundreds of stories and dozens of novels. A precise bibliography of Kuttner's fiction is perhaps impossible. He is known to have made use of some twenty pseudonyms and house names, and much of his writing following their marriage in 1940 was in collaboration (often published under only a single byline) with his wife, the noted fantasy author, C. L. Moore. While an author tends to hide his lesser work behind pseudonyms, Kuttner chose to credit *some of his best-known fiction as by Lewis Padgett or by Lawrence O'Donnell.*

Commercial considerations aside, Kuttner's extensive use of pseudonyms would seem to indicate an author of multiple personalities, and to one extent this holds true: Henry Kuttner was an extremely versatile *writer. Kuttner was to adapt the styles of other favorite writers to his own work, and a reader can examine a cross section of Kuttner's fiction and note here the influence of Robert E. Howard, there Lewis Carroll, or A. Merritt, or Thorne Smith.*

Following the death of Robert E. Howard in 1936, Kuttner filled the heroic fantasy gap in the pages of Weird Tales *with a short series of stores featuring Elak of Atlantis. A shorter series of stories featuring Prince Raynor appeared in* Weird Tales' *pulp rival,* Strange Stories. *"Wet Magic," which was published in* Unknown Worlds, *is a later heroic fantasy piece—one that shows the influence of T. H. White, who had recently published three novels of his Arthurian series:* The Sword in the Stone, The Witch in the Wood, *and* The Ill-Made Knight. *"Wet Magic" is typical of editor John Campbell's insistence upon a modern approach to fantasy tempered with whimsical humor—a formula that characterized the pulp. Despite its initial lighthearted cuteness, as the story progresses Kuttner manages to inject an unrelenting grimness of his own. Fantasy stories set during the age of King Arthur have become commonplace, but "Wet Magic" remains unique.*

Not one to confine himself to one particular genre, Kuttner wrote exceptionally well in the fields of fantasy, science fiction, and mystery. While he is perhaps best remembered for his science fiction work, toward the end of his career much of his writing was devoted to mystery novels. Henry Kuttner died of a sudden heart attack on February 3, 1958, while working for his M.A. at the University of Southern California. He was only 42, and the career of this prolific writer could only have continued to develop and expand. In a recent tribute to Kuttner in the excellent small-press publication, Etchings & Odysseys, *Robert Bloch suggests that "Hank never became a super-star, because he was so versatile. He never became known for one style, one theme, one famous story." It may be said of Henry Kuttner that he was a jack-of-all-trades— and a master of most of them.*

Wet Magic

Henry Kuttner

It happened in Wales, which, of course, was the logical place for Morgan le Fay to be. Not that Arthur Woodley expected to find the fabled enchantress there, of course. He was looking for something entirely different. In a word, safety.

With two Stukas hanging doggedly on the tail of his observation plane, despite the pea-soup fog that shrouded the craggy peaks of Wales, Woodley dodged and twisted frantically, his hard, handsome face set in lines of strain. It wasn't fair, he thought. This crate wasn't meant as a fighter, and needed another crewman anyway. Nazis weren't supposed to butt in on routine transfer flights.

Z-zoom!

Tracer bullets fanned Woodley's helmet. Why wouldn't those Stukas leave him alone? He hadn't been looking for them. If he had thought to find enemy aircraft in Wales, he'd have flown rapidly in the opposite direction. *Zoom* again. No use. The Stukas hung on. Woodley dived dangerously into the fog.

Damn—Hollywood arranged things better. Woodley grinned mirthlessly. In the air battles he'd starred in in Paradox's *Flight Wings,* he had the proper kind of a plane to work in. Say a Spitfire or a P-38. And—

Tut-tut-tut! Double-damn! This couldn't keep up much longer. Those Stukas were becoming familiar with all of Woodley's tricks—the *spang!* each slug made as it struck armor plate unpleasantly reminded him that these were not Hollywood blanks.

Tut-tut-tut-spang! He would have engaged one. Two of them made the odds unnecessarily heavy. Also, in this thick fog, it shouldn't be too difficult to escape—

The engine coughed and died. A bullet had found the fuel line, presumably. Woodley almost felt relieved. He banked the plane into an especially dense bank of fog, glanced back, and saw the Stukas following relentlessly. How far down was the ground?

He had to risk it, in any case. As he bailed out, some bullets screamed past, but none found a mark in Woodley's body. The fog was denser lower down, and camouflaged the parachute so that there was no more gunfire.

The plane crashed, some distance away. The drone of the Stukas grew fainter as the Nazi planes circled away to the east, their job done. Woodley, swaying in the silk shrouds, peered down, straining his eyes to see what lay below.

A tree. He caromed off a branch, in a tremendous crackling and thumping, brought up with a terrific jolt, and hung breathless, slowly revolving. The silence of the fog closed in again. He could hear nothing but the low murmur of a rivulet somewhere in that blanketing grayness.

Woodley slipped out of his harness, climbed down, and drank brandy from a pocket flask before he looked around.

There was little to see. The fog was still thick, though he could make out the silhouettes of ghostly trees all around him. A forest, then. From where he stood, the ground sloped sharply down to where the unseen streamlets gurgled.

The brandy had made him thirsty for water, so Woodley stumbled through the murk till he almost fell into the stream. He drank, and then, shivering with cold, examined his surroundings more carefully.

Not far away grew an immense oak, gnarled and ancient, with a trunk as large as that of a California sequoia. Its exposed roots, where erosion had done its work, made a comfortable-looking burrow—or, rather, cave; and at least it would provide shelter from the knifing wind. Woodley went forward warily and assured himself that the little den was empty. Fair enough.

He got down on all fours and backed into the hollow. Not far. Something kicked him in the pants, and Woodley described an arc that ended with his head in the brook. He bubbled a yell and sprang up, blinking icy water from his eyes. A bear—

There was no bear. Woodley remembered that he had scrutinized the cave of roots carefully, and he was certain it could have contained nothing larger than a fairly young mouse. And mice seldom, if ever, kick with noticeable effect.

It was curiosity that drew Woodley back to the scene of his humiliation. He peered in furtively. Nothing. Nothing at all. A springy root must have snapped back and struck

him. It couldn't happen twice. Moreover, the wind was
growing colder.

This time Woodley crawled in headfirst, and this time
he was kicked in the face.

Rising rapidly from the brook, Woodley thought wildly
of invisible kangaroos. He stood motionless, staring at that
notably empty cave of roots. Then he drank brandy.

Logic came to his aid. He had been through an unpleasant nervous ordeal. Little wonder that he was imagining things
now. Nevertheless, he did not make a third attempt to
invade the burrow. Instead, he went rather hastily down-
stream. The watercourse should lead somewhere.

The parachute descent into the tree had bruised him a
bit, so presently Woodley sat down to rest. The swirling
gray fog made him slightly dizzy. The dark column of the
trees seemed to move with a wavering, half-animate life of
their own. Woodley lay back, closing his eyes. He didn't
like Wales. He didn't like this mess he was in. He—

Someone kissed him full on the lips.

Automatically Woodley responded before he realized
what was happening. Then he opened his eyes to see a
slim, lovely girl rising from where she had knelt beside
him. He had not heard her approach—

"Well—" he said. "Hello!" The girl was singularly
beautiful, dark-haired, with a fillet of gold about her brow.
She wore a robe that reached her ankles, but Woodley
could see that her figure was eminently satisfactory.

"You smell of Merlin," she said.

"I . . . uh . . . I do?" murmured Woodley, feeling
vaguely insulted. He got up, staring. Curious costumes
they wore in this part of the country. Maybe—*yipe!*—maybe
he wasn't even in England!

He asked the girl about that, and she shook her head.
"This is Wales." There was a puzzled frown drawing

together the dark line of her brows. "Who are you? You remind me of . . . someone—"

"Arthur Woodley. I'm flying for the A.E.F. You must have seen some of my pictures—eh?"

"Merlin could fly," she remarked cryptically.

Baffled, Woodley suddenly recollected that a Merlin was a bird—a sort of falcon, he thought. That explained it. "I didn't see you come up," he said. "You live near here?"

The girl chuckled softly. "Oh, I'm usually invisible. No one can see me or touch me unless I want them to. And my name is Vivienne."

"It's a lovely name," Woodley said, automatically going into his routine. "It suits you."

Vivienne said, "Not for years have I felt passion for any man. Is it because you remind me of Merlin? I think I love you, Arthur."

Woodley swallowed. Curious customs they had in Wales! But he'd have to be careful not to insult the girl—after all he was lost, and her services as a guide would be invaluable.

There was no need to speak. Vivienne went on swiftly.

"I live not far from here. Under the lake. My home and I are yours. Provided you pass the testing, of course. But, since you can fly, you will not be afraid of any task Morgan may set you—so?"

"Why—" Woodley hesitated, and then glanced around him at the chilly grayness of the fog. "Why, I'd love to go with you, Vivienne," he amplified hastily. "I . . . I suppose you live with your parents?"

"They have long been dust. Do you come with me of your own free will?"

"It's a pleasure."

"Say it—your own free will," Vivienne insisted, her dark eyes glowing.

Woodley complied, definitely puzzled, but willing to

play along, since it obviously could do no harm. The girl smiled like an angel. "Now you are mine," she said. "Or you will be, when you have passed Morgan's testing. Come! It is not far, but—shall we fly?"

"Why not?" Woodley countered, grinning. "Let's go."

Vivienne obeyed. She lifted her arms, stood on tiptoe, and rose gently from the ground, swaying slightly in the breeze. Woodley remained perfectly motionless, looking at the spot where she had been.

Then he started violently, cast a quick glance around, and finally, with the utmost reluctance, tilted back his head.

There she was, floating down the gorge, looking back over her shoulder. "This way!" her silvery voice came back.

Automatically Woodley turned around and began to walk away. His eyes were slightly glazed. He was brooding over hallucinations—

"My love!" a voice cried from above.

There was a *swoosh* in the air behind him, reminding Woodley of a Stuka. He whirled, trying to dodge, and fell headlong into the stream. His temple thumped solidly against a rounded stone—and unconsciousness was definitely a relief.

He was back in his Bel-Air home, Woodley thought, waking up between silk sheets, with an ice pack on his head. The ice pack was refreshing, almost eliminating a dull, throbbing ache. A hangover—

He remembered. It wasn't a hangover. He had fallen, and struck his head. But what had happened before that? Vivienne . . . *oh!* With a sickish feeling in his middle, Woodley recalled her words, and they had assumed a new and shocking significance.

But it couldn't be true—

His eyelids snapped open. He was in bed, yes; but it wasn't his bed, and he was looking up into the face of a . . . thing.

Superficially she was a girl, unadorned, and with a singularly excellent figure. But she was made of green jello. Her unbound hair looked like very fine seaweed, and floated in a cloud about her head. She drew back at Woodley's movement, withdrawing her hand—which the man had mistaken for an ice pack.

"My lord," she said, bowing low.

"Dream," Woodley muttered incoherently. "Must be. Wake up pretty soon. Green jello . . . technicolor—" He tapered off vaguely, looking around. He was between sheets of finest silk; the room itself had no windows, but a cool, colorless radiance filled it. The air was quite clear, yet it seemed to have—thickened. Woodley could trace the tiny currents in it, and the swirls as he sat up. The sheets fell away from his bare torso.

"D-dream," said Woodley, not believing it for a moment.

"My lord," said the green maiden, bowing again. Her voice was sweet and rather bubbly. "I am Nurmala, a naiad, here to serve you."

Woodley experimentally pinched himself. It hurt. He reached out to seize Nurmala's arm, and a horrifying thing happened. The naiad girl not only looked like jelly—she *was* jelly. It felt like squeezing a sack filled with cold mush. Cold and loathsome.

"The Lady Vivienne ordered me to watch over you," Nurmala said, apparently unhurt. Her arm had resumed its normal contour. Woodley noticed that she seemed to waver around the edges as she went on, "Before sundown you must pass the testing Morgan le Fay has set you, and you will need all your mettle to do that."

"What?" Woodley didn't quite comprehend.

"You must slay that which lairs behind Shaking Rock,"

Nurmala said. "Morgan—made it—this morning, and placed it there, for your testing. I swam out and saw—" She caught herself, with a quick glance around, and said swiftly, "But how can I serve you, lord?"

Woodley rubbed his eyes. "I . . . am I dreaming? Well, I want some clothes. And where am I?"

Nurmala went away, seeming to glide rather than walk, and returned with a bundle of garments, which Woodley took and examined. There was a knee-length blue samite tunic, with gold bands of embroidery upon it, linen drawers, long fawn-colored hose with leather soles, and a belt with a dagger in its sheath attached. On the bosom of the tunic was a design of a coiled snake with a golden star above its upraised, threatening head.

"Will you don them, lord? You are not dreaming—no."

Woodley had already realized that. He was certainly awake, and his surroundings were quite as certainly—unearthly. The conclusions were obvious.

Meanwhile, he'd feel better with pants on. "Sure," he said. "I'll don them." Then he waited. Nurmala also waited, cocking her head to one side in an interested way. Finally Woodley gave up, dragged the drawers under the sheets, and struggled into them in that position with some difficulty. Nurmala seemed disappointed, but said nothing.

So Vivienne's words had been literally true! Good Lord, what a spot! Still—Woodley's eyes narrowed speculatively as he adjusted his tunic. Once you took the initial improbable premise for granted, you were far safer. Magic— *hm-m-m*. In folklore and legends, humans had generally come off second best in encounters with fairy folk. The reason seemed fairly obvious. A producer could usually outbluff a Hollywood actor. The actor felt—was made to feel—his limitations. And supernatural beings, Woodley thought, had a habit of depending to a great extent on their unearthly background. It was sound psychology. Get the other fellow worried, and the battle is more than half won.

But if the other fellow didn't bluff—if he kept his feet solidly on the ground, and used his head—the results should be different. Woodley hoped so. What had Vivienne— and Nurmala, the naiad—said about a testing? It sounded dangerous.

He held out his hand. Quite steady. And, now that he was dressed, Woodley felt more confident.

"Where's a mirror?" he asked. Concentration on such down-to-earth details would help his mental attitude—

"Our queen mislikes them," the naiad murmured. "There are none beneath the lake. But you cut a gallant figure, lord."

"Lake? Queen? You mean Vivienne?"

"Oh, no," said Nurmala, rather shocked. "Our queen is Morgan le Fay." She touched the embroidered snake design on Woodley's breast with a translucent forefinger. "The Queen of Air and Darkness. She rules, of course, and we all serve her—even the Lady Vivienne, who is high in favor."

Morgan le Fay. Remembrance came to Woodley. He had a kaleidoscopic picture of knights in armor, distressed maidens shut up in towers, the Round Table, Launcelot and Arthur—Vivienne! Didn't the legend say that Vivienne was the girl with whom the wizard Merlin had fallen in love?

And Morgan le Fay was the evil genius of the Arthurian cycle, the enchantress who hated the king, her half-brother, so bitterly—

"Look," Woodley said. "Just how—"

"I hight Bohart!"
The words didn't make sense. But they came from someone who, at least, looked human, despite his cos-

tume, almost a duplicate of Woodley's. The man stood
before a curtain that billowed with his passing, and his
ruddy, long mustache bristled with fury. Over his tunic he
wore a gleaming metal cuirass, and in his hand was a bare
sword.

Nurmala bubbled faintly and retreated with a swish.
"My lord Bohart—"

"Silence, naiad!" the other thundered, glaring at
Woodley. "I name you knave, lackey, lickspittle, and
traitor! Yes, you!"

Woodley looked helplessly at Nurmala. "It is Sir Bohart,"
she said unhappily. "The Lady Vivienne will be furious."

But it was the obvious fury of Sir Bohart himself that
worried Woodley—that, and the sharp-edged sword. If—

"Draw!" the knight roared.

Nurmala interposed a tremulous objection. "He has no
sword. It is not meet—"

Sir Bohart gobbled into his mustache and cast his blade
away. From his belt he whipped a dagger that was the
counterpart of Woodley's. "We are even now," he said,
with horrid satisfaction. "Well?"

"Say you yield," Normala whispered. "Quick!"

"I yield," Woodley repeated obediently. The knight
was not pleased.

"Knave! To yield without a struggle—Ha! Are you a
knight?"

"No," Woodley said before he thought, and Nurmala
gasped in horror.

"My lord! No knight? But Sir Bohart can slay you now
without dishonor!"

Bohart was moving forward, his dagger glittering, a
pleased smile on his scarred face. "She speaks sooth. Now
shall I slit your weasand."

It sounded unpleasant. Woodley hastily put the bed
between himself and the advancing knight. "Now wait a

minute," he said firmly. "I don't even know who you are. Why should we fight?"

Sir Bohart had not paused. "Craven dog! You take the Lady Vivienne from me, and then seek to placate me. No!"

They circled the bed, while the naiad bubbled a faint scream and fled. Robbed of even that slight moral support, Woodley felt his knees weaken. "I didn't take Vivienne," he urged. "I only just met her."

Sir Bohart said, between his teeth, "For centuries I have dwelt here beneath the lake, since Arthur fell at Salisbury Plain. The Lady Vivienne loved me then—and in a hundred years I bored her. She turned to the study of goety. But I have been faithful, knowing always that some time I would win her back. Without a rival, I was sure of it. Now you have to come to lure her from me—lackey cur! Ah-h!" The dagger's sweep ripped cloth from Woodley's sleeve as he nimbly dodged and caught up a metal vase from a tabouret. He hurled it at Bohart's head. The vase bounced back without touching the knight.

More magic, apparently.

"Maybe I am dreaming, after all," Woodley groaned, jumping back.

"I thought that myself, for a while," Bohart said conversationally, leaping across the bed and slashing out with his weapon. "Later, I knew I was not. Will you draw?"

Woodley unsheathed his dagger. He ducked under Sir Bohart's thrust and slashed up at the knight's arm. It was like striking at glass. His point slid off harmlessly, and only by a frantic writhe was he able to avoid being impaled.

How the devil could he fight against this sort of magic?

"Look," he said, "I don't want Vivienne."

"You dare to insult my lady," the knight bellowed, crimson-faced, as he plunged forward. "By the spiked tail of Sathanas, I'll—"

"Sir Bohart!" It was Vivienne's voice, iron under the velvet. She was standing at the curtain, Nurmala quivering behind her. "Hold!"

"Nay, nay," Bohart puffed. "This knave is not fit for black beetles to eat. Have no fear for me; I can slay him easily."

"And I promise to slay you if you harm him, despite your magic cuirass that can turn all blows!" Vivienne shrilled. "Let be, I say! Let be! Else—"

Sir Bohart hesitated, sending a wary glance at the girl. He looked toward the shrinking Woodley and snarled silently.

Vivienne said, "Must I summon Morgan?"

The knight's face went gray as weathered stone. He swung around, a sick horror in his eyes.

"My lady—" he said.

"I have protected you till now, for old time's sake. Often the queen has wanted a partner to play at chess—and often she has asked me for you. In truth, there are few humans beneath the lake, and I would be sorry to lose your company, Bohart. But Morgan has not played at chess for long and long."

The knight slowly sheathed his dagger. He licked his lips. Silently he went to the hanging drapery, passed through, and was gone.

"Perhaps Bleys should bleed him," Nurmala suggested. "Sir Bohart grows more choleric each day."

Vivienne had lost her angry look. She smiled mockingly at the green girl.

"So you can get the blood, eh? You naiads. You'd strip yourself clean for a drop of human blood, if you weren't stripped already." Her voice changed. "Go now. My new gown must be ready, for we sup with Morgan le Fay tonight after the testing."

*   *   *

As Nurmala vanished, Vivienne came forward and put her arms around Woodley's neck. "I am sorry for this, messire. Sir Bohart will not offend again. He is fiercely jealous—but I never loved him. For a little time I amused myself, some centuries ago—that was all. It is you I love, my Arthur, you alone."

"Look," Woodley said, "I'd like a little information. Where am I, for one thing?"

"But do you not know?" Vivienne looked puzzled. "When you said you could fly, I felt sure you were at least a wizard. Yet when I brought you here, I found you could not breathe under water—I had to ask Morgan to change you."

"Change me?" Instinctively Woodley fingered his throat.

The girl laughed softly. "You have no gills. Morgan's magic works more subtly. You have been—altered—so that you can live under water. The element is as air to you. It is the same enchantment Morgan put upon this castle when she sank it in the lake, after Camelot fell and the long night came upon Britain. An old enchantment—she put it upon Lyonesse once, and lived there for a while."

"And I thought all that was just legend," Woodley muttered.

"How little you mortals know! And yet it is true—in some strange paradoxical way. Morgan told me once, but I did not understand. Well, you can ask her tonight, after the testing."

"Oh—the testing. I'm not too happy about that. What is it, anyway?"

Vivienne looked at him with some surprise. "An ancient chivalric custom. Before any man can dwell here, he must prove himself worthy by doing some deed of valor. Sir Bohart had to slay a Worm—a dragon, you know—but his magic cuirass helped him there. He's quite invulnerable while he wears it."

"Just what is this testing?"

"It is different for each knight. Morgan has made some being, with her sorcery, and placed it behind the Shaking Rock. Ere sundown, you must go and kill the creature, whatever it is. I would I knew what manner of thing lairs there, but I do not, nor would Morgan let me tell you if I knew."

Woodley blinked. "Uh . . . suppose I don't want to take the test?"

"You must, or Morgan will slay you. But surely you are not afeared, my lord!"

"Of course not," he said hastily. "Just tell me a little more, will you? Are we really living under water?"

Vivienne sighed, pressed Woodley down to a sitting position on the bed, and relaxed comfortably in his lap. "Kiss me," she said. "There! Now—well, after the Grail was lost and the table broken, magic went out of Britain. There was no room for the fairy folk. Some died, some went away, some hid, here and there. There are secrets beneath the hills of Britain, my Arthur. So Morgan, with her powers, made herself invisible and intangible, and sank her castle here under the lake, in the wild mountains of Wales. Her servants are not human, of course. I had done Morgan a service once, and she was grateful. So when I saw the land sinking into savagery, I asked to go with her to this safe place. I brought Bohart with me, and Morgan took Merlin's old master, Bleys the Druid. Since then nothing has changed. Humans cannot feel or see us—or you either, now that you have been enchanted."

"Merlin?" Woodley was remembering the legend. "Didn't you shut him up in an oak—" He stopped, realizing that he had made a *faux pas*. But it was so damnably hard to realize that legend had become real!

Vivienne's face changed. "I loved him," she said, and her lips pinched together. "We will not speak of that!"

Woodley was thinking hard. Apparently he *was* breathing water, though he didn't notice any difficulty with his lungs. Yet there was an extraordinary—*thickness*—to the atmosphere, and a glassy, pellucid clarity. Moreover, the angles of refraction were subtly alien. It was true, then.

"So I'm living in a legend."

She smiled. "It was real for all that, in a way. I remember. Such scandals we had in Camelot! I recall once Launcelot rescued a girl named Elaine, who'd been shut up in a boiling bath in a tower for years and years—she said. I got the truth of it later. It was all over the court. Elaine was married to an old knight—a *very* old knight— and when she heard Launcelot was in town, she decided to hook *him*. So she sent her page to Launcelot with a cock-and-bull story about a curse—said her husband wasn't her husband at all, but a wicked magician—and had a bath all ready in the tower, for the right moment. When Launcelot broke down the door, she hopped into the tub, naked as a needle, and yelled like the Questing Beast. It hurt, certes, but Elaine didn't mind that. Especially when her husband rushed in. She pointed at him and cried, 'The wizard!' So Launcelot drew his sword and made Elaine a widow. Not that it did her any good, with Guenevere in Camelot waiting for her lover. Though Guenevere had reason for behaving as she did, *I* think. The way Arthur behaved with Morgawse! Of course that was before he married, but just the same—

"Legends, indeed," went on Vivienne. "I know legends! I suppose they gloss over the truth nowadays. Well, I could tell them a thing or two! I'll wager they've even made a hero out of that notorious old rake Lot. *He* certainly got what was coming to him. Indeed yes! But bad blood tells, I always feel. There was King Anguish, with his hunting lodge in the forest, and his unicorn hunts. Oh, yes!

"Unicorn hunts, forsooth," said Vivienne. "It's true you need a virgin to lure the unicorn, but there weren't many horns Anguish of Ireland brought home, I can tell you! And look at his daughter Yseult! She was her father all over again. She and Tristran—a minstrel! Everybody knows about minstrels. True enough, Yseult's husband wasn't any Galahad. Not Mark! For that matter, let me tell you about Galahad. It wasn't only the bar that was sinister about *him*. They say that over in Bedigraine Forest one hot summer—"

Nurmala's bubbling voice interrupted. The naiad stood by the drape that masked the door.

"My lady, I have done all that I can to the gown without you. But it must be fitted."

"Lackaday!" said Vivienne, rising. "I'll tell you about Uther and that widow some other time. Ten children, mind! Well, you need not go to the Shaking Rock till after midday meal, so would you like to view the castle?"

"Now wait a minute!" Woodley was beginning to feel anxious. "About this testing, Vivienne—"

"It is simple. You gird on a sword, go to the Shaking Rock—someone will guide you—and slay whatever creature Morgan has created there. Then you come back to sup."

"Just like that, eh?" Woodley said, with rather feeble irony. "But how do I know a sword will kill the thing? Suppose it's a dragon?"

Nurmala gave a quickly suppressed giggle. Woodley glanced at the naiad, remembering something she had let drop earlier. What was it? Nurmala had begun to say that she had swum out and seen—

The creature behind the Shaking Rock? Woodley's eyes widened. He could make use of the naiad!

Not yet, of course. There was still plenty of time. It

would be better to familiarize himself with the aqueous life of the castle first.

Vivienne said, "Shall I have Bleys show you around?"

Bleys? The Druid wizard—not a bad idea. He might be a valuable source of information, and perhaps something more. If one could use magic to fight magic—

Not that Woodley had any intention of visiting the Shaking Rock, he pondered. At the first opportunity, he was getting out of this place. He could swim. If Bleys would show him the front door, he'd show Bleys a clean pair of heels.

"Fine," Woodley said. "Let's go."

Vivienne swept to the door. "Nurmala will take you to Bleys. Do not linger, naiad. The gown must be finished—"

She was gone. Woodley waited till the sound of soft footfalls had died. Nurmala was eying him curiously.

"My lord—"

He stopped her with an outthrust arm and closed the door with the other. "Just a minute. I want to talk to you."

The naiad's green jello face became slightly tinged with blue. She was blushing, Woodley surmised, and gulped. He went on swiftly:

"I want you to tell me what's behind the Shaking Rock."

Nurmala looked away. "How can I do that? Only Morgan knows."

"You swam out there this morning, didn't you? I thought so. Well, I'm not blaming you for curiosity, especially since I need the information. Come on, now. Give. What is it? A dragon?" he hazarded.

The naiad shivered around the edges. "Nay, my lord, I dare not say. If Morgan were to find out—"

"She won't."

"I cannot tell you!"

Woodley took out his dagger and touched the point to his arm. Nurmala watched with suddenly avid eyes.

"Vivienne said naiads were crazy about human blood. Like vampires, eh? Even for a drop or two —"

"No! No! I dare not—"

Woodley pricked his finger—

"Well," said Nurmala some time later, "it's this way. Morgan le Fay created an undine and placed it behind the Shaking Rock."

"What's an undine?"

"It's about fifteen feet long, and—like hair," the naiad explained, licking her lips.

"Like hair?"

"You can't see its body, which is very small. It's covered with long hairy filaments that burn like fire when they touch you."

"I see," Woodley nodded grimly. "A super-Portuguese man-of-war. Electric jellyfish. Nice thing to fight with a sword!"

"It is a demon," Nurmala agreed. "But you will slay it easily."

"Oh, sure. Any idea how?"

"I fear not. I can tell you how to find it, though. Take the root of a mandrake and squeeze out the juice. That will bring the undine posthaste, if it tries to hide from you."

"Catnip," Woodley said cryptically. "Well, at least I know what the thing is."

"You will not tell Morgan I told you? You promised!"

"I won't tell her. . . . *Hm-m-m!* I wonder if—"

Nurmala jumped. "I have kept the Lady Vivienne waiting. Come, now, my lord. Quickly!"

Woodley thoughtfully followed the naiad into a tapestried hall, and along it to a carved door, which Nurmala pushed open. "Bleys!" she called.

"Bip!"

"Drunken oaf of a Druid," the naiad said impatiently. "There is a task for you."

"Has the dragon's fire gone out again?" a squeaky voice asked, rather plaintively. "By Mider, a salamander would be more dependable. But I suppose the water keeps putting the fire out. I keep telling the dragon not to take such deep breaths. *Bip!*"

"This is Messire Arthur of Woodley. Show him the castle. He is the Lady Vivienne's lover," Nurmala added as an afterthought, and Woodley blushed hotly.

It was very dark in the chamber. Sea spiders had spun webs all around, and it looked very much like an ancient alchemist's chamber, which it was. There were stacks of heavy tomes, a crucible or two, several alembics, a stuffed crocodile, and Bleys.

Bleys was a withered little gnome of a man, wispy enough to be blow away by a vagrant gust of wind. His dirty white beard hung in the aqueous atmosphere like a veil before his wrinkled brown walnut of a face. Bleys wore a long mud-colored robe with a peaked hood, and he sat cross-legged, an earthenware jug in his skinny hands.

"Messire Arthur of Woodley," Bleys squeaked. "Greeting. *Bip!*" He drank from the jug. "*Bip!* again."

Woodley said at random, "You've . . . uh . . . got a nice place here." It would be wise to make friends with the Druid, as a first step in enlisting his aid.

Bleys waved casually at the alembics and retorts. "Those. Used to do all sorts of magic with 'em. Philosopher's Stone—*you* know. But not now. I just make liquor. *Bip!*"

"Liquor?"

"All sorts. Mead, wine—all by magic, of course. Real liquor wouldn't last long under water—*you* know. *Bip!* I haven't been drunk since I came down here with Morgan. Magic ale hasn't got the kick of the real stuff. *Eheu!*"

"Bleys," Nurmala murmured.

"Oh, yes, yes, yes." The wizard peered blearily through his beard. "Vivienne wants me to show you around. Not worth it. Dull place, the castle. How'd you like to stay here with me instead and have a few drinks?"

As Woodley hesitated, the naiad said, "I'll tell the Lady Vivienne, Bleys."

"Oh, all right." The Druid stiffly rose and moved unsteadily forward. "Come along, then, Messire Arthur. Arthur . . . Arthur?" He squinted up sharply at Woodley's face. "For a moment I thought . . . but you're not Pendragon. There was a prophecy, you know, that he'd come again. Get along with you, Nurmala, or I'll turn you into a polliwog and step on you."

"You'll show Messire Arthur the castle, now?"

"Yes, yes," Bleys said snappishly. As Nurmala rippled away, he made an angry sound in his beard. "They all kick me around. Even the damned naiads. But why not?" He drank from the jug. "I'm just an old has-been. Me, who taught Merlin all he knew. They hate me because I won't work magic for them. Why should I? I make this instead. Have a drink. No," he added hastily, drawing back. "You can't have any. I made it, and it's mine. Not that it'll get me drunk! Magic ale, forsooth! Sometimes I wish I were dead. *Bip!*"

He headed for the door, Woodley at his heels. "What do you want to see first?"

"I don't know. There'll be plenty of time to look around after I pass the testing. You know about that, don't you?"

Bleys nodded. "Oh, yes. But I don't know what sort of creature Morgan put behind the Shaking Rock." He glanced up shrewdly. "Before you go on—I can't help you. I can't give you any magic, because the queen won't let me, and I've no valuable information you'd be glad to hear. The only thing I have to give is a sword, and I'm holding that for—one who will come later." His voice had changed oddly. "You must meet the testing with true courage, and that will be your shield."

"Thanks," Woodley said, his lips twisting wryly. No information, eh? Well, Bleys must know how to get out of the castle. Yet that secret must be wormed out of him subtly. He couldn't ask point-blank—

"Well," the Druid said, guiding Woodley along the hall, "the place is built in a hollow square, around the courtyard in the middle. No windows. The fishes are worse than mosquitoes. Snatch the food out of your hands. We keep the dragon in the courtyard. Scavenger. He takes care of the garbage problem. *Bip!*"

Vague memories of museums stirred in Woodley. "I don't see any suits of armor."

"Think you'll need one?" Bleys cackled unpleasantly. "They're in the armory." He toddled unsteadily on with a certain grim fortitude. "This isn't Joyouse Garde or the Castle of the Burning Hart. Environment's different. No pots of lead for melting on our towers. We can't be besieged. For that matter, the whole design of a castle is functional, quite useless under the lake."

"Why don't things get wet?"

"Same reason the water seems like air. Wet magic. That type of enchantment was perfected in Atlantis—it's beyond me, but I'm a Druid. We work with fire mostly. Oak, ash, and thorn," Bleys reminisced. "When I was a boy at Stonehenge . . . oh, well. *Sic transit*—you know. *Bip*. Mider curse this ale—it's like dish water. How I've longed for a sippet of dry-land liquor! But of course I can't live out of water now. What are you looking at? Oh, that. Recognize the scene?" The Druid tittered unpleasantly.

Woodley was examining a great tapestry that covered one wall of the room they had just entered. Faded and ancient, but still brilliantly colored, it was covered with scenes that evoked a familiar note. A man and a woman—a tree—a snake—and, in the background, another woman who was strikingly beautiful even through this medium.

"Lilith," Bleys said. "The castle's full of tapestries. They show legends, battles, sieges—*you* know." He peered through the veil of his floating beard. "*Ars longa*—but the rest of the tag isn't exactly appropriate, eh? *Bip!*"

"Come along," he added, and tugged at his guest's arm.

It was not a leisurely tour of the castle. Bleys was impatient, and willing to pause only when he wanted a drink. Woodley was towed about willy-nilly, seldom catching a clear glimpse of anything. But he managed to form some sort of picture of the place.

Built three stories high around a central courtyard, the castle came to a climax in the enormous donjon keep whose great square height dominated one angle of the building. Across the court from it was a barbican—two huge towers with the gateway recessed between them, guarded by a lowered portcullis through which an occasional fish swam lazily, and a futilely lifted drawbridge that had once spanned a vanished moat. Woodley saw this from the tower of the keep—the first time he had emerged from within the castle itself. And the ground was unpleasantly far down.

The lake bottom, rather. What he wanted to find was a door—an exit!

Water was like air to him, Woodley remembered. So a jump from the top of the keep would mean, in all probability, breaking his neck.

"Come on," said Bleys impatiently. "Let's go down."

There were great bare halls within galleries, there were storerooms and kitchens and barracks and dormitories. The

smaller apartments were few. They passed a cobwebby
still room where sea spiders had veiled loaded shelves
behind wavering curtains of web. Bleys remarked that
Morgan le Fay once amused herself by distilling potions
and poisons, but she never used such clumsy devices
nowadays.

An idea was beginning to stir in Woodley's mind. He
asked questions.

"That? An alembic. That? Staghorn with gum Arabic.
For childbirth, mostly. That jar's got dried bedbugs in it.
Mastic, snakeroot, fennel, mandrake, musk, medlar tree
bark—"

Mandrake. Remembering what Nurmala had told him,
Woodley edged closer.

"And that thing over there?"

"That's a Witch's Cradle. It's used—"

Woodley deftly annexed the mandrake, slipping it into
his tunic. So far, so good. All that now remained was to
work out a method of using the root effectively. If only
undines were afraid of mandrake, instead of being attracted to it! Well, if worse came to worst, he might
distract the monster's attention with the root, somehow,
while he made his escape—

"Come along. *Bip.*"

Presently they were on a little balcony overlooking the
courtyard. "There's the dragon," Bleys said. "Draedan.
It's an Anglo-Saxon name, and Anglo-Saxon was unpopu-
lar in our day—but so were dragons. See all that rubbish?"

There were amorphous ruins rising from the silt at the
edge of the courtyard, and a larger mound in the center.

"Stables, falcon mews, cattle barns, a chapel—once.
Not that anybody ever worshiped in *that* chapel. Morgan—
you know. Air and Darkness. *Bip!*" Bleys stared reflectively into his jug. "Come along."

"Wait," Woodley said rebelliously. "I want to look at

the dragon." Actually, he was hoping to find an exit from this vantage point.

"Oh, Draedan. That worm. Very well." The Druid slipped down to a sitting position and closed his eyes. "*Bip*."

Woodley's gaze was inevitably drawn to the dragon—a truly startling spectacle. It looked vaguely like a stegosaurus, with waving hackles on its arched back, and a long, spiked tail with a knob at the end. The head, however, was not the tiny one of a herbivorous dinosaur. It was a mixture of crocodile and tyrannosaur rex, three horns atop the nose, and a cavernous mouth as large as a subway kiosk. It was as long as two streetcars, and twice as high. Glowing yellow eyes glared lambently. A gust of flame shot out from the horror's mouth as Draedan breathed.

Just then, the grimly monster was eating garbage, in a somewhat finicky fashion.

Woodley wondered how its fiery breath could burn under water, and then remembered Morgan's magic. If he could improvise a flame thrower to use against the undine— but how? He watched a gush of bubbles drift up each time the flame rippled out. Hordes of little fishes were trying to swipe Draedan's dinner.

Clumsy on its columnar legs, the dragon would retaliate by breathing heavily upon its tormentors, who fled from the fire. Bleys woke up to say, "That creature's got its troubles. It hates cooked food, but by the time it chases those fish off, all the garbage is well roasted. I'd put its flame out for good, but a dragon needs fire in its stomach to digest its food. Something to do with metabolism. Wish I could put out the fire in *my* stomach," he added, and, after drinking from the jug and bipping reflectively, went to sleep again.

Woodley leaned upon the balcony and examined the dragon with fascinated horror. The slow movements of the

saurian—all dragons are saurians—gave it a peculiarly
nightmare appearance. It looked like a Hollywood techni-
cian's creation, rather badly done, and far from convincing.

At that moment, someone seized Woodley about the
knees, lifted him, and hurled him bodily over the balcony.

He fell with a thud in cushioning soft ooze. A cloud of
silt billowed up as Woodley sprang to his feet. Not a yard
from his nose, a lake trout hung suspended with waving
motions of its fins, eying him thoughtfully. Other fish,
attracted by the commotion, swam toward Woodley, whose
heart had prolapsed into his sandals.

As the silt-cloud cleared, Draedan became visible. The
dragon had turned his head to stare straight at Woodley.

Draeden yawned fierily.

He lifted one tree-trunk leg and began to move ponderously forward.

"Bleys!" Woodley roared. "*Bleys! Help!*"

There was no answer—not even a bip. "Bleys! *Wake
up!*"

Then he ran. There was a closed door in the wall near
Woodley, and he fled toward it. Draedan was not far
behind, but the saurian moved slowly and clumsily.

"*Bleys!*"

The door was locked, quite firmly, from the inside.
Woodley groaned and dodged as Draedan lumbered on,
resistless as an army tank.

"*Bleys!*"

There was another door across the courtyard. Woodley
sprinted toward it. He could hear lumbering footsteps behind him.

But this door, too, was locked.

Flattened against it, Woodley looked back with narrowed, calculating eyes. A trail of silt hung wavering in
the water to mark his trail. Through it Draedan came,

yellow eyes shining like fog lamps, flame bursting from his mouth.

"*Bleys! Wake up!*"

Still no response. Springing away, Woodley tripped over a stone buried in the mud, and a cloud of ooze leaped up around him. As he hastily rose, an idea flashed into his mind.

A smoke screen—

He ran, scuffing his feet. Silt billowed up. Draedan's behemothic progress helped, too. Yelling occasionally at Bleys, Woodley circled the courtyard and then crossed his own trail, stirring up a murky barrage. Within a few minutes the water was as opaque as pea soup.

Yet Draedan did not give up. His feet thumped on, and his glowing disks of eyes swam out of the dimness with horrifying frequency. Woodley was too winded now to shout. But if he could keep on dodging long enough— Draedan could not possibly see him now—

The dragon had other ideas. Abruptly a long tongue of flame flashed out murkily. Almost immediately it came again. Woodley ran.

Draedan breathed heavily. Fire trails lanced through the silt fog. Apparently the dragon had realized that there was more than one way of skinning a cat—or getting his dinner. Once one of those fiery gusts found him, Woodley knew, he would be reduced to cinders. It was ridiculous to be incinerated under water, he thought moodily as he sped on his frantic way.

The silt particles made him cough. He crashed against the grilled metal of the barbican and hung there, gasping. Iron, rusty and weak, bent under his weight, leaving a gap in the barrier.

Draedan's headlight eyes glowed out of the murk. With grim desperation Woodley wrenched at more bars. They, too, were fragile and corroded, and came away easily. As the dragon charged, Woodley dived head first through the hole he had made in the barbican. Flame singed his drawers.

He seemed, however, to be still cornered. The drawbridge was raised, and hung like a slightly slanted wall above him. But the difficulty was only an apparent one, as Woodley found when he slipped sidewise past the edge of the bridge. He was in the open, outside the wall—and there was no moat to keep him from escaping.

He was on the lake bottom. Behind him and above, the castle of Morgan le Fay rose like a crag. It was no longer a prison—

Woodley listened. Draedan had apparently given up the chase. And Bleys was presumably still asleep. Best of all, the way to freedom was open. That tumble into the courtyard had been a blessing in disguise.

Well—fair enough! Woodley sighed with relief. He would not have to face that unpleasant testing involving the undine. Instead, he hurried away from the castle.

Rounded stones felt hard through the leather soles of his hose. The ground slanted up sharply. And, as he went on, he realized that the lake was, as well as he could tell, bowl-shaped, and very deep. The castle was in the deepest part.

He wondered where the Shaking Rock lay. Not that he wanted to go there—now!

Briefly he found himself regretting Vivienne, who had been quite lovely. Her face in his mind was vivid, but not enticing enough to slow down his steady climb. He went through a forest of water weeds—no great hindrance—and was trailed by a school of inquisitive minnows. From above, a cool blue light drifted down.

Higher he went, and higher. Far above, he could see a flat shining plate—a bright sky rimmed by a circular horizon. It was the surface.

His head was almost above water now. He could see a rocky shore, and trees—oddly distorted, with fantastic perspective. A water bug dived to look at him, and then departed hastily.

Then Woodley's head broke the surface, and he started to strangle.

Air gushed into his nostrils, his mouth, his lungs, carrying little knife blades of agony. He coughed and choked, lost his balance, and fell, the water closing over his head. It was pure ecstasy. Woodley sat where he had fallen, gasping, watching air bubbles cascade from his mouth and nostrils. Presently there were no more, and he felt better.

Of course. He might have expected this. But—

Good Lord!

Morgan had changed him, so that water was now his natural element. Air was as fatal to him now as it would be to a fish.

The thing was manifestly ridiculous and horribly logical. Woodley shut his eyes and thought hard. Eventually he remembered that, normally, he could inhale above water and exhale below. He reversed the procedure, taking a deep breath of water and standing up, dribbling slowly.

He was near the steep, rocky bank of a lake, surrounded by high mountains. Not far away a stream rushed through a gorge to lose itself in the mere. Save for this canyon, the craggy walls were unbroken and seemed unscalable.

Woodley inadvertently breathed air, and had to dive for relief. A familiar voice pierced through his coughs.

"Oh, there you are," Bleys said. "What a time I had finding you. Why didn't you wake me up when you fell in the courtyard?"

Woodley regarded the Druid bitterly, but said nothing. Obviously his plan of escape had failed. He couldn't leave the lake. Not unless the wet magic spell was reversed.

Morgan could do that. Probably she wouldn't, though. Vivienne certainly wouldn't if she could. But Bleys was a magician. If he could be induced to reverse the enchantment—

"Well, come along," the Druid said. "I left my jug at the castle, and I'm thirsty. *Bip!*"

Woodley followed Bleys. His mind was working at top speed. It was necessary to return to Morgan's stronghold, but—what then? The testing at the Shaking Rock? Woodley thought of the undine, and bit his lip. Not pleasant—no.

"Draedan can't get out of the yard, you know," Bleys presently remarked. "What possessed you to fall off the balcony anyway? It seems a stupid thing to do."

"I didn't fall," Woodley snapped. "I was pushed. Probably by Sir Bohart."

"Oh?" said Bleys, and puffed at his floating white beard. "Anyhow," he remarked at last, "you can't breathe out of water. It's dangerous to try."

Woodley said slowly, "When I met Vivienne, she was on dry land."

"Morgan taught her the trick," the Druid grunted. "It's beyond me—I never learned it. Any time you want to walk dry again, go see Vivienne." He grinned unpleasantly. "Or Morgan. It's my opinion that Vivienne is Morgan's daughter. That would explain a lot of things. However, here we are back at the castle, and we go in this way." He paused by a door in the outer wall, fumbled with the latch, and stepped across the threshold. "Come along!" he urged. "Don't let the fish in."

He headed along a corridor, Woodley at his heels. Soon they were back in Bleys' apartment, and the Druid was selecting a new jug from his assortment. "Camelot Triple-X Brand," he murmured. "Ninety proof. It isn't, of course, but I label the bottles for old times' sake." He drank, and burst into a furious string of archaic oaths. "Damned self-deception, that's all it is. Ninety proof, hah! Magic never made good liquor, and there's no use arguing about it. *Bip!*'' He glared malevolently.

Woodley was brooding. So Bleys didn't know the wet magic spell. Well, that left Vivienne and Morgan. How he could worm the secret out of either of those two, he had no idea. But he'd have to do it somehow, and soon. When would it be time for the testing? He asked Bleys.

"Now,'' said the Druid, getting up stiffly. "It's nearly sundown. Come along!'' He peered at Woodley with bleary eyes. "Vivienne will have a sword for you. It's not Excalibur, but it will serve.''

They went to a hall where Vivienne and Sir Bohart were waiting. The knight's jaw dropped at sight of Woodley, but he rallied valiantly. "You've come tardily, messire,'' he managed to say.

"Better tardy than not at all,'' Woodley returned, and had the satisfaction of seeing Bohart's eyes flicker. Vivienne moved forward, holding a great sword.

"My lord! With my own hands I shall arm you. And when you return from Shaking Rock, I shall be waiting.'' Her eyes promised much, and Sir Bohart gnawed his ruddy mustache.

Woodley touched his tunic where he had concealed the mandrake root. His lips twisted in a grim smile. He had an idea—

"Fair enough,'' he said. "I'm ready.''

Vivienne clapped her hands. "Gramercy, a valiant knight! I shall summon Nurmala to guide you—''

"Don't bother,'' Woodley interrupted. "I'd rather have Sir Bohart show me the way.''

The knight made a gobbling sound. "I am no lackey!''

"Fie,'' Vivienne reproved. " 'Tis a simple request to make.''

"Oh, well,'' Woodley shrugged. "If Sir Bohart's afraid,

never mind. I can understand how he feels. Even with that magic cuirass, accidents might happen. No, you stay here by the fire, Bohart. You'll feel safer.''

Bohart turned purple. There was, of course, only one answer he could possibly make. So, ten minutes later, Woodley walked beside the red-mustached knight through the ooze of the lake bottom toward a towering pinnacle of stone in the green distance.

Sir Bohart preserved a furious silence. Once he rattled his sword in its scabbard, but Woodley thoughtfully didn't hear. Instead, he remarked, ''I wonder what it is behind the Shaking Rock. Got any ideas?''

''Morgan does not tell me her secrets.''

''Uh-huh. Still, it must be pretty dangerous. Eh?''

Bohart smiled toothily at that. ''I hope so.''

Woodley shrugged. ''Maybe I'd better use some magic. A sword might not do the trick.''

The knight turned his head to stare. ''Goety?''

''Sure. I'm a magician. Didn't you know?''

''Vivienne said . . . but I did not think—'' There was more respect in Bohart's eyes now, and a touch of fear. Woodley chuckled with a lightheartedness he scarcely felt.

''I know a few tricks. How to make myself invisible, for instance.''

''With fern seed? I have heard of that.''

''I use mandrake juice,'' Woodley explained. ''Come to think of it, that gag would come in handy now. In view of what may be behind the Shaking Rock—yeah.'' He moved his hands in intricate gestures. ''Saskatchewan, Winnipeg, Mauch Chunk, Philadelphia, Kalamazoo,'' he added, and deftly slipped the mandrake from his tunic. To the staring Bohart, it seemed as though the gnarled little root had been snatched out of thin water.

''By Atys!'' the knight said, impressed. ''Swounds!''

Woodley lifted the mandrake toward his head, and then hesitated. "Wait a minute. Maybe I'd better make you—"

"Make me invisible also?" Bohart jumped at the bait, after one apprehensive glance ahead at the Shaking Rock. "Yes—that would be wise."

"O.K. Let's have your helmet. Uh . . . maybe you could help me out against this . . . monster . . . if I need help. Though I don't think I will."

Bohart's red mustache did not entirely conceal his sardonic smile. "Well, we shall see. My sword is sharp."

But Woodley's apparent attempt to propitiate him had disarmed the knight's suspicions. He handed over his helmet and watched as Woodley inverted it and used the haft of his dagger to mash the mandrake root into pulp, mortar and pestle fashion.

"There. That's all. Put the helmet back on—keep the mandrake in it—and you'll be invisible."

Sir Bohart obeyed. He looked down at himself.

"It doesn't work."

Woodley stared around blankly. "Where are you? I . . . Sir Bohart!"

The knight was taken aback. "I . . . I'm here. But I can see myself as clearly as ever."

"Of course," Woodley explained, not looking at the other, "you can see yourself, but nobody else can. That's the way the mandrake spell works."

"Oh. Well. Make yourself invisible now."

"Too much bother," Woodley said casually. "I don't want all the odds on my side. It takes the fun out of a fight. If I get into trouble, I'll use magic, but I think my sword will be enough. Here we are at the Shaking Rock."

Far above them, a boulder balanced on the stone pinnacle rocked slowly in the lake currents. Woodley noticed a small cave a few yards away. He stopped.

So did Sir Bohart, who was visibly nervous. "I go no farther."

"O.K.," Woodley nodded, his throat dry. "Just wait here, then. I'll be back in a minute. Uh . . . you wouldn't care to lend me that cuirass of yours, would you?"

"No."

"I thought you wouldn't. Well . . . *adios*." Woodley lingered a moment longer, eying the cave mouth; but there was no way to turn back now. Anyhow, his trick should work. Nurmala had said that undines were strongly attracted by mandrake juice—

He left Sir Bohart leaning on his sword, and plunged ahead into the shadows that lurked behind the Shaking Rock. He felt the ground slant down steeply, and moved with more caution. There was, after all, little to see. It was too dark.

Something moved in the green gloom. A huge ball of hair that drifted past, paused, and then came with unerring accuracy toward Woodley. It was the undine.

Fifteen feet long, shaped like a fat submarine, it was surrounded by a haziness where the filaments grew finer and vanished. It had no definite edges. It simply faded into the green darkness.

It swam by wriggling its filaments, like a ciliate. Woodley miscalculated its speed, and before he could turn, the undine was shockingly close. A tendril whipped across his cheek, burning like a bare wire overcharged with electric current.

Automatically Woodley whipped out his sword, but sanity held him back from using it. Steel would be no good against this creature. Besides, he had a safer plan. If it wasn't too late—

He turned and ran at top speed around the base of the Shaking Rock. Sir Bohart was still standing there, but at sight of Woodley he, too, whirled and made off, forgetting that he was presumably invisible. But the undine was a sight fearful enough to drive any man to flight.

The mouth of the little cave gaped like a friendly mouth. Woodley went into it headfirst, losing his sword and rolling over several times before he came to a halt. Hastily he twisted about and looked at what was happening. Would the undine follow him? Or would it catch the scent of the mandrake juice—the effluvium hanging in the water where Sir Bohart had stood?

The cloud of wriggling filaments was following the trail. The undine torpedoed in pursuit of the knight—

Woodley sighed deeply. He found his sword, went cautiously toward the mouth of the cave, and watched. Now the undine had caught up with Sir Bohart. Those dangerous filaments couldn't harm the man, of course, protected as he was by his magic cuirass. But it must be definitely uncomfortable to be surrounded and smothered by an undine—

A sword flashed. Sir Bohart was fighting at last. Woodley grinned.

He hoped the undine wouldn't last long. He was getting hungry. But, of course, he'd have to wait till . . . er . . . till he had passed the testing Morgan le Fay had set him.

He was presently roused from his reverie by Bohart's yells. "You tricked me! You lickspittle knave! I'll split you from pate to groin! You made me a cat's-paw—"

"Hold on!" Woodley said, nimbly dodging. He still held his bare sword, and automatically countered Bohart's blow. The undine, he noticed, was quite dead about twenty feet down the slope. Small fishes were already approaching it.

"You craven cur!"

"Wait! What'll Vivienne say if I'm found dead with my head lopped off by a sword? What'll Morgan say?"

That sobered Sir Bohart. He paused, his brand held motionless in midair, the red mustache wriggling with fury. His face was beet-purple.

But he didn't renew the attack. Woodley lowered his own weapon and talked fast.

"Don't forget I was there when Vivienne said she'd sick Morgan on you. I still remember how scared you looked. Vivienne wants me alive, and if she found out you killed me—and she'd certainly find it out—"

"You warlock," Sir Bohart snarled. "You warlock devil!" But there was a betraying mottled pallor in his no longer purple cheeks.

Woodley put his sword away. "What are you kicking about? You didn't get hurt, did you? You've got that magic cuirass. Look at me!" He ran his forefinger over the livid welt that ran from temple to jaw. "The undine put its mark on me, all right. You weren't even scratched."

"You made me your cat's-paw," Bohart said sulkily.

Woodley persuasively slipped his hand through the other's crooked arm. "Forget that. We can be plenty useful to each other, if you'll play along. If you won't—I've got lots of influence with Vivienne. Want me to use it?"

"You devil," the knight growled, but he was licked and knew it. "I'll let you live. I'll have to. Provided you shield me against Morgan." He brightened. "Yes. Tell Vivienne that I am your friend. Then—"

Woodley grinned. "Suppose I told her you pushed me into Draedan's courtyard this afternoon."

"But—messire!" Bohart gripped the other man's shoulders. "Nay! I did not! You cannot prove it was I—"

"It was, though, wasn't it? And Vivienne would take my word against yours. But cool off. I won't tell. If you'll remember something."

Bohart licked his lips. "What?"

"That I killed the undine."

"Oh, a thrice thousand curses! But I suppose I must. If I do this, you will use your influence with Vivienne, though. She is capricious, and Morgan has often asked her to . . . to—" The knight swallowed and began again. "Morgan wishes to destroy me. So far, Vivienne has not permitted that. Now you and I can strike a bargain. You get the credit for this testing, and in return you insist that I remain free from Morgan—should that danger arise."

"Fair enough."

"But if Morgan should learn of this deceit we have practiced upon her, we will both die—quite terribly. She is unforgiving."

"She won't find out."

"If she should, not even Vivienne could save us."

Woodley frowned slightly. The risk wasn't alluring. Yet it would have to be taken. Besides, Morgan would never find out—

"It is a bargain," Sir Bohart said. "But remember this: if you should ever seek to betray me, it will mean your own downfall. Your life and mine are one now. If I go down, I drag you with me—because then I shall speak. And Vivienne will weep for you, if not for me."

Woodley shivered. With an effort he threw off his intangible fears. "Forget it," he said. "Dinner's waiting. And we've got to tow the undine back to the castle."

That wasn't difficult, since the dead monster floated easily. Plodding along the lake bottom, Woodley felt his spirits rise. Once he touched the hilt of his sword. Wielding a weapon like that was oddly satisfying. Suppose he had not tricked Bohart into aiding him? Suppose he had battled the undine with bare steel alone? Briefly Woodley half regretted that he had not attempted the dangerous deed.

It *would* have been dangerous, though. Far too much so. And there had been no real need to risk his skin, as he had proved. Calm logic was better. Eventually that would get him out of the castle, and back to dry land, free from Morgan's perilous enchantments.

He had passed the testing. So he was safe for a while. The next step was to learn the wet magic spell that would make it possible for him to breathe air again.

Woodley tugged at the bunch of undine filaments in his fist. Behind him, the lake monster floated slowly in his wake, a comet tail of small fishes veering after it. The castle loomed ahead—

"Remember!" Sir Bohart warned. "Our lives are one now. Here is Bleys. No more talk—it is not safe in the castle."

The lake bottom was shrouded in night shadows. It must be past sunset in the world above. Sir Bohart slipped away and was gone. The brown-robed figure of Bleys was visible ahead, by a door in a tower's foot.

"Here's the prize," Woodley called. "Come and get it!"

The Druid plowed forward through the ooze. His eyes gleamed through the waving net of white beard.

"An undine. And you have slain it—"

Woodley felt an extraordinary sense of shame as he met the wizard's gaze. But that was ridiculous! Why the devil should he feel embarrassed because he had hesitated to commit suicide? Hell!

Bleys said slowly, "I told you that courage was both sword and shield. Magic cannot stand against it. Now I—" He paused, his hand going out in a queer fumbling gesture. "Age is heavy upon me. When I saw you bringing your booty toward the castle just now, it seemed to me I was standing beneath the wall of Camelot, watching Arthur Pendragon—"

The low voice tailed off into silence. Bleys said, *"He was and will be."*

Nurmala's murmur broke the spell that held Woodley silent. The naiad rippled through the door in the tower, carrying a lighted lamp.

"Oh! Messire Arthur of Woodley has slain the monster! My lord!" She curtseyed low. "There will be feasting tonight. The table is laid."

Bleys seemed to relapse into his usual drunken self. "All right," he snapped, and the girl turned and went back into the tower. Woodley noticed that the lamp flame shone through the translucent emerald of her body. It looked rather pretty, or would have, had it not been so disturbing.

"Worse than pyromaniacs, those naiads," Bleys remarked, producing a jug and drinking from it. "Can't leave fire alone. Silly to carry a lamp in the castle at night—the place is lighted by magic. Blood and fire, that's all a naiad thinks of. Horrid wet oozy things," he finished, in an outburst of senile fury. "I hate 'em all. I hate everybody. Come along! Leave your undine here; it'll be safe."

Woodley noticed the sharp glance the Druid cast at him, though, and wondered if Bleys was as drunk as he seemed. Apparently so, for his progress along the passage was punctuated by oaths, groans, and bips. He led the way to Woodley's apartment, where the latter made a hasty and inadequate toilet—for one couldn't wash, under the lake—and then hobbled off to the great hall of the castle. Woodley had not seen this room before.

It was very large indeed, and had a gallery halfway up one wall. There were tapestries, dozens of them, rushes on the floor—presumably weighted, since they didn't float up—and a dais at the farther end. There, seated by a fairly small table, was Vivienne. She looked strikingly lovely, in a gown of applegreen satin embroidered with pearls. Her hair was in braids, plaited with pearls, and she wore a jeweled belt. She, at least, was the essence of magic.

"My lord!" She ran to Woodley. "They told me you were safe. But your poor cheek . . . oh! That horrible undine."

"It's nothing. Doesn't hurt."

"Nothing! To slay an undine . . . yet I knew you would prove yourself a great knight. Come, sit by me here, my love, and we can talk as we sup." Her gaze devoured Woodley, who felt slightly ill at ease.

Grumpily Bleys found a bench for himself and greedily eyed the linen-draped table. "I don't want fish again," he snapped. "Sick of it."

"It's roast pig," Vivienne said, in a glancing aside. "Sea pig. Fowl and pasties . . . ah, my lord! Now that you have passed Morgan's testing, you and I will dwell here forever."

Before Woodley could answer, there was an outburst of music. Slow in tempo, it came from the gallery across the hall, but there was no sign of any musicians. Vivienne followed Woodley's gaze.

"That? Morgan keeps the musicians invisible. They're elementals, and ugly enough to spoil your appetite. The queen will join us later. She does not eat."

A drapery at the back of the dais was pulled aside, and several naiads appeared, each of them, as far as Woodley could make out, exact duplicates of Nurmala. They carried trenchers and trays, serving in complete silence. The food, for the most part, was familiar to Woodley, but some of it tasted strange. The stewed fruit had a definitely uncanny flavor. Nor did he especially like the omnipresent almond-milk flavoring.

Yet he ate heartily, for he was ravenous. And he would

need all his energy to carry out his plan—securing the wet magic spell from Vivienne or, perhaps, Morgan. How—

Bleys drank steadily, and Vivienne picked at her food and languished at her self-chosen lover. She insisted that he learn the proper etiquette of Arthurian times.

"We eat from the same trencher, Messire," she said, with a demure twinkle. "You must cut the choicest portions and offer them to me on the point of your knife. I . . . oh, dear. Here is Sir Bohart."

It was indeed the knight, advancing through the rushes. His eyes, fixed on Woodley's, held a warning message.

"Forgive me for my tardiness, my lady," Bohart said. "I did not think Messire Arthur would return so soon from slaying the monster."

With a certain air of coldness, Vivienne welcomed the knight, and soon Sir Bohart was gnawing on a mutton bone and casting furtive glances at Woodley. The supper went on in silence, broken only by the playing of the unseen musicians. At last it was over, with nuts, highly spiced fruit, and wine which Woodley found mild and tasteless. Still, after those spices, vitriol would have seemed like milk, he mused, nursing his tongue. He felt rather like Draedan.

The naiads whisked away the cloth, leaving a smooth-topped table inset with a chessboard. Replete, Woodley settled back. He had earned a rest. Presently he could begin to work on the next problem—the necessary spell that Vivienne held—but not yet. Better to play along with the girl, get in her good graces, as she laid her burnished head on his shoulder.

"Oh, I was telling you about Uther," she said. "And that widow. Ten children, as I said. What a rogue Uther was, to be sure. It seems—"

And she was off, in a cloud of scandal. Bleys drank. Sir Bohart moved uneasily, as though nervous and worried.

Woodley dozed. Vivienne unfolded the secrets of the hoary past, and the band played on.

Woodley became aware that Vivienne had stopped talking. He shivered, and, with a sudden sense of abysmal shock, sat bolt upright. Briefly he felt an extraordinary vertigo, and a ghastly sensation as though the flesh was crawling upon his bones.

Then he saw a woman seating herself across the table.

She wore a very plain white gown, with long, trailing sleeves, and there was a band of jeweled flowers about her slim waist. Star flowers glinted in her hair, where hints of bronze showed amid the cloudy darkness. Her face was young and very lovely. Woodley found it difficult to see her face, except in sidewise glances. Why?

He—well, he could not meet her eyes.

He *could not* look into them. He found it utterly impossible to meet her gaze. Why this was, Woodley could not in the least imagine. He forced himself to turn his head so that he could look into the eyes of Morgan le Fay.

And his own eyes would not obey. On the very edge of obedience, they rebelled. It was as though Woodley's flesh revolted against the commands his brain issued.

Yet he could see her face, though not directly, and it seemed oddly familiar. Where had he seen it before?

Of course! That tapestry with the tree and the serpent. Morgan had the face of Lilith—

Woodley stood up, rather awkwardly, and bowed. "Your Majesty—"

"No," Morgan said, her voice gentle and abstracted. "You need not rise. I am Morgan—call me that. As I shall call you Arthur." The name lingered on her tongue, as though she were loath to relinquish it.

Woodley sat down. There was a silence. He tried again to meet Morgan's eyes and failed.

She said, "You slew the undine? Because if you have not passed my testing fairly, nothing can save you. Especially since you are named Arthur. I mislike that name—"

Woodley met Sir Bohart's imploring gaze and swallowed, his throat dry. "I killed the undine. Fairly, of course."

"Very well," said the Queen of Air and Darkness. "Let it be forgotten, then. It has been a long time since I saw anyone from above the lake. Sir Galahodin was the last, I believe."

Bohart coughed nervously. Morgan smiled at him. Her slim fingers tapped the table top.

"He played at chess with me," she added, half maliciously. "You see . . . Arthur . . . for a hundred years or so after I came here, I invited occasional guests. I would play at chess with them. Then I tired of it, and only lately have I felt the . . . need again. It does not matter much; I would not leave the lake for such a slight whim. But Sir Bohart is here, and . . . Vivienne, have you not tired of him yet?"

"I tired of him long ago," the girl said frankly. "But I am used to Sir Bohart and his ways."

"You have a new lover," Morgan murmured. "Will you not withdraw your protection from the old one?"

Sir Bohart squirmed. Arthur said hastily, "Vivienne, I hope . . . I mean, Bohart's promised to show me a lot of things, how to joust and so on. You wouldn't—"

Morgan's slow, sweet voice said to Vivienne, "In time you will tire of this new lover, too, and you will not weep to see him play at chess with me."

Woodley gulped.

"I shall always love Messire Arthur," Vivienne contended stoutly. "When I first saw him, he reminded me of Merlin. Also, since Sir Bohart's company pleases my lord—"

Morgan laughed a little. "Merlin! Ay me! Well, I will not touch Sir Bohart without your permission, but—" She shrugged. "It is in my mind that I would prefer Arthur, indeed. Perhaps the name evokes old memories."

"Er—" said Woodley.

Morgan watched him. "You are safe enough for now. As long as Vivienne is here—and she has no wish to leave the lake—she may have her playthings. But she is human, and a woman—therefore capricious. Sometime she will grow tired of you, Arthur, and then you will play at chess with me."

"I . . . I'm not very good at it," Woodley said, and paused, startled by the shrill cackle of laughter that came from Bleys. The Druid subsided immediately to gulp wine.

"Who plays—*chess*—with Morgan—win or lose, he loses," Bleys said.

Woodley was unaccountably reminded of the Eden tapestry he had seen. Well, he'd have to pry the wet magic spell out of Vivienne. Morgan was out of the question. She was too—disturbing.

Vivienne said, "As long as I am here, Messire Arthur will not play at chess."

Morgan smiled again. "All things end," she remarked cryptically. "Let us talk of other matters. Has the world forgotten me, Arthur?"

"Oh, no. You're in Tennyson, Malory—you were even in the movies once."

"Movies?"

Woodley explained. Morgan shook her head.

"Faith! And no doubt they think *I* am a legend."

Vivienne said, "What were you telling me about history and fable, Morgan? I meant to explain it to Messire Arthur, but I could not understand. He did not know how legend could be true—nor do I, for that matter."

"Tell the story, Bleys," the queen commanded.

The Druid drank wine. "Oh, it's simple enough. Something to do with the fluidity of time. Historically, Pendragon was named Artorius, a petty British chieftain who fought against the Romans, around 500. There weren't any castles or knights then—not like this. We're pure Plantagenet."

Woodley looked puzzled, as he felt. "But I thought—"

"Legends can affect the past. Ever write a story, Messire Arthur?"

"Well—I've tried a scenario or two."

"Then you've doubtless gone back to make insertions and revisions. Suppose you're writing a history of the world. You deal with Artorius and his time historically, go on for a few thousand words, and then get a better idea. You decide to make Artorius a great king, and to build up a heroic saga about knighthood and the round table—about Bleys and Guenevere and Merlin and so forth. You just go back and make the insertion. Later on, you have one of your other characters, named Malory, make a number of references to the Arthurian cycle. Law of compensation and revision," Bleys said ambiguously.

"But we're not talking about stories," Woodley contended. "We're talking about real events. Life isn't just a story somebody's writing."

"That's what you think," the Druid retorted rudely. "And a lot you know about it. *Bip!*"

There was a silence, broken when Vivienne began to retail some long-forgotten scandal about Yseult and a Dolorous Knight. As usual Woodley went to sleep. His last memory was the sight of Morgan's half-glimpsed face, lovely, mysterious, and terrible.

He awoke in bed, to find Nurmala peering in through the curtains. "We breakfast early, my lord," the naiad bubbled. "Will it please you to rise?"

"Is it morning?"

"Sunlight shines through the lake."

"Oh," said Woodley, and followed his routine of struggling into his drawers under the sheets. This seemed to baffle Nurmala, who presently quivered out of the room. Sight of her green jello back made Woodley realize that he was hungry.

In the great hall he found only Vivienne. He had a slight headache, and after responding to the girl's request for a kiss, fell to upon ale, rolls, and salt fish. He would have preferred tomato juice. There was no invisible orchestra in the gallery this morning.

"Cozy place," he remarked, shivering a little. "I've never had breakfast in Grand Central Station before."

She caught his meaning. "All the castles had a great hall. After this we can eat in the solar, if you like. In the old days there were mighty feasts. Boards were laid on trestles to make tables—sometimes we have banquets even now."

"Visitors—down here?" Woodley asked, puzzled.

"Morgan raises the dead," Vivienne explained. "It amuses her, at times."

"Well, it doesn't amuse me," said the horrified man. "Where is Morgan this morning?"

"She is—busy. Bleys? Trying to get drunk, I suppose. Senile creature that he is."

"Well, where's Sir Bohart?" Woodley wanted to know.

There was a strange look in Vivienne's eyes. "After you fell asleep last night, and after Bohart had gone to his apartment, Bleys told me how that craven knight hurled you into the dragon's courtyard. So I withdrew my protection from him. Now he plays at chess with Morgan."

Woodley choked on ale. "Oh, my g-guh . . . Vivienne, where is he?"

"He plays at chess with Morgan. You will not see him again."

Woodley put down the drinking horn. His stomach was churning coldly. So the worst had happened. Bleys had remembered, and had talked. Now—

"Vivienne! I thought you intended to keep Bohart alive. You've got to save him!"

"After he tried to murder you? Nay! Besides, it is too late. The . . . game . . . will not finish till sundown, but Sir Bohart is already beyond rescue."

The girl's dark brows drew together. "That reminds me. Morgan wants to see you."

"She . . . she does?"

"Tonight, she said. I do not know why. Something Sir Bohart told her, she said. It does not matter."

"Oh, doesn't it," Woodley muttered, and finished the ale. It didn't help much. He could visualize the future all too well. Bohart, facing destruction, had revealed to Morgan the trick about the undine. And what had Morgan said last night?

"If you have not passed my testing fairly, nothing can save you."

Tonight would be zero hour, then. Woodley had until sundown—perhaps a little more time than that, but certainly not much more.

One day, in which to learn the wet magic spell from Vivienne!

Abruptly Woodley determined on a bold move. An attack was the best defense.

"Vivienne," he said. "I want to go back."

She did not move. "You will stay with me always."

"Suppose Morgan—does something to me?"

"She will not. And—" Vivienne's eyes darkened. "And I would rather have it thus than let you go back above the lake, where other women would have you. Mark you,

Arthur; you cannot breathe above water now. Only Morgan or I can change that. In air you die. *We* will not help you to leave the lake. And if you try—I shall bring you back, messire. Listen!'' She leaned toward him, elbows on the chessboard table. ''You are invisible and intangible to humans. You are one of us. Your voice could not be heard by any but the magic folk.''

''You could change me back, Vivienne!''

''And let another woman have you? I would sooner see you a corpse. Do not speak of this again, messire, lest I change my mood and tell Morgan she may have you for a chess partner!''

''Don't bother,'' Woodley said through tight lips. ''Morgan can take care of herself.''

But he realized he had gone too far, and taken the wrong tack with Vivienne. So he placated her—and she was responsively willing. At last, head on his shoulder, she began to talk about Sir Pellinore and the Questing Beast. ''Glatisant, its name was,'' she explained, all velvet now. ''Old Pellinore got tired of his wife and said he had to go questing. Honor demanded it. So off he went, cavorting through Britain. Nobody ever saw the Beast but Pellinore—and many's the wench who listened to Pellinore's stories about Glatisant, to her sorrow. Forsooth! You could mark Pellinore's trail nine months after he passed. I always say—''

Woodley wasn't listening. He was thinking, hard and fast. He knew now, quite definitely, that he had to get out of the lake before sundown. Morgan . . . she was not, he thought, of human blood at all. And that—chess game!

What nightmare that euphemism masked he could not guess. But he knew very well he didn't want to play chess with the Queen of Air and Darkness, as poor Bohart was doing now. Again, Woodley remembered the Eden tapestry—

How could he escape?

He was invisible and intangible—and dumb—to humans. No one could see, hear, or sense him. Except the magic folk, whoever they were. Moreover, once Woodley got out of the lake, he would strangle.

Wait! There was a thought somewhere along that line. Men could live under water, in diving suits. Presumably Woodley could live in air, if he could arrange to breathe water continuously.

A diving suit was obviously out of the question. But—good lord!—all Woodley needed was a bowl of water to carry with him! He almost grinned at the thought, but masked his face in time.

In this rocky country there were few streams—only one emptying into the lake. But . . . let's see . . . Woodley didn't want to be a water-breather all his life; it would be horribly inconvenient.

And Vivienne would pursue him. She could fly—

Woodley strained his memory. Wasn't there something in the Arthurian legend that would help him? He had a vague glimmer of an idea . . . Merlin.

In his dotage, Merlin fell in love with Vivienne and followed her all through Britain. Finally the girl, tired of her ancient lover, learned a spell from him and used it to shut Merlin up inside the trunk of an oak. If Merlin were only around!

"Good lord!" said Woodley, sitting up. "Uh . . . oh, nothing, darling. Something bit me."

"Poor dear," said Vivienne, snuggling closer. "After killing that undine yesterday . . . well, as I was saying, this knight climbed down from the tower and hid in the moat till—"

Woodley was remembering his experience just before he had met Vivienne—that little cave of roots under an oak tree, where something had kicked him in the pants. Soon after that, Vivienne had said that he "smelled of Merlin."

Merlin—of course!—was in that oak!

And no doubt feeling embittered toward Vivienne. Woodley's memory of Malory told him that Merlin and Morgan le Fay had always been bitter enemies. Usually Merlin had triumphed.

Merlin would help him now, out of sheer gratitude, if he could free the wizard. Certainly Merlin could reverse the wet magic, make Woodley an air-breather again, and protect him against Morgan and Vivienne. Shut up in that oak for centuries—ha!

It was beautifully logical. And all Woodley had to do, therefore, was to learn the spell that would free Merlin.

Bleys was the answer to that.

"Darling," said Woodley suddenly, "what happened to the clothes I was wearing when you brought me to the lake?"

"Why?" Suspicion showed in the dark eyes.

"I want a cigarette." He explained about tobacco. The girl nodded.

"Of course. Morgan can make some, by magic, but it will take time till she finds the right spell. I'll have your things brought here. Nurmala!"

The naiad came translucently from behind the curtain, listened, and went away, to return with Woodley's clothing. He searched for and found the cigarettes, which were magically dry. Of course, it was quite impossible to smoke under water, but . . . Woodley blew a smoke ring.

He glanced keenly at Vivienne. "Try it, darling?"

Under his tutelage, the girl learned about tobacco. Ten minutes later, her face a rather becoming shade of mauve, she interrupted an involved story about Guenevere and Borre to leave the room. She did not return.

Tense with nervous excitement, Woodley found the flask

of brandy still in the pocket of his uniform. It was more than half full. Good!

He went to Bleys' apartment. On the way, he picked up a glazed crockery bowl, which he thoughtfully left just outside the Druid's door.

"May I come in?"

"*Bip!*"

Woodley took this for assent. He found Bleys fuming over a retort and sampling the contents of a jug.

"Dish water!" Bleys shrilled. "Hog slop! Pap for suckling babes! After working hours over the spell, I felt sure it would be at least thirty proof. May Satan crumble my bones! No—" he added hastily, glancing around, "I take it back."

"Try this," Woodley offered, holding out the flask. "I'd forgotten I had it with me."

Bleys' eyes glistened through his floating beard as his clawlike hand shot out. "Dry-land liquor? Messire Arthur, I love you for this! Wine? Ale?"

"Brandy. Try it."

Bleys took one swallow. Then he lowered the flask, his lips twitching convulsively, his head thrown back. A low purring came from deep in his throat.

"Brandy." His voice caressed the word. His eyes opened, a greedy, mad gleam in them. "I shall get drunk! For the first time in centuries!"

"No," said Woodley, who had recaptured the flask. "Sorry. That's all you get."

"B-but—" Bleys' jaw dropped. "Messire Woodley! You jest!"

"Like hell I do," Woodley said grimly.

"Wait," said the Druid, slobbering. "I'll make you wine. Mead. Ale. Tons of it. I'll give you anything."

Woodley waited. Finally he decided he had Bleys where

he wanted him. "O.K.," he said then, "you can have the rest of the brandy. But you've got to pay me for it. I want a certain—spell."

Bleys looked shrewd. "The spell to change a water-dweller to an air-breather? All right."

"No, you don't," Woodley snapped, drawing the flask out of reach. "You told me once that you didn't know it. No tricks, now."

"Well," the Druid said sulkily, "what *do* you want, then?"

"Does Mer . . . did Merlin know the wet magic spell?"

"Yes, he did. Merlin was my pupil once, you know, but he learned far more than I ever did. Why?"

Woodley sighed with relief. "Never mind. Do you know the spell to release a man shut up in an oak tree?"

For a long time Bleys said nothing. Then he whirled to a nearby table, picked up a jug, and drank from it. With a furious oath he sent the ewer smashing against the floor.

"Slop!" he shrilled. "I cannot drink this stuff forever! The oak tree enchantment? Oak is a Druid tree. Of course I know it."

"Then tell it to me," Woodley said. "For the brandy."

Greed triumphed. At last Bleys explained the formula.

"That's the right one?"

"It is. *Bip!* Give me the brandy!"

"Swear it by . . . uh . . . Mider."

"By Mider I swear it," Bleys said angrily. "You are a fool, Messire Arthur. But do as you will. If Morgan slays me, at least I will die drunk."

He drank brandy. Woodley turned away.

The Druid's voice halted him. "Wait. I have a thought."

Bleys was shaking his head, his beard streaming, as he blinked through watery eyes. "This—brandy—clears my brain. Strange. I have been half-drunk for too long . . . a minute." He drank again.

* * *

Woodley hesitated, remembering Morgan. But the Druid's skinny hand clutched his arm. Bleys peered up, searching the other's face with his bleary stare.

"Arthur . . . I should have thought of this before. When I saw you bringing back the undine yesterday . . . Bah, to be in one's dotage—I grow old and stupid. Yet I remember now."

He tightened his grip. "You must listen. It is important. Perhaps because Morgan mislikes you, perhaps because your name is Arthur—listen! Do you remember that I told you the course of history can be changed? That time is fluid?"

"Yes. What about it?"

"Strong characters twist an author's pen and change the story he writes. Artorius of Britain did that. He was a petty chieftain, but he was strong—valorous. So strong that he forced himself into a greater role than he had originally. There was a—revision. This petty chieftain took Excalibur and made a legend. As Arthur Pendragon he saved England from the powers of the dark."

Woodley glanced at the door, anxious to be gone. "Well?"

"On Arthur's tomb are the words—he was and will be. There is a legend that Arthur will come again, in the hour of England's need, to save her once more. Has that hour come?"

"Then—" Woodley stopped, licking his lips. He stared at Bleys.

"Listen again!" The talon fingers tightened. "Any man can be Arthur, if he is strong enough to twist the author's pen. Any man can be Arthur if he dares to hold Excalibur. And your name—

"Your life may not have been a great one, till now. That does not matter. Artorius was not great, till he held

Excalibur. Do you know why I am here, why Morgan has kept me her prisoner?''

"Why?"

"I am Excalibur's guardian," Bleys said. "After Merlin passed, the charge was given to me. Arthur slept in Avalon. Yet the prophecy said that in England's hour of need, he would come again, and I must offer Excalibur to him. I looked to see Pendragon," the Druid went on quietly. "I had forgotten that Pendragon was once merely Artorius. Now I think the time has come. It was not chance that brought you beneath the lake. Excalibur lies here, ready for your hand. With it you can be Arthur."

Woodley's eyes were shining. "Bleys—" He paused, biting his lip. "Morgan."

"With Excalibur you can conquer her—and more. The man who holds Cut-Steel will save England!''

"Why haven't you used it on Morgan?" Woodley asked quickly.

"I am its guardian—the only man in all earth who can never hold that brand.'' There was a strange, deep sorrow in Bleys' voice. It was incongruous that he should seem a figure of such dignity, in his dingy brown robe—

"I know what is in your mind," the Druid said. "Escape and safety. It is not the right way. Excalibur lies ready for your hand. I have seen the portents, and I think the time has come. Remember—any man can be Arthur. If he has the courage to take and wield Excalibur. Artorius had that courage. Gawaine, the son of Morgawse, did not; Cut-Steel was offered him first, and he was afraid. And now—"

"I—can be Arthur," Woodley said, very softly.

"You can change past, present, and future. A strong and brave man can alter history. Your own past does not matter. If you take Excalibur now, there will be—revisions."

*   *   *

Woodley did not answer. He was remembering the way a sword hilt had felt against his palm, and the strange, high excitement that had filled him when he matched steel briefly against Bohart. To hold Excalibur—

To be Arthur!

"You can be the man," Bleys said. "You slew the undine. I should have known then that you were the man for whom I had waited."

But Woodley had not slain the undine. A small cold sickness crawled suddenly in his stomach. He said, "If I took . . . Excalibur . . . what would I have to do?"

Bleys' scrawny body trembled with excitement. "You would know. First, slay Morgan. After that your star would lead you."

Slay Morgan?

Somehow a sword, even Excalibur, seemed a poor weapon against the horror of her eyes. Even now the enchantress might be finishing Bohart and preparing for the next victim.

Suppose Woodley took Excalibur and failed to conquer Morgan? Suppose he couldn't wield the magic sword? After all, he hadn't really killed the undine. He had depended on strategy, which was perhaps more dependable than courage alone.

If Woodley had had no alternative, he would have battled Morgan, and done his best. He thought so, anyhow. But the alternative was so much safer!

Besides—he wasn't Arthur!

Not that he was a coward—no. But Bleys' proposition was a gamble, pure and simple. And why should Woodley gamble with his own future at stake? Merlin was in the oak, and Merlin, with all his mighty powers, was certainly a match for Morgan le Fay. This way was logical, much safer, and with the odds in his favor.

And yet—certainly there was something very splendid

about the alternative Bleys was offering. Excalibur! To
hold such a weapon! Briefly his mind flamed with the
idea. Armed with that enchanted sword, he would have
little need to fear even the Queen of Air and Darkness.

Provided—and that was the hitch!—provided he could
hold Cut-Steel. What if he wasn't the man? Certainly he
didn't feel very much like Arthur Pendragon. In the wrong
hands Excalibur would be worse than useless—probably it
couldn't even be wielded. Woodley's scalp crawled at the
thought of himself facing Morgan's terrible gaze armed
with a useless sword—

No, it was too much of a gamble. Accepting this glittering offer *might* mean finding himself completely defenseless
against Morgan, with all chance of escape gone. The dice
were too heavily loaded. Merlin meant certain safety.

The Druid bent forward, eager-eyed. "Excalibur is hidden in a place where only Arthur would dare enter. Let me
show you that place."

Woodley took a deep breath.

"Bleys," he said, his voice not quite steady. "I think
I've got a better idea. I'm going to try it, anyhow. If it
doesn't work, I'll be back to fight Morgan."

The Druid's figure seemed to shrink in upon itself.
Bleys let fall his hand from Woodley's arm and stepped
back.

"Gawaine," he said. "Excalibur is not offered twice."

"But—I'll fight Morgan, if I have to. Only—"

There was no answer, only stony silence. Woodley
hesitated, feeling, curiously, as though he had failed some
vital test. He turned at last to the door, leaving Bleys
sitting on the floor, pouring brandy down his throat.

For a moment there had been a curious, somber dignity
to the old man; the brandy had paradoxically made him
soberer than Woodley had ever seen him. All that was

gone now. Except for a little discouraged sag to the shoulders, he looked as he had always looked, dingy and drunk.

"Good-bye, fool," he said. "*Bip!*"

Woodley nodded and let the curtain fall back, picking up the crockery bowl he had left outside the door. Then he went in search of the portal by which Bleys and he had entered the castle yesterday. He was thinking uncomfortably of Bleys' proposal—and almost regretting his decision.

But it was much more important to be watching for possible guards. Suppose he encountered Vivienne? Or even Morgan? But not even a naiad appeared. Ten minutes later Woodley was climbing the lake bottom.

Fish swam past. He plodded on. And at last his head broke water.

Well—he had made his decision. He hoped it had not been the wrong one. There was only one way to find out—

He filled the crockery bowl, and, when he had to breathe again, he did so after dipping his face into the water. It worked.

He repeated the process half a dozen times before he felt satisfied. Then he made for the shore. The stream burst out of its gorge a few hundred feet to the left. Woodley reached it and discovered that the canyon, though steep, was by no means unscalable.

He looked back. Behind him, the still surface of the lake shone like silver under the midday sun. Was that—his heart jumped—was that something leaping up from the depths?

Only a fish, thank Heaven. But the sight reminded Woodley of the urgent need for speed. He inadvertently breathed air, and spluttered and coughed for a time with his face in the water. Then he turned to the gorge.

He climbed fast. Nor had he far to go—half a mile or

less, till he recognized the spot where he had first met Vivienne. The oak must be a few hundred yards beyond.

Some instinct made him look up. High above, toward the lake, a bird was wheeling in midair. No—not a bird—Vivienne!

"Lord!" Woodley breathed, and dived under a projecting rock. He lay hidden for a time. When he dared to peer out again, Vivienne had vanished. Luckily she had not yet glimpsed her quarry.

At any rate, Morgan herself presumably wasn't warned yet. That was something. Woodley hurried on up the gorge. He had difficulty in breathing, somehow. The water in the bowl choked him. He replenished it from the stream and went on. He caught sight of the oak.

It was as he had remembered, with the little root-cavern under it. So this was Merlin's prison!

Now for it. Woodley refilled the bowl, climbed the bank, and experimentally approached the tree. There was no sign of Vivienne—as yet.

His skin felt hot and dry. He would have liked to immerse himself in the brook, but it was too small, and, in any case, there was no time to waste. The spell Bleys had given him—

Woodley plucked seven oak leaves and laid them in a row on the ground before the tree. He put his face into the bowl, took a deep breath, and lifted his head. Now—

His skin was burning like fire. Woodley knew he had to get back to the water fast—not merely to breathe it, but to keep himself from shriveling up like a beached jellyfish.

He said the spell, a short one, articulating each word carefully.

There was a clap of thunder, a streak of lightning, and, with a terrific crash, the bole of the oak split asunder.

Woodley had a moment's fear that the commotion would attract Vivienne.

The tree's trunk was hollow. A man stepped out.

It was Merlin Ambrosius, a tall, dignified man with a hooked nose and a long white beard. He looked exactly like a professor of history, except for his brown robe and hood.

"Merlin!" Woodley said, his voice tense with relief, and hastily dipped his face into the bowl. Let Vivienne come now! Merlin was free!

"Oh, dear, dear," said the wizard, in a querulous voice. "You . . . you're not Arthur? But no; I can see that you're not. Why do people meddle so? Why can't you mind your own business?"

Woodley said, quite stupefied, "I . . . I've freed you from the oak where Vivienne imprisoned you."

Merlin threw up his hands. "What in Heaven's name ever gave you that fantastic idea? One of Vivienne's stories, I suppose. She wouldn't want the truth to get out, of course. Name of Mider! For centuries she's been looking for this oak, trying to find me, ever since I shut myself up here."

"You—shut yourself up?"

"I presume you've met Vivienne," Merlin said, with furious patience. "A lovely girl. A charming girl. But she talks like a magpie. Scandal, scandal, scandal, morning, noon, night, and Sabbaths. She followed me all around Britain—I couldn't get away from the wench. How she loved me! And how she talked! I couldn't think straight. Every time I tried to work out a spell, she'd begin babbling about the affair Duke Somebody had with Dame Somebody Else. Oh, no!" Merlin said emphatically. "It wasn't Vivienne who shut me up in this oak. I shut myself up, and I've had a very pleasant time since, thank you, except when Vivienne got dangerously close. I've been napping, off and on, and working out some lovely new magic. But I was always afraid that beautiful, brainless, chattering magpie would find me some day and make my life a hell again.

"But no more," Merlin said very firmly. "I've worked out a new spell for which there's no antidote. It begins *somnus eternatis*, and I'm going to use it to shut myself up again in this oak. When I've done that, not the devil himself can ever open this tree again. I should have used it long ago, but I didn't think a few centuries would matter much, one way or another."

"But!" said Woodley, who had been alternating between the bowl and staring at Merlin. "You won't help me, then?"

"Oh, I'll help you," the wizard grunted. "That'll be easy enough. I'll take off the wet magic and protect you against Morgan and Vivienne—as I read your mind, that's what you want. It won't take long. Then I'll just go back in my tree, and after I've used my new spell, it'll be sealed inside and out. I can't get out, ever, and nobody can ever get in. Arthur won't need me, anyway, when he comes again. He'll have Excalibur."

There was a *swoosh* in the air behind Woodley. He whirled, to see Vivienne flying down at him, her hair streaming behind her. So the thunderclap of the oak's opening *had* summoned her!

"Messire Arthur!" she shrilled. "So there you are!"

Merlin let out a whoop of dismay and stepped back into the tree. His voice rose in a hurried incantation.

"*Somnus eternatis*—"

There was a joyous shriek from Vivienne. "Merlin!" she screamed. "My love Merlin! At last!"

She swooped down, past Woodley, knocking the bowl from his hands. Merlin was inside the hollow oak, frantically intoning his spell. And then Vivienne had reached him, had flung her arms around the struggling wizard's neck, was planting passionate kisses on his bearded cheeks—

Crash!

Lightning blazed; thunder rolled; and the oak slammed shut like two halves of a door. Woodley, automatically holding his breath, stood gaping at the tree. Merlin and Vivienne had vanished.

He scooped up the unbroken bowl and raced back to the stream, where he replenished it. His body was burning like fire, and he hastily splashed water upon himself. Then, the bowl refilled, he clambered up the bank to the tree and plucked seven oak leaves.

He repeated Bleys' incantation, but nothing happened. He tried it again and again—six times in all. No use. Merlin and Vivienne were sealed within the oak.

Woodley went back and sat in a shallow pool, bending forward occasionally to breathe. Where his skin was exposed to the air, it was sheer agony. He longed to immerse his whole body, but the stream was too shallow here, and he could only pour water from the bowl over his skin. It didn't help much.

If Merlin had only had time to take off the wet magic spell—if Vivienne had not arrived when she did—

Woodley gnawed at his lips. If he could only get help—

If he had only accepted Excalibur—

Help was far away. Woodley knew he had to stay near water, where he could replenish the bowl from time to time. With a hollow reed, he might contrive to aerate the water he carried with him, but he could not expose his skin to air for very long. Like a jellyfish, he could not live in sunlight and air.

If he could find a deep pool—

But there was none. The shallow stream raced steeply

down the gorge without pausing. Only in the lake itself could Woodley survive.

"No," he thought. "I'll stay here. It'll be an easier death. Bohart—"

But the weakness of his flesh betrayed him. Minute by minute the burning agony crawling along his skin became worse. It was intolerable—unendurable.

There was no other way. He must return to the lake. And—Morgan le Fay.

Woodley began to stumble down the gorge. After all, he need not go back to the castle itself. He could hide somewhere, under the water, where Morgan might not find him—

The cleft ended. Woodley's feet splashed into deepening water.

For a very brief moment, he saw a mirage. It seemed to him that an arm, draped in white samite, rose from the smooth surface of the lake, and that it brandished a sword that flamed with intolerable brightness in the sunlight.

It was gone. Woodley splashed deeper. It was only a mirage.

No revisions—this time.

The grateful coolness of the water soothed his burning skin. It closed over his head. Woodley dropped flat on the lake bottom, luxuriating in the element that meant relief to his parched throat and lungs. For a long time he lay there, unconscious of his surroundings. It was enough merely to relax.

The lake grew darker. The sun dropped behind the peaks. An inquisitive trout investigated Woodley's hair and flicked away as he stirred.

Merlin—Bleys—no help there. He must find a hiding place. That cave in the Shaking Rock. Morgan might not find him there.

His body was no longer afire. Slowly Woodley rose and

began to descend the slope of the lake bottom. A green twilight surrounded him.

Then he saw—something—slowly stirring at his feet.

For a moment Woodley's shocked eyes could not quite comprehend what he saw. He gave a little choking gasp of nausea. It was not the actual appearance of the—thing—so much as the unmistakable fact that it had once been Sir Bohart.

And it still lived, after a fashion.

Morgan's chess game was finished.

Woodley shut his eyes, squeezing the lids tight together, as he fought down the sickness of his human flesh, revolting from that which Morgan had done. Through the dark came a voice.

"She plays at chess with Bleys now," it said.

Woodley tried to speak, but could not. That which should have had no voice went on thickly:

"She dared not slay him before, since he held Excalibur for Arthur. But the hour for Arthur's coming has passed, she said to me before I died, and she has no more fear."

The thing did not speak again, for it had disintegrated.

Woodley opened his eyes then. The green twilight had darkened. He could see little, except a great black shadow far below that was the castle. To the right was another blot of darkness—the Shaking Rock, perhaps.

He could hide there—

No. Morgan would find him. Woodley half turned to retrace his steps, but remembrance of the agony he had suffered in air halted him. He could not endure that again.

But—it would be better than playing chess with Morgan. Woodley knew, at last, what that euphemism cloaked. Poor Bleys!

He thrust that thought, and the memory of Bohart, out of his mind. He knew, now, what he had to do. It was the only way. A clean, final solution, with sharp steel, thrust through his heart. It would be the period to his failure.

His hand went to his belt, but the sword was not there. He had removed it, Woodley remembered, in his apartment after the slaughter of the undine. Well—the dagger, then.

That, too, was gone. He was unarmed.

Briefly a racking sickness shook Woodley. He dared not remain alive now, to suffer the same fate as Bohart. Again he glanced back.

Well, he would not leave the lake again. It would mean unnecessary suffering. Somehow he would find a way to kill himself. Even if he had to enter the castle again—

It came to that, in the end. There was no other way. No weapons existed under the lake, except in Morgan's stronghold. Woodley knew which door to use—the one Bleys had showed him. He was encouraged by the thought that he was not apt to encounter Morgan. She would be busy—

Nevertheless, he kept to the shadows as he crept along the corridor. A curious darkness seemed to have fallen over the castle. The vague, sourceless light had dimmed. It was utterly silent.

He saw no one—not even Nurmala, as he cautiously hurried to his apartment. But there were no weapons in evidence. They had been removed.

Well—there might be a dagger in Bleys' room. He went there. The door was closed and locked, and Woodley dared not risk the noise of breaking it down.

The armory?

Fear mounted within him as he went through the castle. Something was crouching in the shadows, watching him. Worst of all was the thought that Morgan, somewhere here, was playing at chess with Bleys.

Bleys—Bohart—*Morgan!*

At the end of a hall he saw a door agape, and beyond it the sheen of steel. The armory, then. As he hurried forward, a curtain billowed out at his side, and Woodley froze, seeing what was embroidered on that white surface. A coiled snake, with a golden star above its lifted head. Morgan's apartment.

Somehow Woodley crept past. Somehow he reached the armory, and chose a sword at random. An ordinary enough blade, but sharp. Not Excalibur, though. His lips twisted at the thought.

This would be a clean death. Or, perhaps, a dagger would be better. He selected one.

But his fingers remained curled about the sword hilt. He had forgotten how strangely satisfying it was to hold a blade. The weapon was like an extension of his own body, giving him a power he had not possessed before.

Woodley looked at the dagger. Then he thrust it into his belt. He hefted the sword.

Not Excalibur. He could never hope to hold Cut-Steel now. He could never hope to slay Morgan, or even to face her—

Woodley's face changed. His hand tightened on the sword hilt. He was remembering his last words to Bleys.

"I think I've got a better idea. I'm going to try it, anyhow. If it doesn't work, I'll be back to fight Morgan."

Fight her? Without Excalibur? The thought was mockingly hopeless. Yet, oddly, a curious sort of anger was beginning to glow within Woodley.

From the beginning, Morgan had had it all her own way. Everyone was afraid of her. Secure in her dark magic, she had done exactly as she liked, trampling roughshod over those who got in her way. Perhaps she had felt some fear that Arthur would come again, and destroy her. Now that menace was gone. Morgan was confident—and with reason.

No one had dared to oppose her. The thought of Morgan's triumph now was suddenly unendurable to Woodley. She had not even troubled to follow and destroy him. She knew that he would skulk back, and perhaps kill himself to save her the trouble of . . . of crushing him, as she would crush a fly.

Bleys—Bohart—the thing that had been Bohart.

Why had the armory door been left open? Had Morgan known what Woodley intended to do?

Sudden anger darkened his face. Damn her! He had failed—yes. But this—

Very well. He had to die; there was no possible escape now. But at least he could give Morgan the trouble of having to kill him herself!

Hot with anger, Woodley whirled and hurried back along the passage. At the white drapery he hesitated for a brief moment. Then he flung it aside and stepped across the threshold.

The room was empty. The wall that faced him was not a wall. It was, he thought, a curtain of black cobwebs that hung from ceiling to floor. Or it was a tapestry of darkness, intangible, shifting—more of Morgan's magic.

Damn Morgan, anyway!

Woodley marched forward. Out of the dark curtain two armored knights came pacing, visors concealing their faces. They lifted their swords in grim silence.

Woodley grinned. He had held his own against Sir Bohart—this would be no pigsticking, anyway. He'd give Morgan some trouble before she destroyed him.

He did not wait for the attack; he ran in, lightly as a cat, feinting at one of the knights. A reasonless confidence seemed to distill in him from the feel of the sword against his hand. Arthur must have felt like this, long ago, when he held Excalibur— As the knight's brand swept down

Woodley, unencumbered by heavy armor, sprang aside, and his sword point slipped through the bars of the knight's visor. It stuck there, trapped by bone.

The other attacker cut at Woodley. There was no time to recover a sword; his own was stuck beyond retrieving and the other man's had shattered to flinders against the stone floor. Woodley felt pain bite into his arm. He hurled himself forward, grappling with the cold, unyielding steel of the body before him, fumbling for the dagger at his belt. Almost of its own volition his heel hooked behind the other's ankle. They crashed down together, armor thundering.

Woodley's dagger grated across steel and found that vulnerable spot beneath the arm where the cuirass always fails its wearer. The sharp blade sank and rose and sank again.

Woodley tore the sword from the dying knight's hand and leaped up. Out of the dark curtain of cobweb a serpent came sliding, coil upon shining coil. A point of light danced above its head. Morgan's emblem—Morgan's familiar.

Woodley did not wait for the great coils to loop him— and they were not proof against the sword he wielded. The snake's thick blood poured through its gashed side as it threw itself about him, bruising, tremendous. Woodley hacked blindly.

The flags were slippery with blood when he rose from the loosening folds of the serpent above whose head the star no longer trembled.

On unsteady legs Woodley went forward to meet a laughing, crimson thing that was hideously anthropomorphic. He left it more crimson still, but no longer laughing. And this time nothing else emerged from the veil.

Beyond there was only a faint crimson glow through which shapeless shadows loomed. Dimly in the red dark he saw Morgan at the end of the room rising from a table. Bleys sat across from her, lifting a pale, incredulous face as he saw Woodley. He was apparently unharmed as yet, but Bleys did not speak.

Morgan turned her terrible gaze upon the newcomer. As always, Woodley's eyes slipped away. He could not meet it. But he saw that her strange, lovely face was expressionless. She was not afraid. Of course not. Nothing could harm her—

He moved forward in the gloom, lifting his sword. Morgan's hand rose, and the blade crumbled in his grasp. Woodley stared down stupidly, a dull anger brightening in his mind behind the pain and the despair. He tore out his dagger and lurched forward.

Morgan's hand rose again, and the dagger fell to dust.

Now he stood unarmed, facing Morgan across the gulf of crimson shadows. But the confidence that had distilled from the feel of the sword in his hand remained. He was not afraid. His courage and strength had not lain in the blade alone.

He took a long step forward into the dimness. Morgan burned white a dozen yards away, blotting out everything else. The glimmer of her pale throat made his fingers twitch unconsciously. He stumbled another step forward.

At his knee in the gloom something bulky touched him. He looked down. It was a stone anvil, and a sword stood embedded deep in the stone.

A weapon! A weapon against Morgan. He thought of no more than that as his fingers curled lovingly about the jeweled hilt. There was a moment of hesitation before the blade slid free, and the hilt quivered in his palm as if it were alive.

But when he swung the sword up shoulder high it was as if he lifted a suddenly flaming torch.

The man who held Excalibur stood motionless, squinting against the brilliance of his own weapon, feeling the power that had once gone coursing through Arthur Pendragon's veins flooding his own. The white blaze of Cut-Steel routed the shadows of the room. Bleys slipped down from his stool and knelt, head bowed to that strong pale fire.

There was utter silence.

Then Morgan said: "You have come again, my enemy. No magic of mine has power over you now. The lake is no longer a prison for you. Your star rises. The sword Excalibur is drawn again to save England, and it will not fail." Her calm voice deepened a little, revengefully. "But you will not live to take joy in your triumph, Arthur, my enemy! The touch of Excalibur's hilt is as deadly as the touch of its blade. When all is won, on some dark tomorrow, you shall die."

The sword was a flame of living light. The man who held it did not answer for a moment. Then—

"Yes," he said, very softly. "But you shall die today."

He moved forward.

CONAN

- ☐ 54238-X   CONAN THE DESTROYER $2.95
     54239-8   Canada $3.50
- ☐ 54228-2   CONAN THE DEFENDER $2.95
     54229-0   Canada $3.50
- ☐ 54225-8   CONAN THE INVINCIBLE $2.95
     54226-6   Canada $3.50
- ☐ 54236-3   CONAN THE MAGNIFICENT $2.95
     54237-1   Canada $3.50
- ☐ 54231-2   CONAN THE UNCONQUERED $2.95
     54232-0   Canada $3.50
- ☐ 54246-0   CONAN THE VICTORIOUS $2.95
     54247-9   Canada $3.50
- ☐ 54258-4   CONAN THE FEARLESS $2.95
     54259-2   Canada $3.95
- ☐ 54256-8   CONAN THE RAIDER   (trade) $6.95
     54257-6   Canada $8.95
- ☐ 54250-9   CONAN THE RENEGADE $2.95
     54251-7   Canada $3.50
- ☐ 54242-8   CONAN THE TRIUMPHANT $2.95
     54243-6   Canada $3.50
- ☐ 54252-5   CONAN THE VALOROUS $2.95
     54253-3   Canada $3.95

Buy them at your local bookstore or use this handy coupon:
Clip and mail this page with your order

TOR BOOKS—Reader Service Dept.
49 W. 24 Street, 9th Floor, New York, NY 10010

Please send me the book(s) I have checked above. I am enclosing
$ _____ (please add $1.00 to cover postage and handling).
Send check or money order only—no cash or C.O.D.'s.

Mr./Mrs./Miss _____
Address _____
City _____ State/Zip _____
Please allow six weeks for delivery. Prices subject to change without notice.

THE BEST IN FANTASY